DARK
THINGS

DAVID M. HUMPHREY, SR.

MOODY PUBLISHERS
CHICAGO

All Scripture quotations are taken from the King James Version.

Library of Congress Cataloging-in-Publication Data

Humphrey, David M.
Dark things / David M. Humphrey, Sr.
p. cm.
ISBN 0-8024-1252-1
1. Washington (D.C.)—Fiction. 2. Spiritual life—Fiction. 3. Rape victims—Fiction. 4. Demonology—fiction. I. Title.

PS3608.U48D37 2005
813'.6—dc22

2005002188

ISBN: 0-8024-1252-1
ISBN-13: 978-0-8024-1252-2

1 3 5 7 9 10 8 6 4 2

Printed in the United States of America

To my mom,
who went home to be with the Lord in 1999.
How do I thank you? Mere words are not enough.
You gave me life, and then introduced me
to the Lord of Life, Jesus Christ.
You are a true Warrior of the Kingdom
whose encouragement, prayers, sacrifices and selflessness
have helped to mold me into the man I am today . . .

CONTENTS

ACKNOWLEDGMENTS

TO THE MANY over the years who have contributed in ways great and small to this project, thank you for believing in me and in my dream . . .

Our Heavenly Father, the Lord Jesus Christ and the Holy Spirit. My wife, Velma, whose prayers, words, encouragement, patience, and giving spirit made this book possible. Mrs. Jennifer Ferranti, my early mentor and an excellent writer in her own right. Mark Littleton, your words of advice, praise and hope sparked a fire that God wouldn't let die.

Cathy, Monique and Twinkle Toes, Donna Lee, Cynthia Johnson, Cynthia Ballenger, Tanya Harper, Elya and Jerice Williams, Mai Li and Phyllis, Ms. Emma Leech, Elaine, Sylvia (Syl) Washington, Paulette, Brent and Persia, Steve Wistar, Janet Andrews, Leni Houser, Jeff Wright, Horace and Pat Drumming, Ron and Natile Yarborough.

Rosanne Thompson (I did it Chief!), Peggy and Noah (God bless you guys!), Judy, Sheila Farthing and all those at Greenberg and Traurig Law Firm, Will Landsperger, David and Diana Mollon, Marcy and Ron Williams, Valerie Hartridge, Jessica and Ron Dyson, Col. Omar and Family, Gen. Gary McKay and Family (Keep writing Brandon!), and Janet Hall.

And last, but definitely not least, my sons, Brian (El), Eric Jonathan, David Jr. You make me so very proud. The whole Rainbow Family Christian Center Church and many, many others . . . And all the Anointed people at Moody who contributed to this book and made it possible. God bless you . . .

1
DARK THINGS . . .

THE DOORS EXPLODED at St. Michael's emergency room as if they had been hit by a bomb.

Two grim-faced paramedics erupted through the open doors and down the crowded gray corridors at speeds reserved for the dying and those as good as dead. Patients and doctors alike scrambled out of their way like nervous matadors before a raging bull.

Using the gurney as a lifesaving battering ram, they blasted through door after door until at last they reached the emergency operating room. The OR's faded and pockmarked green walls stood like ancient sentries overseeing this latest victim of man's inhumanity to his fellow man . . .

The sparse but clean room quietly welcomed this new critical patient with the strong smell of anesthesia, urine, and sweat. Blood lay on an operating table still warm from the last fruitless attempt to save a life but seconds before. The warm pool was quickly sponged away, and fresh, taut sheets briskly shrouded the table.

Doctors flung aside the straps that secured the unconscious woman and lifted her quickly from the battered gurney to the operating table. They worked feverishly to stop the profuse bleeding and revive her.

"All right. We'll take it from here," said Will Jefferies, dismissing the paramedics out of the operating room.

"Make sure you swab her out for semen samples for the police," snapped a nurse to her trainee, who instantly obeyed. "Good. Now bag it quickly, mark it, and get back over here and give me a hand."

Darting around the operating table like bees in a hyperactive hive, within seconds the young black female was attached to monitors that beeped her weakening condition to the hospital room staff.

Dr. William Jefferies studied her declining heart rate on the monitor with quiet dismay, then shouted for an injection of epinephrine. Instantly, nurse Angeline Winters, gray haired and in her late fifties, prepared and injected the powerful heart stimulant. Nurse and doctor both watched the monitor and held their breath.

Mildred Hartley was the RN on duty, a flaming redhead in her forties who was known to have a temper as fiery as her hair. The pert and attractive ex-marine drill instructor was also a Vietnam medical vet. She quickly searched the patient's body for obvious and hidden wounds. She ripped open the already torn and bloody blouse, revealing a snow-white bra, now tie-dyed red, the left cup nearly filled with the victim's blood.

Mildred surveyed her quickly as she tossed the soiled bra to the side and shouted, "I've got multiple stab wounds here—looks like *two* near the heart! Let's clean her up and see what else we've got!" She barked orders as if she were still a drill instructor in boot camp and expected them to be obeyed just as quickly—and they were. Her shoulder-length hair, snatched back hurriedly into a ponytail, snapped like a red whip as she whirled about working frantically to keep this woman alive.

The stimulant, once given to the patient, still had no effect. Her heart rate fell like a wounded star. Voices shouted information back and forth as they fought desperately for this woman's right to survive . . .

"I've got the bleeding stopped, Doctor. Total of four stab wounds to the upper chest and one to the scalp, down to the skull, deep bruises on the throat and inner thighs. By some miracle the stab wounds to the chest all missed the heart, but they're 'danger close'!"

"Good—let's hope her luck holds out," said Dr. Jefferies, but he knew they were losing her. He looked at the blood pressure gauge to his left, and his heart sank.

"Doctor, her pressure's down to 40 over 20!" said a masked attendant excitedly.

"I know—I can **see**," snapped the young doctor testily. He bit his lip in growing frustration, and the others watched him as they flew about their duties, looking to him for leadership.

He'd been under tremendous pressure of late, working double shifts to cover his bills and expenses from med school. Having a mother in a nursing home who called every day to say how much she missed him didn't help any either. The guilt of that alone was eating him alive.

And the malpractice insurance! It was cheaper trying to pay off the Mafia! Sometimes the pressure was just too much, and he felt as fragile as a glass of fine crystal beneath a sky that threatened violent winds and hailstones. He felt as if his troubled mind were a dam that could burst at any moment. But, still, somehow, with Sam's help, he kept it all together.

He watched the monitor while he quickly pondered his next move.

"Pressure down to 30 over 10!" said a tense voice, trying to remain calm.

The monitor stared back at him, reflecting all of the victim's depressing vitals. She was sinking fast. "Nurse, give her another shot."

She quickly and efficiently obeyed. Nothing happened.

Nothing . . .

They worked another twenty minutes, to no avail. "I don't understand it—nothing's working," he said aloud, half to himself. He wished Sam were here.

"Her body's not responding to *anything*. It's almost as if she's lost the will to live," remarked a young intern a lot louder than he had intended. Jefferies shot him a cold stare. The young man quickly wilted under the piercing gaze.

The body was a machine and nothing more, as far as young Will Jefferies was concerned. Fix the machine, and you fix the problem. The will, the soul, the psyche, and all other so-called spiritual aspects of life had absolutely nothing to do with it.

For Dr. Will Jefferies, there was no room for philosophy, conjecture, or anything else that couldn't be proven by medical science in his operating room. He wouldn't have it. He'd learned that lesson well in medical school.

The young intern swallowed hard and quickly looked away to the comfort of his monitor.

Jefferies sweated, pondering what to do next.

What would Sam do if he were here? Always solid and self-assured, unshakable, he always held the answers to everything—the right answers. If there indeed had ever been a God in this "godforsaken" universe, He would've been like Sam Hardison.

But Sam wasn't here now. He was on vacation.

Think, Will—think!

Jefferies stood silent briefly, feeling for all the world like some kind of medical bandit. Somehow he must steal back the life that death was working so fervently to steal away from them. He stared at her inert body, a body that now lay perfectly still.

Too still, he noted.

He glanced up at the monitor to confirm her vitals once more.

Suddenly, Virginia Sills' body lifted in a twisted arch and pounded the table violently several times, then slipped into a grand-mal seizure. Her slim brown body hammered the table unmercifully, like a jackhammer gone mad or a woman possessed. For several long minutes they fought to get control of her. The whites of her eyes glowed eerily in the OR's ancient fluorescent lighting. Jefferies and the other staff responded quickly and battled earnestly to hold the unconscious woman down.

Then, as suddenly as it had begun, it was over, and the OR fell strangely sullen and quiet. They all breathed a huge sigh of relief as they slowly released her and returned to their positions.

Then: "*EEEEEEEEEEEEEEEEEEEEEEEEEEEEEE!*"

Abruptly the stillness was shattered again as the monitor erupted into a persistent and unnerving screech.

One minute after the massive convulsions had stopped, so had the victim's heart.

Again the staff exploded into a frenzy of action as the life of Virginia Sills, like water from a broken cistern, began to slip through their fingers and seemed to fade away into the very air around them . . .

2 DARK THOUGHTS . . .

VIRGINIA HEARD VOICES as her life slipped away.

"Doctor!" said a faraway voice. "We've lost all vital signs and she's not breathing!"

The hospital room erupted into activity. Faintly, as if from the opposite end of a tunnel, she heard a frantic metallic-sounding voice say, "CODE BLUE, EMERGENCY ROOM! CODE BLUE, EMERGENCY ROOM!"

And without quite knowing how, she knew they were talking about her.

Two young nurses new to the ER whispered furtively to each other as the others worked frantically to revive the comatose woman.

"I don't think she's gonna make it," whispered short, petite, blonde-haired Cathy Starks. The pert young Peter Pan look-alike was rotating out today to Capitol Hill General.

"I don't either," responded slender Andrea Robins, both unaware they were overheard clear as a bell by Mildred Hartley, who instantly shot them a look that could wither stone. They also were heard by Virginia Sills.

Is it true? Am I as good as dead? Never to see my mother and father again? Never to prove my father wrong about what he'd said to me? Is this it? pondered Virginia.

"No!" said a powerful, thunderous voice in her ear, in direct opposition to the others—a voice, it seemed, that only she could hear. It continued, *"It is not yet your appointed time to die."* The voice was emphatic, almost angry, as if it knew a defiant secret the other voices did not.

Jefferies was already up on the table, straddling Virginia's body, pumping the chest rhythmically, sweating profusely. Blood, like red tears, streamed from the chest wounds with each powerful push of his hands. He called loudly for the defibrillator.

The room had become a mass of confusion as doctors and nurses poured in, wanting to help save this unknown woman. Surprisingly, among them came senior staff cardiologist Samuel Hardison, a huge bear of a man. He pounded into the room, casting his topcoat aside, buttoning his hospital coat up over his twelve-hundred-dollar navy blue Canali suit. Back one day early from his vacation, he had walked through the hospital doors but moments before when the code blue call came. "What's the status here?" he shouted above the melee at Jefferies.

I can't lose another, Jefferies thought to himself as he continued the rhythmic pressure. *I just can't!*

"Will!"

Will looked up suddenly, startled and relieved to see his mentor and friend back. He would know what to do. He would save her. "I thought you were—"

"We'll talk later, Will. Right now—status!"

"Rape victim, Sam," he shouted, swallowing hard as his

huge friend pulled alongside to help. "Blood pressure dropped to 30 over 10, grand mal, then cardiac arrest."

"Shame, what a lovely girl," noted a young blonde nurse quickly, her eyes taking in the bruises on the otherwise attractive face—a face surrounded by a dark waterfall of black hair, hair that now lay tangled and matted with congealed blood. The young blonde was rotating out of St. Michael's today also, and was glad of it. *Just too many gunshot wounds, stabbings, and drug overdoses,* she thought to herself. St. Michael's was the charity hospital, so they always got the worst cases, the ones nobody else wanted or the ones that had questionable coverage.

"No time for chatter!" snapped Mildred to another young trainee who tried to join in the whispered conversation. "Help me with this darn machine!"

A young Carolyn Hodge, an X-ray tech just getting off from duty, rushed into the ER, hoping to be of some help. She was nervous and a little unsure of herself. Nevertheless, she darted to the older woman's side and lent a hand. She too became swept up in the swirling frenzy to save this woman's life.

This was her first week working at St. Michael's, and the atmosphere was electric. Her first time working in an inner-city hospital, she found it an arena of constant excitement. Her heart was pounding a river of adrenaline through her veins. It was awesome to think that at this very moment someone's life was in their hands, that whether this person lived or died depended on what she did or didn't do. Her brown eyes flashed with excitement.

This was so cool!

Meanwhile, Jefferies continued to pump frantically and to brief Sam at the same time, his words now coming in strings of hurried gasps at odds with the rhythm of his strong hands upon her chest: "They found her . . . in an alley . . . deep shock

. . . WHERE'S THAT DEFIBRILLATOR!! I CAN'T KEEP THIS UP MUCH LONGER!"

"It's still not worki—There it is! *Clear!!*" shouted the fiery-haired RN as she extended him the two paddles.

"Sam . . ." Jefferies gasped weakly, in a voice barely above a whisper. It sounded more like a forlorn prayer as Jefferies looked imploringly at his mentor. He didn't have to say any more.

Jefferies jumped down from the table, and Sam shot past him like a sprinter in the Olympic track and field competition. He snatched up the two high-powered voltage paddles from Mildred, who yielded instantly and melted away to other vital duties.

"I've got it, Will! Take a break," ordered the older, more experienced doctor.

Will always marveled at how swiftly, expertly, and confidently Sam worked. He was awesome to watch.

Well, she was in god's hands now—*his* god, Samuel J. Hardison, the only god he knew.

Exhausted from his intense thirty-minute dance with death, Will collapsed against the nearest wall for support. His handsome black face was glistening and pained, his shirt and white coat soaked with fresh sweat, his chest heaving from the effort as Sam shouted in his deep baritone voice, "CLEAR!!" He slammed the two paddles on Virginia's chest, and 650 volts of electricity surged into her tired and weary heart. Her body convulsed from the power and heaved itself up off the table and back down again—as still and as silent as death itself.

"CLEARRRR!" shouted the tall, gray-haired black heart specialist again. He would not be denied. She must live.

"ZZZZZZZZTTT!" The bolt of primal power pounded the heart muscle, slamming it with an elemental surge of energy that could not be denied. But death's grip was at least as strong

as this powerful force of nature, and death seemed to be the one force that would not be denied this day . . .

"Give me 20cc of epinephrine."

"But Doctor Hardison, she's already had—"

"Now, Nurse!"

"Yes, Doctor! Right away!"

"My God, please don't die," whispered Angeline, almost moved to tears by the woman's pitiful condition, strangely moved by this single tragedy out of the hundreds she saw daily. She clasped the tiny crucifix around her neck and squeezed it so hard that she thought the metal might break. Her lips silently mouthed the words again that her heart prayed in secret, "Please God, don't let her die . . ."

Unseen, in the far corner of the crowded room, a small shadow seemed to twitch and wince, as if in pain, then scurry away . . .

Virginia slowly opened her eyes and looked around her. She didn't hurt anymore, she noticed. All the pain was gone, the excruciating pain that had plagued her head, chest, legs, abdomen, and beyond.

Where was she?

The commotion and shouting of the hospital room echoed strangely beneath her. She looked down. There, on the table, surrounded by an army of doctors, nurses, and worried-looking attendants some twenty feet below, was she—or rather her body . . .

"It's true," she said to herself. *"I'm dead!"*

"No," said a deep voice from somewhere above and behind her. "Not yet."

She had heard that voice before, telling her . . . telling her . . . ? Ah, yeah! It had said that she couldn't die yet.

"That's correct. I said that to you. And it is true. Not yet, Virginia—not yet. It is not yet your appointed time . . ."

She whirled around to see the speaker. He stood above her in midair, where the high hospital ceiling should have been, but there was nothing, only space—broad, dark, empty, and boundless.

He was dressed in a broad-shouldered white robe over which he wore an engraved solid-gold breastplate. The white robe was cinched at the waist with a wide, and what must be priceless, engraved gold belt. From it hung a long golden scabbard and sword. It too was engraved with the same strange letters as the belt, strange yet soothing letters that seemed to move when she tried to focus on them.

He stood with massive arms folded, looking at her as if perturbed by something. His skin was dark and golden, an eye-appealing shade of tanned gold.

She'd never seen anything like him before. His hair glistened like gold. It was dark, wavy, and shoulder length, and it shimmered as he moved. She gasped, fascinated. His features were sharp and chiseled, almost sculpted: a strong jaw, prominent forehead, and deep-set eyes—he was stunningly handsome. His eyes pierced her soul. They were a dark and brooding purple, and like magnets they drew her into them.

She thought about all the stories she'd heard in Sunday school as a child and had dismissed as she grew older. Her mom had also taught her about the good "Lawd."

Hmph—maybe Momma wasn't so out of touch after all.

But then doubt, like an insidious weed, sprang up in her mind. Maybe she was just having one of those out-of-body experiences that scientists say is brought on by oxygen deprivation.

Is there really such a thing as God or not?

Who is right?

She became even more frightened and confused. After

several minutes, she found her voice and began to speak. "Are you . . ." she queried nervously, "God?"

The sternness seemed to leave his face for a moment and spread into a slight smile of tolerance for her naïveté. Amazingly, his eyes flashed golden then, the pupils reflecting his amusement, their color changing briefly to match the color of his skin.

Virginia gasped again, captivated.

"No, I am not the Holy One, though glory and honor ever be to His throne," he said, bowing his head slightly, in seeming reverence at the mention of the Supreme Being.

"Are . . ." She swallowed hard. "Are you *Jesus?*" she said hesitantly.

"No, I am not the Blessed One, though glory and honor ever be unto His name." Again, the reverent nod of the head.

"Who—who are you, then?"

"I am Mahatiel, your personal guardian angel."

It was then that she saw the wings. Neatly folded, graceful, rounded, large feathered curves that appeared over each shoulder. How could she not have seen them before now? "My God, you're an angel," she said in hushed awe.

He frowned at the casual use of his Creator's name, his eyes flashing white for a moment in obvious displeasure, but he said nothing. Unfortunately, using the Creator's name so frivolously was a rude habit developed by humans and encouraged by dark things over the centuries. "You must go back now," he said gently but firmly.

"But I don't understand what's happening! I—"

Suddenly, he stiffened. She saw his whole expression change so quickly that it alarmed her. He stared off into the distance, and his face became like stone. His eyes became a smoldering green.

She followed his fierce gaze but saw nothing, only blank

and empty space. While he was distracted, she looked down at herself. She was dressed in some type of off-white gown. She touched it. It felt cool and smooth to her fingers, and for some reason it seemed to give her comfort to stroke the beadlike material.

"You must go back, and you must go back now," he said without looking at her, without moving his eyes for even a moment. It was as if he were watching something at such a great distance that it strained even his eyes to see it. Or, was it that he found it so disturbing that he couldn't look away?

"But who are you, and what's your name, and how did I get here, and—"

Humans. He had tried to be patient, but—"I have told you my name already, BUT THERE'S NO MORE TIME FOR TALK!" he shouted in a voice that demanded immediate silence and instant obedience. His eyes, changing back to a compassionate gold again, now looked deeply into hers. She trembled for a moment in fear, confused about everything going on around her.

Then, her mixed black and Irish-American blood began to rise to the surface. It was an old habit from childhood, and she knew it was a bad one. But she couldn't help it. Whenever she got frightened or dismayed, she got angry. She was starting to get her ire up. Just who did he think he was, her father?

"No! I do not think I'm your father," he remarked tersely, interrupting her thoughts. Then he descended several feet to her level and took her gently but firmly by the arm. It was then that she noticed how huge he was—incredibly tall and powerfully built, more than any man she'd ever seen, his bare arms massive coils of thick and rippling muscle. She'd thought at one time that there couldn't be anyone in the world more gorgeous than John, but—

"I am your angel. Virginia, you are in mortal danger. They come—those that seek the dead and dying. Your life is forfeited if you do not listen to me. I am sent here to keep you alive—if you will hearken unto me. Return to your body immediately. We must get you back into your body before they arrive.

"These are they who smell death, and seek to come and claim what has not already been claimed by Him Who Was and Is and Is to Come. They seek you, Virginia, and are on their way here—now. So, come quickly!" he repeated again.

"You're able to read my thoughts!" Virginia said, blushing with sudden realization. "Who's coming, and what are you talking about, *they* can smel—"

"Virginia! Listen to me! They tried to kill you before, and they will try again and again until they succeed! Therefore, we must get you back! Now come with me," he said firmly, his eyes flashing purple determination. He pulled her back down into the hospital room to hover just above her bruised and battered body.

"They tried to kill me before?" she said, puzzled, "and will try to do it aga—?" Then it hit her, like a punch in the stomach, at the exact same moment she looked at her limp and wounded form on the table. She gasped as the flood of revolting memories came racing back and dashed like breakers over her being.

She had been raped!

Her hands flew to her mouth in horror as if to cover a silent scream. She backed away from Mahatiel and snatched herself free of his powerful grip.

Above them, in the distance, there was an uncanny rustling sound.

Mahatiel felt deeply for her. He sincerely sympathized with her pain, but each moment she remained outside of her body she put them both in increasing danger from those that hunt the undecided.

She was unaligned, unprotected, and unmarked, had not declared herself for either side, and by that, she defaulted and made herself fair game. They would rip her soul apart as they dragged her down to hell. He didn't want to see that.

"Virginia, come!" He extended his hand. She gaped at the hospital floor in horror, reliving in her mind's eye the events that had happened but hours ago.

"Virginia! ***Come!***" he said, reaching desperately, the desperation showing clearly in his voice. He, like the young black doctor leaning against the wall, had recently lost a soul in this deadly game of life and death. And again, he too felt that he must *not* lose another. The screams—he couldn't *stand* the screams, and as an angel, he heard them forever . . .

The rustling sound grew noticeably louder.

Virginia looked up deliberately, past his outstretched and frantic hand, into his eyes. "*You*—how could you just—just let that happen to me?"

Her sorrowful eyes nearly broke his heart. However, he didn't have time for this lengthy foray into the land of "why," and neither did she!

Above them, the sound drew nearer—a sound he knew: the flapping of leathery wings.

Though he hadn't been responsible for her at the time of the attack, he included himself in his final response to her. "We tried to warn you," he said hurriedly, "this morning, at breakfast. Still, like most humans, Virginia, you didn't listen then, just as you're not listening now. And the result was tragedy. If you do not listen to me now, the dreadful tragedy you experienced today will be nothing compared to the grisly end that awaits you. Now, do as I *say!*"

Too late.

Mahatiel saw them then, in the distance, at the far end of the hospital. Swooping low and passing through walls as easily as a dream does through the mind of a sleeper, they sniffed the air, scanning left and right, heading their way.

He watched as they flowed through a far room where an old woman sat arguing with her husband over the phone. She fiercely upbraided him for using her new credit card, which had arrived in the mail yesterday.

It had been relatively quiet in room 201 North, the cardiac wing. Martha Vincent thanked the Lord that she would be going home tomorrow and was looking forward to seeing her grandchildren. The IVs were out, and her heart had responded well to the ACE inhibitors and Coreg. Her frightening bout with heart failure was over, and being a good girl and taking *all* of her medicine would be the order of the day this time around. She had learned her lesson.

Her stay in the hospital had not been that bad. She had made a new friend, Frances, the woman in the next bed who was talking on the phone to her husband. The woman could be a bit testy at times, as sometimes those her age could be, but otherwise she seemed rather nice.

"Roger Williams, you old *fool!* When I get outta here, um gonna slap you! You know better than to use my new credit card while I'm in the hospital! Why, I ain't even had a chance to use it myself yet!" Martha heard Frances say. She watched as the elderly woman fussed and sputtered over the mouthpiece of the phone, flailing her right arm angrily. It smashed into the glass that contained the woman's dentures and it went sailing across the room into the opposite wall, shattering both glass and dentures into pieces. A slimy plastic piece of denture with a single tooth attached landed wetly at the foot of Martha's bed.

Martha felt concern for the woman, and after a few moments, she tried in vain to get her roommate's attention. "Frances! Frances! *Frances Williams*, calm down, girl—it's just a credit card. Now, calm down! You know what the doctor said. Your pressure—"

"You shut up! This ain't none of your business!" the woman said fiercely. "And *you*, Roger, you wait till I get up outta here and I get home! Um gonna make you wish—"

Martha Vincent, embarrassed, fell silent. She put her earphones in her ears and turned up the volume of her TV. She turned her back to the melee and quietly tried to ignore the rantings of the woman she'd thought to be a new friend. Gradually she drifted off into a deep sleep.

Mahatiel watched intently what happened next . . .

The dark things went to the bed of Martha Vincent and sniffed her eagerly. They recoiled instantly, their nostrils burned as if by sulfur. It was then that they took notice of the Bible that lay on the woman's nightstand. Quietly, Martha's angel stood in the corner unseen, out of sight, sword drawn, ready to attack if *they* moved to try and claim her.

"Not her," whispered one of them in a raspy voice. "Let's take the other one." They backed away from Martha Vincent cautiously, then turned their full attention to Frances D. Williams. Their shadows touched the enraged woman as they circled her.

Suddenly she clutched at her chest, her voice coming in tragic gasps. Sudden pain began twisting her face into an ugly sputtering mask. Saliva drooled from her mouth as the numbing shadows of the depraved disseminated death into the room like a fine mist in the air.

The phone slid from Frances's disabled fingers with a soft

thump to the bed, unnoticed by her husband. He held the phone several inches away from his ear. His eyes were padlocked onto the Baltimore Ravens–Washington Redskins game. The picture was bright, beautiful, and stunning on the new 52-inch screen TV.

The Skins made an interception on Baltimore's fifteen-yard line. Roger's screams of joy drowned out Frances's sputtering outrage. The sudden and brief strangling gurgle at the other end of the phone escaped him entirely. It would be several minutes before he sensed something was wrong.

Frances's eyes grew watery, and she struggled for breath that wouldn't come.

The massive coronary that shook Frances Williams's body would later be explained as an "unfortunate and unexpected tragedy." The hospital monitor dutifully beeped its urgent and alarming message, but it was too late.

Carnivorous opportunists, the host of dark things leaped at this chance to feast on such sweet human misfortune. The rest of the demonic horde wheeled in motion like a single, ravenous, multiwinged beast as Frances breathed her last. They waited and watched impatiently as her soul gradually emerged from her body into this strange new world, like a frightened butterfly from the safety of its cocoon.

They devoured her instantly. Like piranha at a feast, they tore at her, dislodging and devouring large chunks of ethereal flesh. What was left of her, two of the brood dragged downward—screaming into hell. There, their compatriots would gnaw eternally on the cognizant "scraps" of her being.

Slowly, the other thirty or so dark things turned to follow the trail of the original scent of death that had drawn them here.

Mahatiel knew his time was short, that he had seconds at best. Their chance diversion with the old woman had bought him mere precious moments, not nearly long enough to argue with this stubborn young black woman about the value of her life.

He had to act, and act immediately.

He thrust the young woman toward her body—violently. Her head whipped backwards from the quick and forceful shove. The moment her soul made contact with her flesh, her body held it fast, like an insect stuck to flypaper. Then, hungrily, it drew her spirit being within itself, as if it knew that without it, there could be no life.

Though the pull was irresistible, a stunned and angry Virginia Sills tried to resist. She struggled stubbornly to be free—to continue her debate and inquisition of Mahatiel.

The struggle between the two dynamic forces—her body, craving life; and her soul, frustrated and rebellious—resulted in a dramatic slowing of the absorption process.

She continued at first to ask him why this had happened to her; then she demanded to know. She felt all the fury and anxiety exploding within her of everyone who had ever wanted to ask God why. And though He wasn't there to answer, she was determined that Mahatiel would have to answer in His stead.

Mahatiel was dismayed at the sight of her. Her soul was sinking so slowly back into her body, like a woman fighting the inevitable effects of quicksand. He watched her, counting the seconds and holding his breath. That she didn't understand what was at stake was evidenced by the scowl of resentment on her face as she strove to resist her body's powerful pull on her being.

Just then, there was a howl ahead of him in the distance.

They had been found.

The horde of dark beasts streaked toward them to reach the girl before her soul slipped back into the safety of its temporal home.

Mahatiel steeled himself as dark things launched themselves in his direction in a burst of dark energy. Draped in black cowls, all but one surged in his direction. The remaining one stood pointing at him, his eyes like red coals glowing eerily beneath the cowl's hood. The long, bony, skeleton-like finger, green with ethereal fungus, stabbed accusingly in their direction.

Mahatiel glanced down at the woman he was assigned to protect. Her absorption was nowhere near complete. He had to stave them off until all was done.

Stubborn girl—she reminded him so much of Kathleen. But she would not end up like Kathleen, by the Son of the living God! He would see to that!

His face turned grim and his eyes a terrifying luminescent green. Furious at their intrusion yet again into the affairs of God and man, he drew his weapon and stood firm to face his enemies.

They surged at him like a swarm of malevolent cockroaches. Chittering away in their own language, they suddenly encircled him and prepared to attack. They were drawn by the smell of death, like a pack of great white sharks drawn by the scent of blood in the water. They came to feed and were furious that this lone angel dared stand in their way.

They eyed him resentfully. They were obviously stunned to see him here.

What could He want with this one? What could God want with such a person that He would have a guardian angel of this order assigned to protect her? This did not bode well. This did not bode well at all.

The information was quickly relayed back to their group leader. He in turn sent one of their number to inform their higher order. This was valuable intelligence, and a ruler would need to be informed immediately.

They knew the reputation of this breed of angel. There was something quite different about this particular one, however. He wore the specialized armor of a guardian angel; the spread wings carved intricately on the front of his breastplate betrayed that.

But . . . but, his sword was that of an Ariye—a Lion of God, a higher rank of war angel, dispatched by the Holy One Himself to execute final judgment against the enemies of God. So what was he doing here, dressed as a guardian angel?

These angels were known to be incredibly fierce fighters. Thus, no one of their group wanted to be the first to rush in and attack. No, they had best wait for reinforcements.

The scent would draw more—and it did. They came from everywhere with anticipation and eager for a feast. They growled like wild animals, resentful that this lone creature of courage stood in their way. They grew more resentful by the minute. Their growing numbers bolstered their courage, and they began to press closer.

Mahatiel noted that one of their number flew back swiftly in the direction that they had come. To report his presence, no doubt, Mahatiel thought to himself.

Then, a particular group arrived. He watched these very closely. They were Kra-Duul, Dung Eaters—the lowest form of demon spirit. The Holy One had alluded to them once in His Word and warned Israel of their existence when He said, "They eat up the sin of my people, and they set their heart on their iniquity." They were sin eaters.

Nothing had changed; the same was still true today. These were the bottom-feeders, which fed on sin and the spirits of the dead vehemently. They were so repugnant in character that even other demons despised them. They were extremely dangerous and not particularly bright, which made them all the more menacing. While other ranks of demons would pause for fear and weigh their chance for success, this class of spirit was populated by the original fools who would dare rush in.

Mahatiel found his perimeter shrinking rapidly on all sides. His sword sang a strange song as he began to weave an intricate pattern with its tip in the air and to pray softly in an angelic tongue, his personal battle language. He prayed for strength and guidance. Opposite him, intensely ferocious appetites guided his growing hordes of enemies. Appetites unrestrained by conscience or anything else, they reeked of excess. He knew them well.

They had one goal—to kill with expediency.

One desire—to savor the fear and torment of their victims.

One mind—no mercy, ever.

One thought—to please their leader.

They lived to kill, to destroy an unaligned soul's very essence, and to intern the rebellious and cognizant remains in torment, forever.

He watched as they conversed briefly in guttural tones. Mahatiel recognized the speech as pure Hellian. They resorted to this language when they wished to communicate in secret.

Mahatiel steeled himself for the onslaught he knew must come. They would not steal this ward, by heaven! Not while he was alive.

Aye. He'd give his life if necessary to protect this woman—and her unborn child.

"It's been longer than fifteen minutes since the last heartbeat. I'm sorry, Doctor. I'm afraid she's gone," said Mildred Hartley sadly. The redheaded RN had observed a lot of people expire in the ER over her twenty-one years of nursing, but for some reason that she couldn't quite explain, this one disturbed her more than most.

Dr. Hardison tossed the two paddles bitterly to the side and said tersely, "Note the time of death as 8:30 p.m."

He hated this part of his job. He took it personally, as if it were a contest between him and death to see who would claim the most—he in the name of St. Michael's and medicine; or death in the name of grief, pain, and suffering.

Bahh . . . He needed a drink after this one. For some reason he felt particularly bad. As if—as if she were *supposed* to live. But, they all were, weren't they . . . ?

Hmph. Enough, for now. He had his own "dance" to attend. He left the ER in disgust, heading for a doctor's appointment of his own. "Seeya, Jeff," he said over his shoulder to his young friend. "Tough loss," he added by way of consolation. But he made sure to avoid all eyes as he plodded from the room, head down. His mind was already troubled by the fog of other things.

Will Jefferies stood in momentary shock. Everyone in the room could feel it, but few wanted to speak for fear of sounding foolish. But . . . she was supposed to live! She was just not supposed to die! Why she, more than Mrs. Ellison yesterday or Mr. Klein last night, no one could say or put into words. It just was not supposed to end this way!

But who could stop it? Who could close the chapter on this woman's life in a way other than it had ended?

Who? Jefferies thought to himself. Who? Them?! The medical profession? Ha! What a laugh. Impotent gods they had turned out to be. They couldn't even cure the common cold, much less stop death head-on, when it was determined to snatch someone away from this earth as it obviously had this young woman. They were powerless, and for a moment, as never before, he felt as if death himself walked into the room, grabbed him by the throat, and told him face-to-face that he was utterly useless, that in this never-ending battle, he was doomed to lose, again and again. Sure, they saved a few lives—for what? Only to have them die anyway a few years later!

Like Mrs. Gibson, who'd had a successful liver transplant after a massive search for a suitable donor, but who died of a surprising and particularly virulent form of lung cancer less than a year later!

Or the Jefferson boy, a drive-by victim they had pulled back from the brink of death itself, who overdosed one week after leaving the hospital. What was the use?

He felt frustration boiling inside of him as he looked at the woman's lifeless body. Attendants and nurses began cleaning up as others flowed from the room deflated, in silent procession, their demeanor a quiet testimony to the tenacity and efficiency of death. He watched silently as Mildred drew the blood-spattered sheet over the woman's head. He slowly took the chart handed him for his signature and final comments.

"You did everything you could," whispered Carolyn, touching his arm for a moment, as if the touch might offer some consolation that words could not. But for the young doctor, this was his second failure in twenty-four hours. He stared straight ahead, teeth clenched. Her words fell on deaf ears . . .

He couldn't take this much longer. His second patient in twenty-four hours, and the fifth one this week. Some were already starting to call him Dr. Death, in secret.

He had come back to D.C. to make a difference—back to his city, his people, his old neighborhood, to help change things, he'd hoped, for the better. His mentor and father figure, Sam, had encouraged him to. But what good had it done? He'd been back six years now and was more frustrated than ever.

Sure, Sam and he had been good friends ever since his years in medical school. In fact, Sam had been his favorite teacher. He'd followed his advice faithfully down through the years, but . . . he felt that even Sam had failed him today. The man whose confidence had been unshakable, shook today. He was human after all. He'd seen Sam do medical miracles before, but . . . as much as he looked up to Sam as a medical god, there was definitely no indication of any spark of divinity today.

He turned and started from the hospital room. He remembered Mildred's prayer earlier.

Hmph. Where was a real God when you needed one?

A powerful spirit named Bellinus, holding the rank of Oppressor, arrived. He immediately ordered something tersely in Hellian speech, and five demons broke like angry bats to Mahatiel's right. This was a decoy maneuver to draw the angel from the woman's body, one of many in their arsenal.

Five more moved like swift darts to wedge themselves between Mahatiel and Virginia as Mahatiel turned to faced the first group and defend his right flank. The rest continued to surround the two, to prevent any escape and to prepare for what should be a worthwhile kill and feast.

Mahatiel, familiar with their tactics, would not budge nor leave his charge.

This was a battle that had gone on for eons. It had not begun with the creation of man—it had simply intensified. The stakes were much higher now; lives were in the balance.

After years beyond number and battles beyond count, their initial assault plan was well-known to him. Only their superior numbers gave him pause for concern.

He remembered an incident from Africa many years ago

when he had been assigned to protect a native missionary there. As his charge slept, he had stood guard over the man. He watched with fascination as, in the distance, a daring battle developed between a young lion, which stood over his charge that night—a wounded lioness—and the ravenous pack of hyenas that had surrounded them.

Hyenas, he noted, would attack and eat anything, even beasts they feared, if their numbers were great enough. Cowards alone, they were ruthless and relentless killers when their bravado was bolstered by the presence of other ravenous members of their pack.

He had admired the young lion's courage. The beast had fought all night keeping the jackals at bay, only to find in the morning that his female companion had succumbed to her wounds. And he, valiant but completely exhausted, collapsed. He succumbed perhaps as much from grief as from fatigue, and was rewarded for his gallantry by being instantly devoured.

He knew now how that brave animal must have felt on that chilly African night, surrounded and outnumbered. A single soul, against so many . . .

He recalled a conversation he had had with Uriel several days earlier when he had been given this particular assignment. Help had been offered him, and he had refused it.

"Mahatiel," his commander had said to him, "this has come from the hand of Michael himself. He requested *you* for this assignment. A second chance . . . yes?"

He searched the eyes of his commander and friend, then nodded affirmatively. "A second chance, yes. I won't fail again," Mahatiel said firmly.

Uriel put a comforting hand on his friend's shoulder. "All the mistakes of the past are forgotten," he said quietly and for Mahatiel's ears only.

"Not all," said Mahatiel, looking down as his jaw tightened.

"It is said that you were specifically requested by the Holy One for this," Uriel said in whispered tones, hoping to encourage his friend. He moved closer, then continued. "Michael was *told* to assign you. In addition, I know for a fact that he offered no objections to the Master's choice. It was felt that you deserved a second chance. You are harder on yourself, my friend, than anyone else has ever been. Also, I and Raphael are available and will help—"

"No—no help," Mahatiel had interrupted. "I must do this myself."

His friend's grip had tightened on his shoulder, but the look of sympathy and concern never left Uriel's golden eyes. Mahatiel dropped his eyes in embarrassment as he said, "I'm sorry, sir. I did not mean to be so abrupt, but this is something I must do—alone." He looked into his friend's eyes again.

"I understand. Mahatiel Ben El, your determination is your greatest asset. But your stubbornness is your greatest point of vulnerability. If you need us, Mahatiel, Raphael and I stand ready to assist you." He then clapped his friend on the shoulder and pointed a scolding finger in his face and said, "And if you ever call me 'sir' again, I will chase you across the heavens!" He chuckled and continued, "You taught me everything I know, my friend, and I told you that I hold this position only until all is well with you again. I feel that this assignment will be the thing that will make all things right for you once more."

Uriel stopped suddenly and listened. His face went pale, and he spoke urgently to his friend and mentor. "You must leave quickly. Paltiel is already down, and the girl is at the point of death. Her name is Virginia Sills. You know as much as I do at this point, but I'm informed that you will be told more later.

"Slean—the Striker—leads their attack. There are currently fifteen in number surrounding her—five controlling the rapist, a man named Pitt. The other ten are attacking Paltiel himself to keep him at bay. Yoel will accompany you for the initial assault and recovery of the girl." He held up his hand as Mahatiel's mouth opened in protest. "Orders," he said matter-of-factly, assuming his full authority once more. "After that, I promise you, you will be on your own. Yoel will return. The Lord says that there are also two lessons that you need to learn during your time on earth, lessons that He has been trying to teach you for a long while. You will learn them during this time. But enough for now—you'll learn more about that later. Here, take your sword and hurry. Godspeed, my old friend."

They had embraced, and Mahatiel turned and ran swiftly from his old command room with its plush royal blue and gold trimmings and diamond-encrusted windows.

He raced down the rich and plush corridors of heaven to the parapet that led to earth. He immediately leaped from it into the realm of space with a grace and style like that of an Olympic diver, scoring a perfect ten. There was a slight ripple in the sea of time as Mahatiel entered the atmosphere of earth.

Thus had begun one battle, but here he faced another. And in this one, unlike the other, he had exactly what he had wished for—he was entirely alone.

The celestial blade hummed in the hand of Mahatiel, as if the sword were eager for battle and hastened to dispense a taste of divine justice.

All it took was one—one dark thing more adventurous and foolish than the rest. Daegal, Dweller by the Dark Stream, was such a one.

In a flash, celestial weapon met demonic flesh, and there was a yowl of pain from Daegal, the first dark thing foolish enough to rush the gold-skinned angel. A dark and withered hand lay severed, a deadly testimony to the accuracy of the weapon and the skill of its user.

First, they scattered, then darted at him like a horde of angry cockroaches.

Mahatiel's thrusts and parries were like lightning. There were sparks as the weapon bit deeply into the curved khukri-like blades of the dark hosts.

Ting!! Ting!! Tang!! Ting!!!

Heavenly steel bit into and clanged its defiance against Hellian iron as the weapons rang out in frenzied testimony to the fervor and rage of the battle. Sparks from the weapons showed in a kaleidoscopic and deadly wonder.

This was not going quickly enough, thought Bellinus, the newly arrived dark thing that held the rank of Oppressor, one of a sadistic class of higher-level spirits that all the lower ones feared.

They could smell the scent of death, as appealing to them as ever any fine steak was to humans, but the scent was growing fainter and fainter as her soul eased slowly inside her body at the chest. He knew once the head was submerged, the prey would become conscious again, and there was no telling how long it would be before they'd have another chance like this, where she was so close to death.

Unless . . . unless . . . she committed *suicide.* He smiled evilly at the thought. *Hmmm, a good backup plan should something go wrong here now.*

Or they could arrange for her to meet with some unfortunate accident. He frowned. That was always pleasant, too, but that could take days, months, or even years to arrange and implement! No, now was their opportunity to strike, and they must seize it.

Bellinus watched as his hordes ebbed and flowed like a

vengeful sea around the two. They flowed forward at a perceived opening, then fell back at the razor cuts of Mahatiel's sunlike sword with its liquid three-foot arcs. Here it parried a thrust; there it shattered a blade. *Ta-clang!*

As one of the chief ruling dark lords, and regarded as one of the most elite of those who stalk the earth for souls, it had been many years since Bellinus himself had joined in active battle. He had become better known for his evil genius for the past many years than his strength.

But he had missed the taste of blood in battle. He missed it desperately. His own weapon literally ached and throbbed at his side to get into the fray. It had indeed been a long time since it had tasted the bittersweet wine of blood, a Hellian delicacy.

"Perhaps you are right, my venomous friend," he said idly to the blade, as if talking to an old friend, and yet stroking it gently in its scabbard as if it were a most dear and sensuous lover. "We should show our minions how a real son of darkness deals with an intruder into our affairs and domain. Come, let's wet your tongue in angelic blood.

"Broga!" he shouted, as a creature of huge proportions and twice the bulk of Mahatiel lumbered to his side. The head was massive, with jaws that unhinged like a python's and enabled it to swallow its prey whole. Long, hairy, apelike arms nearly drug the ground, and filthy nails, like the claws of a wolverine, glistened from constant licking. Like shredders, they were used frequently to rake the captured souls of men, the taste of their fear and misery tangible and delicious.

"Yessss, master," Broga the Terror hissed, snakelike. His bloodred serpentine tongue flicked between his steel-like incisors.

"Broga, I have a mission for you."

The large, pupil-less, murky yellow eyes of the creature showed no interest.

"Would you like to know what it is?"

"Yessss . . ." The creature wheezed, as if exhausted from having to move about its huge bulk, but his eyes still revealed no interest or expression.

Bellinus pointed to the angelic maelstrom in the distance hacking away at his troops and said, "I wish you to destroy that creature. You may have whatever remains of it when you finish."

For the first time, emotion registered within the depths of the empty eyes. A deep grunt like that of a rhino in heat escaped the creature's lips, and bloodlust shot fire through its veins.

"Broga, I wish you to rake from that creature the same agony and terror you have raked from the hearts and souls of men. But can you imagine how sweet it would be to rake such from the heart of a lone angel, eh?" he said cooingly, watching the towering beast's yellow eyes glow with growing hunger and bloodlust.

Broga grunted again, louder, then looked briefly at his master for assurance, like a child with a long-held wish that had finally come true. Bellinus smiled lasciviously and nodded his affirmation.

Broga stared at the whirling angel, like a pedophile eyeing his first victim. Delighted, he looked at Bellinus yet again, a dog glancing at his master for final approval. They could both clearly hear the sounds of battle as Broga darted an intense and hungry look at Mahatiel in dizzying pleasure and disbelief, much like a crack addict does the pipe.

He began to drool. The spittle fell slowly from his open mouth like clear syrup. It ran lazily down his black cloak and dripped to the ground.

"Go, join the fray—you have my permission," said Bellinus. "Capture him; kill him. Cannibalize him. I don't care. Or you may send him back so broken-winged and bloodstained that even his Creator will be unable to mend him! Either way, go!"

In one awesome motion and with stunning speed, the man-beast turned and pounded his way toward the huge knot of warring creatures, like a starving animal to a feeding frenzy.

Bellinus smiled sadistically.

Stupid beast.

Ruled entirely by his appetite, Broga was too stupid to see that he was being used. While the man-beast attacked from the front and distracted the angel, Bellinus himself would attack from behind.

Broga hammered his way through his comrades like a rogue elephant. They parted like the Red Sea before Moses as he tossed and heaved his way through them to get to his prize. Twice their size, none dared say anything as he brutalized a wide path through them, though many cast resentful glances his way. All knew his reputation for savagery, even with their own, and none dared say a word in protest. In brutal fashion, he forged his way through his evil companions right into the thick of the battle.

As Mahatiel turned to blunt an attack from his right flank, Broga charged right up to the surprised angel, grabbed him by the throat, and lifted him high into the air.

Bellinus, in the meantime, circumvented the preoccupied group, and unseen, began running up behind Mahatiel like a madman. His padded boots ran on air as easily as a child's on freshly cut grass, and just as silently. His teeth were bared in a tight deathlike grin, the kind of maniacal grin one sees on a bleached skull. His dark parchment-colored skin enhanced his evil grin all the more. His cape and cowl were flowing in the ethereal breeze of the spiritual realm like a living thing. He was as silent as a bat on the wing at midnight . . .

He leapt like a panther high into the air, intending to fall like an arrow from hell, blade first, from a great height into Mahatiel's exposed back.

He vaulted over his own companions who watched him in admiring wonder, silently cheering him on with their guttural growls of assent. His leap was high into the air, well above the engaged angel's peripheral vision.

"Char taack cha cuul!" whispered a dark thing in pure Hellian speech and great delight, as his leader fell toward the angel unawares. "Death has wings!"

Meanwhile, they had all but overlooked the girl. This maddening angel had severely injured so many of their number that now he became their main focus and the object of their venom, their hate.

Virginia Sills couldn't believe her eyes. Wha . . . what were those things? They were so, so ugly, so inhuman. In her horror, she shivered all over, and since she was nearly completely absorbed and reunited with her body, the shiver was translated there.

Back in the hospital, Carolyn was charged with wheeling the body down to the morgue.

"Oh, look!" gasped the young nurse wide-eyed as she saw the body tremble. "She moved! She—she's alive!"

"That's impossible," protested another nurse.

A shriek pierced the air of the ER—chilling in its intensity, terrifying in its volume, gripping in its strength.

It came from Virginia Sills.

Virginia watched stunned as Mahatiel, this massive being, placed himself between her and the charging minions of darkness. They look like misshapen shadows, she thought to herself.

Suddenly, en masse, they charged. They were stumbling over themselves and leaping upon the bodies of the fallen to get at this whirling guardian and ultimately—her! She shivered as she watched them beyond the silvery arcs of Mahatiel's warring blade. They charged, slashed, stabbed, and hacked at the brave creature with murderous intensity.

But he, the angel, was compelling to watch! He was fighting for his life and hers, but he seemed . . . indignant somehow, not frightened, though heavily outnumbered. More of these things were arriving by the minute, drawn by the sounds of combat. He parried, slashed, dodged, and cut furiously, much as a man would fight off a horde of vicious wolves or animals. He reminded her of some ancient gladiator in a Roman arena.

There were hideous creatures of every sort and size and shape. She had seen such things in her nightmares as a child! She would imagine seeing these creatures under her bed and in the closet at night after Mommy and Daddy had tucked her in. She had had no idea they were real!

Suddenly a venomous man-beast, as tall as Mahatiel himself but twice his sizable bulk, burst through the crowd, thrusting aside his own, and leaped upon the angel. The beast's robe parted briefly, and Virginia could see a dark coat of sharpened, spiked armor underneath. It roared its triumph and defiance, then opened unhinged jaws.

Gripping Mahatiel by the neck with imposing strength, it lifted the angel off his feet. The wide-open mouth revealed rows upon rows of serrated teeth. They lined not only its jaws, but its huge throat as well! He made as if to consume and swallow the angel, much as a man would dangle a piece of meat above his own mouth before devouring it.

"My name is Broga the Terror, and you are not enough to share, Weak One of heaven! I shall have you all to myself! The master says so!" He laughed like one demented, like an evil child preparing to rip the wings from a fly.

Mahatiel, his face a grimace of frustration, anger, and pain, looked down at him. He was impassive for a moment; then his brow knit together, and his entire face twisted into a mask of indignant rage. His eyes exploded into an angry white, then jade. And Virginia knew, somehow deep within, that a line had been crossed, and massive though he was, she knew the man-beast was in trouble.

The angel's voice started out quietly from deep within, like a rolling thunderstorm gathering strength, then rose to a deafening peal that threatened to burst her eardrums! "There is but one **Master.** And I am a servant of His. But you—you **dare** touch a servant of **the living God!**"

Each word rose higher in volume and strength and syllable than the last, until the very atmosphere rang with his indignation! He stabbed at a snarling attacker to his right, even as his left hand shot out and grabbed the throat of the huge monster, and with a tremendous battle cry of rage—he crushed it.

She saw fear in the beast's eyes in that moment, stark terror in the luminous yellow eyes of one who had terrified so many. She heard the neck *snap,* a gut-wrenching sound, from a twist of Mahatiel's powerful wrist. The huge ogre fell to the ground with a tremendous thud, his eyes bulging. He clawed at his throat, gasping repeatedly as his head rolled uselessly to one side. It hung at a bizarre and obscene angle as Mahatiel shouted with cold intensity, "Back to hell, where you belong, and leave the innocent alone! This is kingdom business, and no business of yours!"

Mahatiel briefly remembered the old days and fought back the rampant rage within him. He had not felt this way since the days before he become a guardian angel. *This* was the way it had been! He felt the fire of battle raging within him again but strove to keep it under taut control. It must not get away from him again. That one time it did had cost him too much. It had cost him everything . . .

But one thing still held true: Those who showed no mercy received none.

Disheartened briefly, the surrounding horde paused for the space of a heartbeat. Then, immediately they surged forward again over Broga's body in renewed fury—relentless.

It suddenly dawned on Virginia that this person, this angel that moments ago she had been berating, was risking his very life against these—these dark things—to protect *her.*

She had seen enough. She stopped resisting then, and her soul began to slip back into her body as easily as a slim foot into its favorite shoe.

Her heart went out to Mahatiel. Was this what had gone on when she was being . . . raped? Had her angel been under attack then too? If so, why? Was there something she could have done? What had he meant when he said, "We tried to warn you this morning, but you wouldn't listen"? And where was God in all of this? And—

"Enough questions, Virginia!" said the battling angel, turning to look briefly at her.

Ting! Ting! Clangg! He blocked two blades and cut through a third. There was a frustrated yelp and screech of pain as a creature fell back with two stumps now for arms.

Mahatiel turned again quickly to Virginia to urge her on. "All the way in, now! We'll discuss it later—" The brief second he turned was all the time Bellinus needed.

"Nooo!" she screamed as Bellinus fell, like cursed lightning with fluttering black-and-red robes from nowhere, blade first. "Look out!" She screamed too late and shrieked in panic as if she herself had been stabbed, as the cold blade sank deep into the back of its target. She struggled to reach him, to help fend the dark things off as they surrounded the wounded warrior, smelling blood, as a shimmering substance oozed gracefully from the wound.

"Nooo!" she screamed again and reached out to him, wanting to pull away the venomous beasts from her angel, but instead she awoke to find herself clutching Dr. William Jefferies by the collar, in a grip that terrified him. He stared at her in unbelief and struggled vainly against her iron grip.

She had been dead for more than twenty minutes!

Bob Little stood outside the door to the ER, ogling the pretty nurses that walked by as he answered the blue-suited detective's questions as best he could. "Yeah," said the youthful ambulance driver, while his eyes rocked and swayed with the hips of a red-haired nurse who rushed past him into the ER with an IV bottle in hand. *Not bad,* he thought. *A little old for my tastes, but she sure keeps herself in great shape.*

"Hey," said the impatient detective. "I'm over here," he remarked pointedly. He still had another crime scene to get to after this, and he didn't have time to waste.

"Sorry," purred the driver with an apologetic smile. "But not bad, huh?" jerking his head in the direction of the fleeing nurse.

"Yeah. Great. Now, tell me what you saw again when you got there."

Little tugged nervously again at the ring in his left ear and took off his cap and scratched his blond crew cut. "Well, like I said, when Mike and I pulled up—he's in the bathroom now, should be back in a minute—we saw a fire in the alley behind this pile of trash. And then, there she was—in a pool of blood and out cold. We thought she was dead at first. And ya know, it was really odd . . ."

"What was odd?" asked the salt-and-pepper-haired black detective, his sizable middle-aged gut pushing against his belt buckle in formal protest. It rumbled in anger like a California thunderstorm. He rubbed and patted it absentmindedly. Something had warned him about that last chili dog. Now he wished he'd listened. *Better get some Pepto on the way home tonight. Hmph. Late tonight, too, by the look of it.*

"Well, there was no one else around for blocks. The perp appeared to have been long gone. At least that's what the first officers on the scene told us. It's just a miracle we found her alive. For one, because as many times as the perp stabbed her, by rights, she should be dead. Plus, with all of that flammable material nearby, it could've combusted. Naw, I don't recall offhand the officers' names, but it's in my report. She was in such bad shape we just rushed her here.

"What they told us was that they spotted a fire while on routine patrol. Over there, where the *Evening Star* newspaper used to be. You know, where they used to keep all of their newsprint before they went out of business? So there are still huge amounts of trash, old newspapers and rolls of newsprint paper, rags, chemicals, etc. The homeless use it from time to time too. She was kind of surrounded by this stuff, with this small fire burning at her feet.

"Nothing else was burning, though there was plenty to burn. Funny, 'cause where she was, we couldn't see her at first. She was in this kind of enclave back off of the main alley. You know, behind the warehouse? Nobody's been back up in there for years 'n years. Nothing but a fire hazard. Fire chief says he's going to investigate and bring charges against the property owners for allowing the conditions to get so hazardous. The Hazardous Disposal Unit has already started carting away some of the chemical waste and flammable liquids that were found there. Anyway, it's a real miracle that the fire didn't touch off a major blaze or something. Thank God it didn't, 'cause if it had, the whole block would've gone up. But the two officers on patrol said that if it hadn't been for the fire, nobody would've ever found her, as far back up in the alley as she was. You think the rapist dragged her up in there and set the fire, intending to burn her up or something sick like that?"

"That still has to be determined, but it's a thought, and it's under investigation."

"Man," said Bob, his face twisting into a mask of disgust. "That's *really* sick. Bad enough to rape, but to do that would really take a sicko."

"World's full of 'em, kid. I see 'em every day."

"Yeah," said Bob in deep thought, "I bet you do."

Detective Trumball continued his questioning. "So what's this again about lightning—is that how the fire got started?"

"Well, that's what two of your officers surmised," Bob answered. "Either that or the attacker did it. Apparently there was a sudden thunderstorm in the neighborhood or something. And not too long after that, they noticed the smoke. Didn't really rain in the area tho', just a lot of thunder and lightning. You should really ask *them*. They would know more about that. Any other details other than her condition, when we picked her up, etc., we couldn't help you with. I'm just telling you what they told me."

"Well, right now I need to ask *you* because they got snatched to work a hostage situation on New York Avenue. So, do me a favor—tell me what they told you they found, and then I'll catch up to them later," said Detective Trumball without looking up from his pad. He hated being distracted and preferred to concentrate on one thing at a time. So he always wrote without so much as a glance at the speaker until he was completely through with his questioning. He liked doing his interviews this way, one thing at a time, neat and orderly.

He chewed rather than smoked the stogie in his mouth. He preferred to talk around the cigar. His breath and crumpled suit reeked of onions, sweat, and quiet frustration at a twenty-case workload. *Gotta quit smokin' these things,* he thought to himself.

"Well, they said that from a block away they saw what looked like a lightning strike behind the warehouse and went to investigate, and that's where they found the girl, raped and unconscious. Then, they called it in, and dispatch called us."

Detective Bill Trumball stopped writing and looked up. He reached up and took the wet stogie out of his mouth. His stale breath wafted an incredulous question to the young man's ears and nostrils. Trumball's bloodshot and watery brown eyes held the young fidgeting driver in their grasp for a long moment. "Are you trying to tell me that they told you this lightning strike just happened to hit in this particular alley, on this particular night, and turns the corner in this alley? Then, it strikes a piece of trash, lights it like, uh, some kind of a beacon or somethin' so this lady can be found?" remarked the heavyset detective. He punctuated each syllable with a stubby, stogie-holding finger to the chest of the young driver.

"Whoa, hey, don't bust my chops, man," Bob said, raising his hands in mock surrender. "I'm on your side. I didn't say anything about all that. In fact, all I'm saying is what the officers told me. I'm not inferring anything or whatever. I'm just doing what you requested—repeat to you what they told us when we hit the scene, all right?"

"We'll see about that," the detective said matter-of-factly.

Trumball pumped the soggy stogie back into his mouth and resumed the position. "All right—that's all for now," he said, still writing as he abruptly turned on his heels and headed out to his car. He had to get out of the Sex Crimes Unit. He was getting sick of this stuff. They had as much chance of finding this perp as a man on the moon. He hoped his transfer to Homicide came in soon. At least there the victims were out of their misery. Rape victims, on the other hand, had to live with theirs—forever. "If I have any other questions, I'll be getting back to ya," he said around the piece of smoldering wet mush in his mouth.

"Gee whiz, what a piece of work," Little said under his breath as he watched the detective climb into the banged-up blue cruiser outside, flip the lights on, and screech away.

D.C.'s finest.

What the heck was Lew doing, taking an all-night dump? Geez! They had to go. With all the crap going down in this city tonight, it's just a wonder that they hadn't gotten another call already! But he knew for sure it wouldn't be long until they did.

He stepped to his left to the Coke machine, punched it in just the right spot, and out popped a Coke. He threw a smile at a candy striper as she walked by.

She threw a smile back, asking, "How did you do that?"

Maybe it wouldn't be such a bad night after all. His smile broadened. Let Lew take as *lonnng* as he wanted.

"Well, you must be new here, if you don't know how to do *that.* Everybody knows that trick," he said, putting on his most disarming grin. *In fact, I hope Lew has diarrhea,* he said to himself as he offered the Coke to the cute dark-haired wonder. Her smile deepened, and so did the cutest pair of dimples he'd ever seen. He popped the top on the soda in a gesture of pure chivalry designed to impress. "Here, take mine; I'll just get another one." With that he extended his hand with the Coke.

When it hit him, he spilled the soda down the front of her sparkling starched-white uniform. He was horrified, and so was she.

Like a living thing, the sound crawled up his back, gripping and shaking him. Even as he apologized profusely to the startled young nurse, like a magnet it drew him—no, pulled him—through the ER doors and into the room beyond.

"It" was a scream. "It" was a terrifying screech unlike anything he'd ever heard before in his life. It was beyond the shrieks he'd heard from people pulled from burning cars, or even the agonized cries of the crushed and dying. It was bloodcurdling. Startling. Frightening. Horrifying. Even as he ran and threw himself through the doors toward the source of the sound, he knew in his heart that it came from the woman they'd brought in that night. The rape victim, Virginia Sills . . .

He arrived at a melee. Nurses stood shocked and stunned; doctors poured in past him to pull at the steel-like fingers and flailing limbs of his victim.

The powerful, scraped, and bleeding fingers held in their grip the collar of a struggling and frightened-looking Will Jefferies while that unnerving and nerve-racking shriek shattered and silenced the normal pain and suffering of the bustling ER and its other patients. It put to shame all other noises and sounds of suffering. It screamed a name—"Mahatielll! Nooo! I Must go to him and help him! Let me go! Mahatiellll!"—as they struggled to get her under control and back down on the bed. Limp and broken straps spoke of their own impotence in the face of such desperation and fury.

Bob leaped into the fray with the knot of doctors and nurses who flowed in from all over the hospital, drawn, like him, by the powerful force of the primal, gut-wrenching cry: "They're killing my *ANGEL!* Let—me—go!"

Doctors, nurses, and equipment were sent flying everywhere—until they attacked en masse.

Unbelievable! he thought. *When we brought her in here, she was near death! What kinda shot did they give her?*

The serpentlike point of the blade penetrated Mahatiel's back with a searing pain that made him scream. Entering at the wing root, it lodged right between the shoulder blades, slithering in until it hit bone. It burned and smoked as it entered, searing skin and muscle horribly.

Mahatiel involuntarily drew a deep breath as he felt the dark blade attempt to suck the life force from him. It felt as if fire was being raked from his very bones. It was the most painful and debilitating experience he'd ever had in his existence. "Arrgghh!" He pitched forward and caught himself on one hand before he fell face-first to the ground. He turned then, stabbing fiercely upward in a surprising stroke that caused his secret assailant to leap backwards several feet, sword at the ready. Then, their eyes met.

"You!" said Bellinus in complete surprise. "It's you," he said again; then a dark and arrogant grin began to spread across his shadowed face, and he began to laugh. It was a deep, evil, chilling laugh, with an uncharacteristic high-pitched titter at the end.

Mahatiel momentarily forgot his pain. He forgot the surroundings and the imminent danger. He forgot everything but the one that stood before him. "So it's *you* again," he said through gritted teeth and jade green eyes, using his sword to steady himself.

Bellinus continued to laugh, a slow and surly laugh.

"By the power of God, I tell thee," said the enraged angel, pointing his sword at his nemesis, "things shall be different this time. Much different," Mahatiel said with feeling and a certain fierceness of heart and eye that made the encroaching circle of dark minions hesitate for a moment.

From whence did the master know this one? Had they met in battle before? Obviously he remembered their meeting well.

And so did the angel, though obviously not with the same fondness.

Bellinus' head lowered like that of a hooded cobra preparing to strike, his eyes fixed on his bleeding enemy. Around him his minions began to snarl ferociously, edging closer to the crippled angel with every second, waiting only for the slightest hint of approval from their master to tear this being apart.

Bellinus couldn't help gloating over this most choice moment and prolonging it. "How's Kathleen?" he said mockingly. "But oh, that's right. You wouldn't know . . ." He paused for effect as he slowly circled the wounded creature, being careful to stay out of range of his sword. "She committed suicide under your watch. A fine piece of work, even if I do say so myself," Bellinus chuckled.

He smiled, and a substance like stale saliva dripped slowly from his mouth over his chin. His incisors, like wet steak knives, showed themselves, glistening.

There was a jostling of wings as laughter echoed around the ever-widening ring of several hundred creatures as they joined in their master's mirth.

"What a tasty morsel she's been these many years." He laughed openly. "She still screams your name. Ha ha ha ha ha hee hee hee! Wishing she had listened to you. And in the next breath she curses you in the vilest of ways. I love it when they don't listen, then wake up in hell with their sad, pitiful little faces and say, 'Oh, you mean it was true? There is a hell—you mean they were right?' Ha ha ha ha ha ha hee hee hee! Fool! She wouldn't listen to you on earth, but suddenly wishes she could listen to you now. Ha ha ha ha ha he hee heee!"

Mahatiel hated that laugh. Had hated it over the centuries —a deep, sadistic belly laugh followed by a high-pitched titter at the end. It was a laugh that seemed more suited to a mischievous little girl than for a malicious evil spirit.

The air grew dark and malevolent as Bellinus continued to savor the misfortune of his vanquished foe.

Soon dark things had gathered as far as the eye could see. Bellinus, always the showman, took the time to humiliate his foe even further. "Should I tell them all how long we've been friends, Mahatiel?" he said, turning and letting his eyes sweep the crowd. Broga's body had been drug away long ago, still twitching, by Dung Eaters eager to relieve him of his armor and his ethereal flesh. His vanquished spirit was immediately translated to the dreaded Abyss . . .

"I am no friend of yours, you foul servant of death!"

"Please, no need to be so formal," Bellinus chided.

Suddenly a large and dark shadow swooped down and hovered over the gathering, a shadow so large it covered the entire group of unclean things. Bellinus looked up, startled for a moment.

It was a ruling spirit of Dominion, one of his superiors, one of those the apostle Paul had called the **rulers of the darkness** of this world. He was a **watcher** who constantly patrolled the realm of darkness to keep Satan himself informed of all activities and progress that had been made. A voice, deep and unnerving, that sounded as if it came from the darkest cavern of hell said, "**What do yeee?**" The voice was slow and rumbling, like an echo of distant thunder.

Bellinus bowed to one knee and answered, "We have captured a guardian angel for the master's use and entertainment, sire."

"Where iss his charrrge?"

"The girl? She, uh, has returned to her body, sire."

"Foolll! Slean the Striker thinks she may be pregnant by his creature."

"The man thing, Pitt?"

"Yess."

"Is that not good, master? Her life, reputation, and if all goes well, her mind will be ruined? Another example of some of our finest work?"

"Fool! If it were that simple, do you think that he would be here?

Bellinus turned and looked at the wounded angel who hadn't moved. Archas was right. Bellinus had let his personal pleasure and pride get in the way. There were bigger things afoot this night. His personal pleasure would have to wait.

"There is too much activity in the heavens over thiss one woman and her child that does not bode well for ussssss. If the Holy One is interested in thiss woman, there are reasonss that bode ill for our cause. The master has bid me, and I hereby bid you. Find the woman; kill her and the unborn one. We must kill this plan of theirs before it even beginsss."

"And this thing?" he said, nodding toward Mahatiel.

"Extract what information it has regarding the woman and the Holy One's plans for her. Then, dispose of it. Do not play with it. Do not amuse yourself with it. Extract what we need, and destroy it. They are too dangerousss."

"Yes, sire."

The monstrous creature flew away on massive black wings, but not before a final warning: **"Damnation awaits those who fail . . ."**

Mahatiel had sat quietly during their discourse, gathering strength, secretly listening and formulating his plan. Now, as Bellinus turned to face him once again, he was prepared to implement it.

"Well, it appears that you have information, my friend, that must be extracted from you as painfully as possible, I'm afraid," Bellinus said with a huge smile, meaning every word. But as he leaned forward to taunt the wounded warrior, he moved unwittingly within striking distance.

"Enough!" Furious, Mahatiel leaped up and struck! The blow struck Bellinus near the shoulder, penetrating the leader's body armor. Bellinus howled in excruciating pain.

Numerous curved swords like scimitars and half-moons struck for Mahatiel's body. He cringed briefly—and then disappeared in a sudden flash of light.

"He's gone!" uttered a minor dark thing incredulously. "Quickly, we must search and find him. Find him immediately! He must not escape!" he said, leading a surge of dark things like a band of evil locusts forward.

"Wait!" said a vast voice that seemed to shake everything around them. The sea of creatures parted to reveal chisel-featured Bellinus, calmly tasting the foul-smelling blood that oozed from his wounded arm. His coal black eyes bored into those of his cohort. "Don't pursue him. Let him come to us. Go to the girl, and watch her carefully, for he will come for her."

"Even severely wounded, my lord Bellinus?" He forgot for a moment that there were creatures for which self-preservation was not the first order of things.

Bellinus cut him a glance that withered him. "Move to earth," the leader ordered his horde. "Wound for wound, strike for strike, and I will have my vengeance upon the golden one, but not at the cost of our mission."

Like swarms of flies rising in dark clouds from a carcass, they moved to the passageway to earth. . . .

Virginia was in complete panic. Where was she? And what had happened to her angel? Was he all right? She must get to him! She must help him! Must get back! She screamed his name again.

A bevy of gawking doctors, nurses, attendants, and others had come running. Some stood staring at her in stark disbelief. Then, like a sudden wave, they all moved forward to restrain her.

She fought, scratched, bit, and screamed that she had to get back to help her angel. But of course, they didn't believe her. They pinned her to the bed.

Still she fought them for the right to go and rescue Mahatiel. Her only thoughts before the sedative took full effect were that she regretted not believing him at the very first, for doubting him, not listening to him.

Her limbs became tree trunks then, and she could no longer lift them to fight. Her eyelids became too heavy to keep open. She cried silently the hot tears of frustration and helplessness, the tears of a little girl.

The tears pulled her back to the time in childhood when she had watched her best friend get killed by an automobile that had careened out of control. She was denied the chance to save her by an adult's restraining hand, a hand as concerned about her safety as she had been about the friend she watched die.

She cried those same bitter, heart-wrenching tears once more. She was kept, once again, from saving the life of a friend.

But this time she must succeed, and she would not be denied.

She seemed supernatural in strength and determination at that point, until the group of struggling doctors and nurses punctuated their efforts with a second dose of powerful and swift-acting sedative.

"They're killing my angel," she protested in sleepy despair. "And you," she mumbled to Will, "won't . . . won't let me go . . . help . . . himmmm," her voice trailed off into the dull, gray world of chemical unconsciousness. Tears, like water in a glass too full, brimmed again at the corners of her eyes, then flooded down her flushed and swollen cheeks.

"My God! She was like a madwoman!" blurted out an exhausted Bob Little who had been standing outside the ER, then rushed in to assist. "Haven't seen anyone this strong since that guy we found strung out on crack last month. Whew!" he exclaimed, collapsing briefly into a nearby chair.

Jefferies removed a clawlike hand of Virginia Sills from his now wrinkled, ripped, and torn shirt. "Thanks for the help, Bob," he said in a raspy whisper, rubbing his throat.

"We thought she was dead."

"She *was* dead," interjected Carolyn as she noticed several scratches on the young doctor's neck. "Come here; let me have a look at that."

"It's nothing," he protested weakly. "We'd better start cleaning up this stuff," he said, indicating the overturned equipment, chairs, tables, and scattered supplies.

Just then Bob Little's beeper went off, and the ambulance attendant checked the code number showing on the tiny alphanumeric pager. "Oh-oh, gotta roll, Doc; got another one. So you guys gonna be okay here with her?" he queried, adjusting his askew cap.

"Yeah, sure," came the weak but unanimous reply.

He landed in a brief but blinding flash of blue light. His skin was tingling from the searing sensation. He shuddered uncontrollably for a moment. It had been over two millennia since he had appeared on earth in human form. The last time had been at the tomb, when he, along with Paltiel, had spoken to the woman from Magdala who came looking for the body of the Lord Jesus Christ.

The last time had been at God's command. This time had been a matter of survival.

His skin crawled. The earth itself was much different than what he remembered. It had changed so drastically in such an incredibly short time. Someone privy to his thoughts might have believed he was speaking of earth's modern devices and extraordinary technological advances, but he wasn't.

He had been a guardian angel for centuries now and knew about the development of these devices well before the inventors did. These were trinkets compared to the things he had seen and experienced in the kingdom.

The kingdom of heaven was advanced beyond anything man's mind could imagine, conceive, or comprehend. Travel was at the speed of thought, faster even than the speed of light.

It had the most precious metals, such as gold, so refined and pure that they were rendered translucent. Such a process on earth would cause a stock market crash and financial revolution the likes of which the world had never known. There were metals, gems, and elements so priceless and rare that no man on earth since Adam had seen them, and some had never been seen by human eyes at all.

Gold itself was a metal so common in the kingdom that, after refining, it was used as an ordinary building material, or for mere pavement, much like asphalt and concrete are used on earth today. Pearls so large that two-hundred-foot-tall gates were carved from their precious substance. Diamonds were as common as pebbles on the shoreline or sand on the beach.

For the few precious gems and metals that God had sprinkled just beneath the earth's surface, men through the centuries had fought and died. The opulence that was commonplace in heaven would give every billionaire on earth a heart attack.

Some of these processes God had deemed to send to earth. But regrettably, the ideas, along with the bearers, had been killed off long before their time and many times over.

To help man along, these ideas were planted before birth in the hearts and minds of those who would grow up to become earth's most brilliant inventors, scientists, doctors, humanitarians, and scholars. There were ideas for cures and inventions, remedies for overpopulation and drug abuse—ideas that could end poverty and much human suffering.

That is, had they lived long enough to share them. The answers that man was seeking for himself and his planet were being sent to earth daily, wrapped up in the hearts, minds, and spirits of the unborn.

He shuddered.

How many Louis Pasteurs, Albert Einsteins, Thomas Edisons, George Washington Carvers, Frederick Douglasses, Martin Luther King Jrs., Sojourner Truths, Mahatma Ghandis, and the like—gifts to mankind—had been silenced by the millions before they could ever see the light of day . . .

The very atmosphere of the planet reeked with agony and suffering.

Sadly, a mother's womb had now become the most dangerous place to be on earth . . .

No, it was not the technology he considered amazing, but it was the depravity that mankind had allowed itself to be driven to by the very ones who sought its destruction.

Dark things.

Depravity and apathy hung in the air about him like a thick mist. Dark things had been furiously at work over the centuries to make the atmosphere around earth more hospitable and palatable to their tastes.

In the past, he had more than once battled his way right up to the gates of hell itself, and he noted now that the feel of the earth's atmosphere reminded him very much of what it was like being near those evil portals—too much.

He began to survey his surroundings.

He was crouched in the corner of a restroom. From the sound of tinkling glasses and plates, he gathered that he was in a restaurant somewhere. Getting here, though not difficult, was taxing.

He reached over his shoulder and ran a finger down the long bloody gash between his shoulder blades. He winced and concluded that pain here, in this realm, was considerably more intense than in his own.

How did humans stand it?

He looked at his hand and rubbed the blood between his strong fingers. In the earthly existence, the human body was created by God to rapidly regenerate itself. So his hasty retreat to earth to appear in human form was a strategic move on his part to escape his encroaching enemies, locate Virginia, and allow his body time to heal. He still stubbornly refused to call for help, even though this physical existence held its own inherent dangers for him, as he well knew.

In addition, wounded as he was, he could not phaze back now anyway. He'd have to wait until he was fully recovered, and then he'd be able to phaze and receive his powers back. Phazing was an angel's way of moving quickly between the spiritual realm and the natural realm, earth. One was allowed use of it very sparingly, for in the past, an angel's phazing chanced upon by a human had been the start of many a false religion and idol worship. Except for extraordinary strength and an intimate knowledge of both prayer and his nemesis, he was as helpless and as vulnerable now as any human.

He had no wings. He had no sword. He had no armour.

In addition, he had no ability to travel from one location to another instantaneously.

No, now he had to walk or catch a bus like everyone else without a car. That struck him as incredibly ironic. He would also have to rely on the God who had created him to assist and see him through.

His senses were reeling. He'd almost forgotten what an extraordinarily sensory planet this was. Sights, sounds, smells, touch, feelings . . .

He'd have to watch the feelings.

Now he would have a chance to see what it was like living as a twenty-first-century human.

He sensed danger. He knew dark things would be searching for him everywhere. Bellinus and those of lower rank would continually seek to invade the bodies and minds of unaware humans in order to use them to do their dirty work.

They constantly sought to cultivate such human chalices and vessels for just such usage. They usually picked their subjects carefully: those with just the right belief system, or rather lack of one. They were unaligned, having no allegiance to God or His Son. These choice individuals were then subjected to constant stress and pressure: financial, political, medical, emotional, psychological, physical, and spiritual. The spiritual pressure was the capstone; all other pressure was designed to force itself ultimately upon the spirit of the individual.

They were aware that man's spirit was created by God to turn inward and upward under moments of extreme stress.

Inward, because man's spirit, the core of his inner being, the heart of his very nature, was designed to be a place of individual residence for the Most High. As one man had said, "There is a God-shaped vacuum on the inside of every human being."

Under times of great pressure, the soul turned inward to the spirit, seeking comfort, wisdom, answers, and love. Then the spirit of the man or woman reached upward to touch the heart of God Himself. Dark things, however, worked diligently to convince man that other things could fill such a vacuum.

Consequently, many humans, when pressured so severely, turned inward, and finding nothing there, turned outward—not upward. They sought to make other things, objects or even other people, such as their gods, their primary sources of comfort, love, support, and answers. And there, with open arms and ravenous appetites, stood dark things by the millions, waiting to enter in . . .

He rose to his full height of seven feet. He looked around him and caught sight of his face in the small, chest-high mirror.

He was brown skinned, African American, well built, every muscle perfectly toned. He should blend in well, unnoticed by the populace.

Just then the restroom door opened, and in strode a woman of huge bulk, sweating profusely. She spied him and screamed.

Well, maybe not entirely unnoticed.

Matilda Gray's eyes were locked onto the small compact mirror, fixing her makeup as she entered the ladies' room. It was a moment before she felt someone else's presence in the well-lit room. She looked up to see a huge, not unattractive, well-built black man looking at her.

And he was completely naked.

"Rape! Help! Rape! Help!"

She walloped him with her pocketbook—a formidable weapon, filled as it was with four pieces of cheesecake she was taking home for later.

He rushed past her, embarrassed and chagrined for forgetting that in this realm they were extremely body conscious, and in addition, here one had to clothe oneself. In the spiritual realm, one never had to consider such things, for one was always clothed from within, simply by using one's will.

He raced down a hallway and suddenly burst into a room full of dinner guests who all froze in disbelief at the sight of him.

In the far corner of the Four Seasons Restaurant, a dark thing, invisible to the humans, squatted on a table whispering dark words and thoughts into the mind of a bejeweled woman of about sixty as she contemplated the murder of her wealthy invalid husband. Subtle but suggestive evil thoughts, like dark gray smoke, passed from the demon's mouth into her mind and stayed there—revealing that she was pondering the suggestion seriously.

Across from her sat her young lover, his mind already filled to the brim with the same gray ideas. He sat urging her to give in to the evil suggestions. "We can do this, baby," he said, taking her hand and stroking it seductively. "Trust me; I wouldn't steer you wrong."

Mahatiel stood confused for a moment, looking for a way out. He garnished stares, glares of outrage, guffaws, and one outright look of admiration.

The demon, hearing the commotion and feeling a strange presence, snapped his head in the angel's direction.

His dark eyes grew wide as he saw the angel and instantly knew who he was, even though he was in human form. And it was that particular revelation that caused him even greater concern. A lower-ranking spirit of little to no power, he nonetheless rose to his full three-foot height and from the table pointed a crooked finger in his direction and screeched a warning clarion that could be heard by his compatriots for miles.

Suddenly, other dark things, previously hidden from view, rose from all over the restaurant and added their voices to the fray and confusion. Dozens of demon fingers, like crooked knives, pointed accusingly in his direction and like radar followed him as he raced toward the nearest door.

On his way out, a patron sitting at a table near the door shouted at him, "Hey man! Here! Catch!" and tossed him a raincoat, which he hurriedly snatched on as he ran out into the damp night air. He waved his thanks as the young man's date smiled and kissed him on the cheek for being so chivalrous.

Ten minutes later, the young man cursed loudly.

"What's wrong?" his date asked.

"I forgot—my wallet was in that coat! See that? No good deed goes unpunished," said the exasperated young man wryly.

"What happened here?" Summoned by a page, which now no one remembered placing, Sam Hardison stood in the doorway aghast, staring, as they placed new IVs into the arms of a heavily sedated Virginia Sills. His heart leaped, and a long brown finger pointed at her sleeping form in protest. "That woman was legally dead! What's going on here? Will someone please answer me? Will, what's going on here?"

William Jefferies, though visibly shaken, helped the startled nurses cover the unconscious woman with taut sheets, using some to tie down and secure her arms and legs.

"I—I don't know, Sam," said Jefferies, now beside his mentor, his eyes never leaving the sleeping woman. "Uh, one—one minute she was dead, then the next she was alive and screaming something about her needing to save her angel and grabbing my collar like this," he said, demonstrating on Sam's shirt collar suddenly.

"Okay, okay," said the older man, gasping, "I get the picture. You needn't be so demonstrative, Will." He rubbed his own throat now.

"Oh—sorry, Sam, but it was the most frightening thing I'd ever seen in my life! One minute I'm signing off on her chart and standing over the body, and the next minute she's screaming at me and choking the life out of me! We had to give her two doses of—"

"Well, you just made an error in your pronouncement, that's all. Obviously she wasn't dead. It can happen to anyone—"

Will was incredulous.

"Sam! You know very well I didn't make a mispronouncement in diagnosis! In fact, I wasn't the one who told the nurse to put down 8:30 as the time of death! You did! And the record reflects that, Sam. You and I both know she was dead a solid twenty minutes!"

Will was furious that Sam would say such a thing, to try to blame him for a wrong pronouncement. It could literally destroy his career, open him up to lawsuits, and at the very least drive his insurance rates higher than what they were now!

He eyed Sam suspiciously. His discerning eye for the first time picked up something in Sam's face that he had not noticed before. Or then again, perhaps he had. It was a strange look that he at first had assumed was the result of the shock that they all had felt at the astonishing—dare he think it?—

resurrection of this girl, but now he saw that it was something more.

To try and shift blame was not something that Samuel Hardison, the most prominent doctor in his field, was inclined to do. It didn't fit in with his well-known and exemplary character. Now, however, this outstanding scholar, the most respected cardiologist in the country, had a decidedly worried look on his face, a look that Will sensed had nothing to do with the shocking events that they had all witnessed tonight.

"Sam—what's wrong? This isn't like you. We're not only colleagues, but friends. Something's wrong, and it's got nothing to do with this. What is it?" He watched as all the color drained from Sam's face and the older man began to apologize.

Will grabbed his friend by the shoulders to steady him as the others in the room busied themselves with the sedated young woman and prepared to assign her to a room.

Only Mildred Hartley saw and watched with interest from Virginia's bedside the unusual interaction between the two men.

"I—I'm sorry, Will. I . . . I guess I just forgot for a moment that I . . . You're right, Will. I was the one who made the pronouncement that she was dead. Not you." Sam began to rub his forehead as if trying to rub away a sudden massive migraine, but it was in actuality some decidedly troublesome thoughts. He swayed slightly.

This was too much, just too much to bear alone. He had to tell someone —but whom could he trust? Will?

He looked into his young friend's eyes and searched out the concern he saw there. Yes, it was genuine. Even as a child Sam could always tell the sincerity of those around him by simply looking deeply into their eyes.

Sam suddenly fell back against a postered wall for a brief moment of respite as if the wall could support not only his weight, but the tremendous burden of his heart as well.

Deep concern like a bird on the wing swept over Will's face. He turned to call a nurse for assistance as he watched Sam collapse against the Healthy Heart poster on the wall behind him.

"No, Will—don't. I'll be okay. I'm—I'm fine. Just a little dizzy for a moment, that's all. Give me a minute, and I'll be fine. Help me to that chair."

Will pulled the worn but sturdy bare metal green chair nearer for his mentor, who settled his sturdy frame into it with a powerful grunt and sigh. The next three words that came out of the mouth of Samuel Hardison almost made Will collapse just as suddenly as his friend.

"I'm dying, Will . . ." Sam confessed in a defeated whisper. "Advanced, inoperable cancer. Next week this time, it could very well be me up on that thing," he said, gesturing with a nod toward the bloodstained gurney that had wheeled in Virginia Sills.

The words were a small nuclear device in Will's chest that exploded with an intensity that almost suffocated him. It was several long moments before he could breathe again.

No—it wasn't possible!

Slowly in stunned silence, he knelt beside the man who had been a professor to him in college, a mentor to him in medicine, and a father figure to him in life.

"*No*, Sam!" His voice was a tense, fierce whisper. He was angered, hurt, and horribly shaken by the gut-wrenching confession.

"Shhhh. There's nothing to be done."

"But there must be! Are they sure? It can't be, Sam! Why didn't you tell me?" He gripped his friend's hand so tightly that it almost hurt, so tightly that the grip alone must hold his friend here.

"Shhhh . . . Will, no one else knows, and I want to keep it that way."

"But there must be some mistake, Sam." Tears now brimmed the edges of Will's eyes.

Sam patted Will's hand sympathetically. "No, Will. No mistake. The extended leave I've taken over the past few weeks has been to see the best specialists in the country. Batteries of tests have all confirmed the same thing. I have maybe days or, at most, weeks to live."

Will's mind was a tornado of thoughts. Had he just won one soul back from death only to turn around and lose another? And that one, his best friend? No! It wasn't fair!! It was like some weird trade-off. No! Let the girl die then, but give him the life of his friend—a man who had saved the lives of hundreds, thousands!

What kind of sick twist of fate was this? Will closed his eyes as if to gather his composure. It didn't work, and instead he wept bitterly.

Nearly everyone was gone now. Even as Sam and Will spoke, nurses were wheeling Virginia out of the ER to her own room on the fifth floor.

Mildred lingered a few extra moments until she was noticed by Sam, who gave her a look that pleaded for privacy. She read it well and left.

The only permanent white nurse in an all-black hospital, she sometimes felt like an outsider, an interloper into a private world of sadness and heartache. But the thing that kept her at St. Michael's was the fact that she felt genuinely needed here. Not like Capitol Hill General, where she'd felt like the proverbial fifth wheel.

At age forty-two, still single, no children, and no living relatives, she needed to feel a valuable part of someone's life.

The people here—doctors, patients, and nurses—were her family. St. Michael's wasn't much, but it was all she had.

No one else had dared say anything, counting the interaction between the two physicians as too personal to disturb. Besides, they thought, the hospital grapevine being what it was, they'd know all about it within a few days anyway.

Will was terribly shaken and wept openly, his head lying on Sam's hand as Mildred reverently closed the door, feeling as if the grand struggle between life and death that had transpired in the room today had somehow made it sacred.

"It's not fair, Sam!"

Sam rubbed away the tears from Will's upturned face. The young man had become like a son to him over the years, replacing the one he'd lost in a car accident.

"It's not fair!" he said again fiercely.

"Son, life's not fair," responded the older man by way of consolation.

But Will would have none of it. He rose to his feet. He paced back and forth; anger was like a caged tiger within him. He muttered distressing words, talking as much to himself as to Sam in a low and increasingly disturbing tone.

"And here we were fighting to save this woman's life, a woman I don't even know, while my friend—my best friend, a man who's been like a father to me, who is standing right next to me, helping me—is dying of cancer! It's not fair!" He shouted bitterly at the heavens and hammered a metal table full of medical instruments so hard that it bent under the impact, launching scalpels, sutures, forceps, and tongue depressors into the air like angry missiles.

Sam leaped to his feet. "William Jefferies! Control yourself!"

Will collapsed to the floor like a puppet whose strings had suddenly been cut. Weeping, he held his right hand at the wrist. When his friend knelt beside him and hugged him, he laid his head on the older man's chest like a little child and wept great heart-wrenching sobs.

"It's not fair—it's not fair—it's not fair! All that time we spent working on her we—we should've been working on a cure, a cure for you! What am I going to do without you! What am I going to do without you, Sam?"

"Shhh, Will, don't talk such foolishness. You're a doctor," he said, rocking the young man back and forth slowly in his arms like a small child. "It's your duty to save lives. Mine, you cannot save, but hers . . . I was very very proud of you today, son. You made me very proud indeed," Sam said, his own eyes filling with the tears he'd managed to fight back until now.

"It doesn't mean a thing anymore . . . Besides, we both know I had nothing to do with saving her life," came the hollow reply.

"It does mean something, son. You don't mean that. You—"

"No! I mean it. Without you, it doesn't mean a thing anymore," came the reply with a frightening intensity and bitterness.

A titanic struggle seemed to go on within the younger man. Abruptly, Will became intensely animated. It was as if his puppet strings had suddenly been snatched up by another puppeteer.

"I did it all for you," said Will with furrowed forehead and reddened eyes above an accusing finger. "I wanted to be just like you. I wanted you to see me. I wanted to make you proud of me. All to honor you. You were like a god to me! Your approval meant life. Your disapproval was like dying a little each time.

"I was never one of the best students in class, but I always made sure I was the hardest working, to make you proud of me. Always staying late, working hard for your approval. And now, for what?" The last words hissed out of the young man's mouth like the flickering tongue of a venomous snake.

"Will!"

"All the people you've helped and saved over the years, all the lives you've saved over the years, for what?"

"Will!"

"For nothing. All for nothing."

The deep bitterness in Will's voice disturbed him—no, more than that, frightened him.

"Will, get a hold of yourself. I've never heard you speak like this before. This isn't like you. You're just overwrought from the day and deeply grieved by what I've shared with you. But Will, you've got to realize that you've got your whole life ahead of you. Son, my life may be over, but yours isn't."

"It might as well be," came the tiny childlike reply.

"Will, what is wrong with you? Get a grip on yourself, young man. You've got a lot of people in this hospital that count on you, Will, including me. So you've got to carry on. Do you hear me?" He shook Will by the shoulders, stood him up, and looked him square in the eye and started to speak. "Will, I want you to promise me—"

He stopped.

Will slowly raised his eyes to Sam's, his head lowered still, but looking for all the world like a hooded cobra preparing to strike. The fifty-three-year-old doctor felt a shiver go up his spine.

As Will's eyes looked at him, Sam saw a dark and irate despair in them—swollen, bloodred, hate-filled eyes that frankly scared him and made him concerned for the younger doctor's health—and his sanity. Perhaps he shouldn't have told him after all.

"Will?"

"What . . ."

"Are—are you all right? I'm—I'm sorry; maybe I shouldn't have told you. I know that you have a tremendous amount of pressure on you already, but, I felt you should know. I knew you would grieve, son, but I didn't know you would take it this hard. I'm sorry, I—"

His eyes searched the soft brown face for the compassion, solace, and tenderness that had always been there. It was gone—all gone. In its place now was a decided hardness, a severity in the reddened eyes that disturbed him. He took a step back, visibly shaken.

They didn't even look like Will's eyes anymore.

"Will . . . ? Will, maybe you need to talk to Dr. Stanley. I'm sure, son, he can help you put all this into perspective. I've had to talk to him myself over the past few days, and I must admit I feel much better about—"

"I don't need to talk to any psychiatrist," came the husky and disdainful reply. A dark thought, like rancid oil, slowly seeped into Will's mind, gradually filling it, crowding out all logic, all compassion, and all reason, filling it instead with quiet and twisted thoughts.

His work done, the seed planted, Bellinus whispered one last word in Will's ear, and then, smiling, he melted back into the shadows unseen, to watch his handiwork.

"She should've died, not you . . ."

"Why, Will, you talk as if I'm already dead," Sam said with a fainthearted laugh, hoping a bit of levity would pull the young man out of his doldrums. Failing that, he took a sterner tone.

"Will Jefferies, you listen to me. How dare you talk like that about a patient! That's not what I taught you in medical school. Remember your Hippocratic oath! Now, you get a grip on yourself, young man, and go home and get some rest. It's been a long, hard day on all of us. Obviously, you've been under a very heavy strain all day and, from what I hear, over the past several weeks. You have been under an excessive amount of pressure, without a break, much more so than the rest of us. Go home, Will, and get some rest—now. And that's an order."

Bellinus grinned at the older doctor's quiet anxiety over his young friend and proceeded to whisper into Will's mind, "*It's not fair, it's just not fair! She should've died, not him—with all the people he's helped over the years. It's just not fair! There has to be something that can be done.*"

"There just has to be!" Will's lips moved mechanically, like a mannequin's. His mind—in its anguished state—adopted the subtly induced thoughts as his own. His eyes, watery and grief-filled, were glazed and glassy. He returned to his former lethargic, zombie-like state. He mumbled, "I—I've gotta go, Sam. I feel strange. I don't feel well—"

"It's okay. I understand—you've had a full plate today."

Sam suddenly felt horribly guilt ridden. "I'm so sorry I had to tell you this, Will, but you asked, and I thought you should know. I didn't—I didn't want my death to come as a sudden sh—"

"I gotta go," Will interrupted. He pushed past Sam and left the ER. He staggered past the older doctor, through the door, and out into the bustling corridor. Sam watched through the glass doors as the badly shaken young doctor fell up against a wall and clung there for a moment like a sick fly. A business card fell from Will's pocket and floated to the floor like a single cream-colored snowflake.

Will bent over, picked it up, and read it as he leaned against the wall. Felicia had given him the card this morning, before he had left her place for work. Their torrid one-night stand had been sizzling and haunting at the same time.

"Try it," she had said. "I'm sure he can help you. Trust me." Her dark and mysterious green eyes had hinted at further mysteries, but her lips had stopped midword as if not to tell too much. He had completely forgotten he had the card. He read it once again.

"Marcus S. Talbert, Psychic. A Doorway to Your Past, a Gateway to Your Future . . . "

Then, seeming to gain strength, he roughly brushed aside a nurse's helping hand and strode erect and purposeful from the hospital, never to be seen or heard from by the staff again.

A dark and quiet whisper escaped from Sam's trembling lips.

"What have I done . . ."

3

DARK TIMES . . .

SHE FLOATED UP to consciousness slowly, like a bubble in a bottle of viscous liquid. Her eyes opened sluggishly, as if resistant to her will.

The light from the window blinded her, and her lids quickly slammed shut, pulling darkness like a warm blanket around her again. She turned over reflexively to place her back to the stabbing light.

She couldn't move.

Slowly, her eyes—thin slits—opened again and looked down at herself. Starched sheets like white serpents intertwined around her arms and legs and held her fast to the side guards of the bed.

A sharp pain through her back caused her to jerk violently and gasp in quiet agony.

Back at the nurses' station, the monitor beeped dutifully to the day nurse that its patient was active.

"Ethel!" crackled the voice from the nurses' station over the small intercom.

"Yeah!" responded a tight voice from down the hall in room 212.

"Check on 216B when you get a chance. Her monitor is going off."

"Can't you do it? I'm changing Mr. Klarn's bedpan right now!"

"No, I can't, because I'm the only one on the desk."

"Fat, lazy wen—"

"Look who's talking! Just do your job, okay? Don't worry about mine! Now hurry up and go check it out!"

"Sorry, Mr. Klarn. There you are. You okay now? Good. I'll be back later to check on you."

Nurse Mars smoothed the wrinkles from her uniform as she moved quickly down the hall a few doors to the psycho's room. *Oh Lord, forgive me, I shouldn't call the poor girl a psycho,* she thought to herself. The girl had been through a tremendously traumatic experience. Enough to affect anyone mentally, to one degree or another. ,

She put on her best smile and strode into the room.

"Hi there!" she said cheerfully, pulling back the curtain around Virginia's bed. "So, how are we feeling this morning?" noting the girl's look of bewilderment.

"My back—," said Virginia, her voice so hoarse it startled her. It sounded as deep as a man's. It sounded so unlike her own, she hesitated before speaking again.

"Where—where am I?"

"You're fine," Ethel said, beaming, keeping up her happy persona. "You're in St. Michael's, and your back is just sore because you haven't been able to move around for a while, that's all. Girl!" Ethel continued excitedly, "you were pitchin' a fit for a while! So we just had to restrain you, so you wouldn't hurt yourself. That's all."

She fluffed Virginia's pillow as best she could and got her

a pitcher of fresh water as Virginia looked down again at her bounds, gently testing them. She asked drowsily, "What time is it?"

"Seven o'clock a.m."

"How long have I been here?"

"Six weeks," replied Ethel, cheerfully.

Stunned silence swallowed up the bright sunshine from outside. The big bay window by her bed, which displayed a beautiful view of the Shrine of the Immaculate Conception and the Washington, D.C., skyline, served only as a poor distraction in the face of such alarming news.

Where had time, and her life, gone?

"I . . . I've been here six weeks?"

"Yeah! Not to worry, though. Your folks know where you are and have been here to see you, actually."

"What? How come I don't . . ." Her voiced trailed off.

"Remember any of it? The mind's a funny thing, girl. If it gets under too much strain, it checks out. Stops working and takes a rest for a while. Don't worry. It'll all come back to you shortly."

"Did . . . did my father come?" she asked timidly.

"Yes, girl, sure. Was here every night for the first three weeks. Momma too. In fact, she's still here, in a motel nearby, but Daddy had to get back to Baltimore."

The portly, dark-haired nurse adjusted the curtains so that Virginia could have a better view of the Shrine and the D.C. skyline. A brief summer shower had left everything looking fresh and shining. Pools of clear water sparkled like little blue mirrors everywhere, reflecting the open and cloudless sky. Too bad the construction on the first floor of the far wing and the dumpster spoiled the otherwise perfect view. Piles of sand and bags of concrete mix were everywhere on the ground below.

"I'm surprised he showed up at all," said Virginia in a dry

whisper. "May I have some water please, and can't we take these off now?" indicating the serpentine bed sheets restraining her.

Ethel looked unsure for a moment as she poured the glass of water, her face a cute, chubby puzzle. "Well, I don't know . . . ."

"Please, they're hurting my wrists. I won't try anything; I'm too weak as it is," she said, her eyes pleading as earnestly as her voice.

"Well, really I'm not authorized to untie you," said the tenderhearted nurse as she tugged at the knots, carefully avoiding the IV tubes flowing into Virginia's arms. "Because, girl, you was talking crazy," she continued, all the while explaining why she should not be doing what she steadily was.

Virginia didn't hear a word she said. Like a kid at Christmas, she was eagerly watching Ethel untie the myriad of knots, wishing she would hurry up. She felt like a prisoner. So, she completely ignored the woman's every word. Until . . .

". . . and when you was hollering and screaming. Talkin' about 'they killin' my angel.' That's when we really thought you was nuts." She chuckled, then looked Virginia in the eye teasingly, winked, and said, "But me guess you're all right now," with just the hint of a Jamaican accent slipping through. Ethel tried hard to hide it, but whenever she got nervous or excited, she forgot herself and lapsed back into her native accent. Embarrassed, she shone a big gold-toothed grin.

Virginia sat up abruptly to ask a question. Then, feeling a little dizzy, she lay back down, the question unspoken.

Ethel had just untied the last knot when the doctor walked in. She felt more than heard the soft footfalls. Then she caught sight of him out of the corner of her eye and froze—unsure of what to do next. She was caught.

She stood bolt upright, her heart in her throat.

She saw her job going right out the window. She had disobeyed a direct order from Dr. Bondsor. Everyone knew what a stinker he could be. He walked around with a huge chip on his shoulder.

The doctor was from southern India, with an accent as thick as Louisiana gumbo. It took a full ten minutes to understand anything he said. However, he was on the hospital's board of directors and had plenty of clout, enough to get her friend Mavis fired when he overheard her making fun of his accent in the nurses' lounge, though he pretended it was for other reasons.

Oh, no, she'd blown it now. She had better try to explain.

"Me sorry, Doctar Bondsorr, but she said dees' tings' be hurr'tin' her limbs," she rattled on, losing all semblance of unaccented English.

But it was when she finally gathered enough courage to turn and face him that she found it wasn't who she thought.

"Waate. Waate a minut. Yu're not Dr. Bondsorr. Yu're not supposed to be in n'ere. Dis is a private room. You haf to go— Waait . . . I know you!" Though he wore a brimmed hat pulled down low over his eyes, a surgical mask that covered most of his face, and a scraggly beard, she knew.

It was the eyes . . .

Virginia sat up in bed in an effort to see the doctor that puzzled the nurse so. But he stood just out of sight behind the curtain at the edge of her bed. Suddenly, she felt an inexplicable uneasiness emanating from this unseen presence behind the curtain.

Something within told her she needed to run—to remove her IVs and run.

She hesitated. Why? And what if the nurse and the doctor saw her remove them?

But the inner voice, the inner something would not leave her alone.

Virginia had just decided to obey the insistent nudging when she looked up at Nurse Mars—and screamed.

Abruptly, from behind the curtain, appeared a surgically gloved hand holding a hypodermic needle like a lethal weapon.

She screamed again and watched in horror as the air-filled hypodermic plunged into the stunned nurse's jugular vein like the deadly fang of a hungry cobra. The vicious impact of the stroke shook Ethel's whole body and caught her completely by surprise.

A latex-gloved thumb quickly flattened the plunger, pumping the fatal air bubble deep into the vein, distending it horribly. The left hand fastened tightly around her throat kept the woman from screaming and ensured that she would not twist away from the powerful impact.

The gloved hands then cruelly shoved Ethel Mars backwards over a chair into the far corner of the room to meet death on her own, the needle still deeply imbedded in her neck. With one last horrible gurgling sound, the spirit of life within her struggled to be free . . .

Virginia, paralyzed with fear, screamed at the top of her lungs. Then she panicked, and as she jerked the IVs from her arms, two brief geysers of blood sprayed across the surrealistic scene, tie-dyeing sheets and splattering the floor.

She forced her limbs, stiff from weeks of inactivity, to move. They responded like two lead weights.

The gloved hands then reached for Virginia Sills as she, screaming, swung her limp feet from the bed, slipped in her own blood, and tumbled helplessly to the floor with a loud smack, with nowhere to run.

In the hall outside, a rising tide of curious voices could

be heard along with a distant pounding sound, persistent in its rhythm and increasing in its volume.

The single nurse on duty put in a hurried call to security, just as something rushed past her so swiftly that reports and sheets of paper were wrenched from her desk in the awesome swirl of its wake.

Virginia screamed repeatedly, her only weapon, as the masked attacker dropped his full weight and knee on her chest, knocking the wind out of her and pinning her to the floor. He quickly pulled another hypodermic from his trench coat and prepared to make her his second victim of the morning.

Just then the door to room 216 exploded off of its hinges as if hit by a mad elephant. The huge wooden door flew across the room and sunk a foot deep into the far wall, grazing the silent killer and narrowly missing the flaccid body of Ethel Mars.

Virginia watched in shock as through the shattered doorway charged a giant of a man wearing a London Fog raincoat. This black man leaped through the air and caught the upraised gloved hand plunging toward her as she lay helpless with numbed legs on the cold hospital floor.

His face twisted in anger and covered with sweat, the killer struggled with her rescuer. Several buttons popped off of the killer's trench coat from the force of the struggle and ricocheted like bullets off the wall. Two more dangled from his coat tenuously.

Her rescuer lifted the man off her chest by his wrist alone. She heard it snap with a dull crunch and then watched as he flung the murderer aside like a rag doll.

He then bent down quickly to see to her. He was the biggest man she'd ever seen. She shrank from him, terrified. His faced warmed into a compassionate stare as he bent to pick her up, and for a moment she could've sworn that his eyes changed color! And, within that instant, he somehow seemed familiar.

She screamed, however, as the deadly hypodermic was plunged into her rescuer's neck from behind.

The surgically masked figure, mysteriously filled with new energy, leaped on her defender's back and drove the plunger home with all the strength of a madman. Choking him with his other arm, the broken wrist seemed to have no effect on the homicidal maniac whatsoever.

The powerful seven-foot giant reached over his shoulder, grabbing for the man's head but instead only managing to rip the hat and mask off the face of Dr. Will Jefferies.

The giant grunted in obvious pain. He purposely fell backward, slamming the insane doctor into the huge bay window, breaking it. The physician's grip loosened, and he fell backwards out of the fifth-floor window.

Now it was he who screamed as he tumbled toward certain death.

The giant distended the muscles in his neck. Flexing them in an amazing display, he forced the needle out. It clattered to the drab hospital floor and shattered into several pieces.

That's—that's not humanly possible! Virginia thought to herself.

The giant extended a powerful hand to her, ignoring the stinging sensation in his neck.

"Virginia, come," he said in a tremendously deep but familiar voice.

"I *know* you!" she shouted excitedly as he snatched her from the floor and quickly used some gauze nearby to bandage her bleeding arms. That done, he snatched her up into his massive arms and fled out the door and down the hall.

Shocked onlookers scattered like pool balls at their approach, then, as they fled past, stared and chattered after them.

Tumbling out of the shattered bay window, Will Jefferies clung tenuously to the one-inch ledge and stared at the giant circular air-conditioning unit five floors beneath him. The huge funnel-like intake looked like a giant metal cavern, yawning and hungering for him. He was dressed in scrubs and a trench coat that billowed and flapped around him in the sudden breeze, like the wings of a great bat.

He glanced furtively about him. Far from being frightened of plummeting to his death from this height, he was angry now, furious at himself for having failed. He growled something unintelligible and spied a communication wire strung between floors, two floors below him.

He released his grip from the ledge and fell toward the thin wire thirty feet below.

"We underestimated them," he said to himself as he fell like a stone dart.

Above him, several security people and one police officer burst into the bloodied hospital room. Quickly surveying the damage, they rushed to the body of Nurse Mars.

Will hit the wire with all the precision and grace of a professional gymnast, though he'd never done anything more athletic in his life than be a water boy in college. One end of the wire snapped under his weight, and he held on tightly as it swung him out over and well beyond the intake unit of the giant air conditioner and above a large battered green dumpster. Sixty feet above the dumpster, he released his grip.

"We must do better next time," he whispered in vicious tones as he fell easily toward his target.

Officer Phil Patterson, his 9mm pistol drawn, approached the shattered and jagged bay window with caution. He looked pensively at the ledge, his weapon and arms extended in front of him like a deadly antenna.

Jefferies, his mind clouded with impotent fury, spread his arms wide to guide his descent.

Officer Patterson looked right, then left, assuring himself that no one was standing on the ledge outside.

Far below, unconsciously, without thought, reflexively, like an animal, Will's muscles tensed for impact. He hit the pile of wet sand behind the dumpster with enough force to stun a rhino, but felt no ill effects in the least. "We will not underestimate them again," he mused angrily. Scanning the area around him with hooded eyes, he quickly turned a corner out of sight, his coat dancing and twisting eerily in the sudden morning breeze like a tortured soul in hell's flames.

High above him, Phil Patterson looked over the ledge of the window of room 216, endeavoring to see what, if anything, had fallen through the huge window. "Nothing out here," he said, looking down and seeing nothing but the intake unit, a dumpster, and piles of construction sand far below. "Must've been broken in the struggle. Call homicide," he said to his partner who'd just arrived.

He holstered his weapon and continued. "Put out an APB on a black man, big guy, about six foot four to seven feet. Traveling with a woman, five six. Possible kidnap victim."

He looked at Ethel's body crumpled in the corner and turned reflective. The duty nurse had said that the scream occurred before this guy raced past her desk.

He caught his partner by the arm.

"Add, 'or possible accomplice.' Suspects wanted for Murder One."

Several blocks away and exhausted, the fugitive pair darted down an alley between two brownstone apartment buildings, then quickly down a short stairwell.

Behind one of the buildings, Mahatiel took the eight stone steps downward in one bound. Virginia, still recovering from six weeks of being comatose, stumbled down the steps after him, landing on the last step with a muffled grunt and thud. Mahatiel quickly checked her bandaged arms. She remarked breathlessly, "I'm not sure which hurts worse—my butt or my legs."

Mahatiel's massive back was toward her as he retrieved some clothes he had secreted earlier behind a loose concrete block. He turned and gave them to her. At her complaint, he knelt and began massaging her atrophied lower limbs. "I am sorry—I realize that must have been rather hard on you, but we had no other choice. I—"

"Hey! *Hey!*" she said, holding the clothes close to her bosom and using the other hand to slap his hands away. "Hey! I don't *know* you. Don't be *feelin'* on my legs like that!"

It had actually felt great, but still . . .

Mahatiel straightened up, bewildered. His massive frame made him look all the more helpless as his powerful brown eyes radiated confusion and innocence.

"I am sorry. I did not mean to offend. I just wanted—"

"That's my problem," she said excitedly as Mahatiel sensed panic slowly beginning to rise within her. "I don't know what you want! I don't know what anybody wants!" Her voice rose another two octaves. She clutched the clothes to her chest as if somehow they were her last hold on reality. "I don't know why that man was trying to kill me! I don't know why he killed that nurse! Stop trying to *shoosh* me!" she screamed as Mahatiel had motioned to her to keep her voice down. Tears gushed from her eyes as the terror of the day began to overwhelm her.

"Shhhh, Virginia, everything will be okay. I am here to help you. I know it has been difficult for you, but—"

"Difficult!" she said at nearly the top of her lung capacity. "You call this *difficult*? I'm nearly *killed* by some maniac with a hypodermic, and all you can say is that things have been difficult? And stop shushin' me!"

Down the street, a D.C. Metropolitan Police car approached at the speed of light. Mahatiel heard it coming and instinctively put his hand over Virginia's mouth to quiet her. This just seemed to infuriate her all the more.

How dare he try to shut her up like some mere child by putting his hand over her mouth!

So, she bit it—hard.

He looked at her with a look of annoyance as the police car, siren off but lights flashing, streaked by. He peered over the stairwell wall in time enough to see the black-wall tires dart by. Virginia tried to peer over the wall too, but he kept her head down.

And in return, she kept her teeth sunk into the palm of his hand. She tasted blood, his blood, strangely sweet and strong. Still, he refused to release her.

The car flashed by the alley, and he breathed a huge sigh. Then he heard a horrendous screech of tires and the ripping clunk of a powerful engine being thrown into reverse.

Screaming tires squealed in protest like stuck pigs, as the powerful cruiser surged back toward the alley's entrance. Mahatiel was already up and running with Virginia in tow, screaming protests of her own. As he raced up the alley, he felt eyes upon him and glanced upward.

In the second-floor window above them, frail, toothless Aggie Heron, hair raised high by the brisk wind that day, sat gnawing a chicken leg already slippery with her saliva. Haggard as death itself, "Crazy Aggie" eyed their flight with more than just a hint of satisfaction. Mahatiel caught a flash in her eyes that for a second reminded him of glowing embers. She grinned as she threw the bone, stripped of meat within seconds, out of the window and watched amused as it clattered mutely to the alley floor, just missing them. From her neck swung a familiar pendant, an upside-down star with a goat's head on it.

The goat of mendes, a symbol of pure satanic worship.

"You didn't really think that you could get away from me that easily, did you, Mahatiel?" said a deep male voice through Crazy Aggie's cracked and ancient lips. She laughed heartily as they raced beneath her window. It was a deep and sadistic belly laugh, with a high-pitched titter at the end . . .

"This is Forty-six! This is Forty-six! I got 'em, Central!" screamed Officer Brown as he slammed the car into reverse, hit the siren, swung the car around, and screeched down the alley after the two fleeing suspects. "The tip was good! I got 'em from Park Street in an alley parallel to Irving, head'n in the direction of Warder Street!"

The emotionless voice of the dispatcher intoned caution from the other side of the two-way radio. "Watch yourself, Forty-six; tip says they're armed to the teeth and dangerous. Take no chances—just pursue and wait for backup. Copy?"

Michael Brown looked at the radio in disgust for a moment. He looked at the fleeting pair. *Hmph, some ex-basketball player and some basket case from the hospital. Hmph! I am Mighty Mike. I don't need any help. Wait for back up? Please! They'll spoil my fun!*

"Central, this is Twenty-one. I'm two blocks away and en route to lend assistance."

"Copy that, Twenty-one."

"Central, this is Eighty-three of 5D; I'm two minutes away and en route."

"Copy that, Eighty-three."

In all, six more cars responded, everyone nearby wanting to get in on the excitement of the hunt. The District of Columbia was divided into seven police districts. Three of those districts converged nearby at North Capital Street and Michigan Avenue, and sometimes the activities of the 3rd, 4th and 5th districts overlapped. It appeared this would be one such day.

Mighty Mike scowled at the radio. Everybody wanted a piece of *his* action, *his* bust. He glanced at the fleeting pair again.

Naw, this was his collar. He flipped a switch on his hand mike. He shouted, then sang, "Bad boys! Bad boys! Whatcha gonna do? Whatcha gonna do when we come for you?" The sleek cruiser's loudspeaker squawked out two quick lines of the song, then shouted for them to drop their weapons. He gunned the engine up to sixty-five miles per hour in the narrow alley until he was right on top of them.

He laughed and got an idea. Time to play a little "chicken."

He gunned the engine until the red, white, and blue police car was right on their heels. He looked around quickly. No one was watching. They'd spent so much time chasing drug dealers up and down these alleys that the residents were jaded and treated the roar of a police engine beneath their windows like the occasional barking dog—nothing to get excited about.

He licked his lips. Nobody watching but that crazy old lady back there who had called in the tip. Yeah, it was time to have a little fun.

Officer Brown skidded to a high-powered stop just behind them with a nerve-grating screech of rubber, then gunned the engine again immediately. He played this nerve-racking cat-and-mouse game several times, then gunned the engine once more as the cross street, with its speeding traffic, rapidly approached.

He gunned the engine one final time, leaning out of the window to holler like a black cowboy herding cattle. He was "herding" them exactly where he wanted them to go. He ran the car right up on their heels and nudged them roughly with the car's hood. Virginia nearly fell under the hungry black tires.

Up ahead, the end of the alley seemed years away as Virginia struggled to keep her aching legs working. Mahatiel's limbs and long legs felt hindered by the tight garments and shoes he wore. He'd gotten the pair of pants and shirt from a street mission he had been staying at for the past several weeks. He still wore the same coat the restaurant patron had thrown him over a month ago. The coat fluttered behind him like a dark cape as they ran for their lives.

The pain in his palm began to aggravate him. The roar of the engine nipping at their heels and bumping them annoyed him. Their antagonist's ranting and raving on the speaker frustrated him.

Nothing had gone right for him this day. If he had only been there moments earlier, he could've saved the nurse's life. "I grow tired of this," he suddenly growled aloud.

"What—?" gasped Virginia as she lost her balance and stumbled in front of the car's churning wheels.

Mahatiel suddenly snatched her roughly up under his arm like a bag of groceries. He turned the corner at the end of the alley as it flowed into Warder Street and leaped like an angry panther over the hood of a swerving police car. It careened around the corner and slammed head-on into Mighty Mike, thus abruptly ending his game of cat and mouse.

As he fully turned the corner, Mahatiel found himself amidst a waiting gaggle of police cars and officers waiting just out of sight. Leaping again, he hurdled over the barricade of cars like an Olympic finalist while Virginia gasped in wonder and pain as her leg muscles cramped uncontrollably.

Officer Tony Dowel of the 3rd District screeched onto Warder Street just in time to see Twenty-one swing left into the alleyway and crash head on into Mighty Mike. Mike had a thing for singing on the "mike" and loudspeaker when running down suspects, hence the nickname. He never really liked the loudmouth antics of his fellow 3rd District officer. He was like the Dennis Rodman of 3D, but he didn't want to see him hurt, either. The guy was so busy singing that he didn't hear Twenty-one from 4D say he was coming around the corner.

"Lord Jesus," Dowel prayed aloud, "I hope none of those guys is seriously hurt." He saw Twenty-one's Tom Handy and Mark Galloway stagger out of their cruiser and then Mighty Mike get out of his, fussing at the two officers and raising Cain.

He smiled. Same ol' Mike. "Thank You, Lord, that they're all okay. Now, Lord, let's catch these two sus—pects . . ." His voice trailed off as he watched the male suspect leap successive cars, including Eighty-three, with a female under his arm like she was a sack of wheat.

Impossible!

They were trying to make it to those deserted buildings across the street. Only he stood in the way. He had to stop them.

Tony Dowel floored the powerful Ford engine. The car lurched forward like a stallion on drugs. He watched the speedometer jump and rocket its way up to 85mph. He nearly lost control of the wheel once, regained it, sped ahead of them, then swung his car hard to the left, blocking their path as other arriving officers blocked off both ends of the street, drew their weapons, and hunkered down behind their cars. His radio squawked a steady staccato of voices.

"I see 'em! Hold your fire. Tony Dowel's in the way!" He slammed on the brakes, threw his vehicle in park, rolled out of the driver's side, hit the ground, and came up in a kneeling position—weapon drawn, ready to fire.

"You! Freeze!" He shouted, but the huge stranger was already upon him. Take the shot, he told himself. Take the shot! He began to squeeze the trigger.

This guy was *big!* The woman seemed so helpless, now slung over his huge shoulder as Dowel watched this man leap over his own cruiser as effortlessly as he had the others.

Then, everything seemed to stop—and then grind forward in slow motion. Every detail before him became crystal clear. It was as if Dowel's entire life had been lived out of focus until this moment, this second, and then someone snapped in the correct lens and his eyes clicked from 50/20 to 20/10!

The assault on his senses stunned him. He blinked his eyes; he couldn't believe it! Every color suddenly became instantly brilliant in its hue. Reds were stunning, blues were astonishing, whites were almost blinding, and blacks were absorbing, pulling him into them. Even the cold metal blue of his gun was fascinating.

He realized suddenly that he not only viewed colors more brilliantly, but he felt them! Reds were warm, blues were tingling, greens were cool, pastels fuzzy and comforting. Browns were rough and edgy; blacks were weightless and light. Grays were coarse, grating. It was astonishing! What was this? Dear God, what was happening to him? *Jesus, help me!*

And his vision! What was happening to his vision? He could see things clearly, even miles away!

He reeled under the sudden sensory assault, but his reflexes, programmed with five years of intense training, still performed on target. The gun barrel of his 9mm Beretta followed the target unerringly and never wavered, not once. He drew a bead on the giant even as he leaped his vehicle.

"Shoot, Dowel, shoot! Shoot!"

"Shoot!"

He could hear the voices of his fellow officers shouting behind him. The gun, like a steel finger, followed the giant through the height of his leap, though Dowel's senses still recoiled under the impact of what was happening. He was acutely aware of everything going on around him.

He heard the shouts of his fellow officers. He then saw Mighty Mike breaking off the argument with Tom and Mark, and now running toward him and drawing his weapon. His sergeant also screamed his name, urging him to fire. He saw the little boy behind him across the street on his red and white ten-year-old Schwinn bike that his mom had bought for him at a thrift store on Saturday. His name was Ronald Hamm; he had a little brother named Raven because his father was such a rabid fan of the Baltimore team.

He was four years old.

How did he know that? *Lord, what's happening to me?*

At that exact moment, at the height of his slow-motion leap, the giant looked at him. Then, two things happened that were forever burned into Tony Dowel's consciousness. He saw the man's eyes—the pupils—flash purple! Then, he smiled!

He's smiling at me! Why? I've got a gun trained on him and he's smiling at me!

He heard the female whimper as she grabbed at her legs. He felt his gun hand lower against his will, but he couldn't resist. Then, the man landed, and just as suddenly as it had begun, everything snapped back to reality.

It was over. It was suddenly gone just as quickly and as inexplicably as it had begun—whatever "it" was, and so were the giant and his companion.

Dowel staggered and grabbed his head and reeled from the rush as the giant scurried through the doorway of an abandoned apartment building and disappeared from sight.

He heard urgent footsteps catching up to him, and six officers brushed past him in hot pursuit as Sergeant Conway Thomas Henderson cursed angrily and said, "How come you didn't take the shot? Come on!" He ran toward the doorway after the others.

Dowel stood for a brief moment, unable to move, almost paralyzed.

"Come on, Dowel!" shouted Henderson over his shoulder. "Move it! They're getting away, thanks to you! We could have taken a shot if you hadn't been in the way!"

Lord, what's wrong with me? thought Dowel as he heard shouts and angry voices. Cops from the other end of the street tried to outflank the pair.

He shook himself into a loose run after his fellow officers. They paused at the door of the complex briefly, then vanished into the same shadows that had swallowed the giant and his whimpering and exhausted accomplice. They combed the abandoned apartment buildings and the empty row houses for hours.

Not a trace of them was found.

Sergeant Henderson was also the watch commander, and he was furious. He stood at the makeshift command post on Warder Street, pounding the hood of his car. "They just couldn't vanish into thin air! Find them!"

"We've looked everywhere, Sarge—twice. They're just not here," said Smiley Roberts. He was the shortest guy on the force, barely regulation, but he made it, and he was the toughest thing in 3D.

Henderson cursed profusely. "Keep looking anyway and bring me Dowel! Where *is* he?"

"Over there, by his cruiser," said an officer nearby.

"Dowel!" yelled Henderson. "C'mere!"

Dowel walked slowly toward his sergeant as his fellow officers cringed for him and discreetly began to melt away—all except for Mighty Mike. He wanted to see and hear every word. He wanted to see Dowel get his just due. He hated the guy—couldn't stand him. Just another crumb-suckin' religious fanatic as far as he was concerned. He couldn't stand that "Jesus this" and :Jesus that" business.

Hmph, well, this . . . this should be good, he thought, smiling coyly, his chocolate face sliding into a malicious grin.

"How come you didn't take that shot like I told you to?" Henderson began. "You see how many man-hours we're havin' to put in here because you were too doggone scared to do your job? What's your problem, Dowel? All you had to do was take that stupid shot and this would've all been over—finished by now!"

"I was afraid of hitting the woman, sir."

"Afraid of hitting the woman?" Henderson rolled his eyes.

"Yes, sir. She appeared to be a hostage."

"She *appeared* to be a hostage," Henderson repeated, mockingly. He got nose to nose with Dowel. "That's *not* what Command says!" Henderson shouted in the five-year veteran's face. "Command says she's a suspect! A *suspect!*" the sergeant roared, and tiny flecks of spittle, like repulsive rain, peppered Tony Dowel's face.

Dowel's jawline tightened, and his teeth hurt from being ground so tightly together. *Lord, help me, because I don't know how much more of this guy I can stand. Help me out here,* he prayed silently while he forcefully bottled his silent rage.

Henderson continued. "Now I've got *two* cars down, two officers I had to send to the hospital to get checked out, and *nothin'* to show for it! *Why?* Because *you* can't follow orders. I *told* you to shoot! You disobeyed a direct order!"

"I didn't want to hit the hostage sir," Dowel said again, firmly. It was the first thing that had come to mind, and it was the truth. She did seem to be more the hostage than a willing accomplice. It was obvious to anybody with two eyes and a brain! And good Lord, he dare not tell him about his "experience," or he'd think he was a nut case for sure then, and knowing Henderson, he'd try to have him bounced off the force.

"You say she's a hostage. *Command* says she's a suspect. Who knows best, Dowel? Huh? You or Command?" With that, he abruptly turned on his heels and pounded away, still furious. "Tell you what—we'll let a board of inquiry decide. Consider yourself written up and on suspension until further notice and until such a board can be convened. And no need going to the union; you're a pariah as far as they're concerned," he shouted over his shoulder.

"And Mighty Mike! Wipe that stupid grin off your face. I wanna know why you were so busy screwin' around on your loudspeaker that you didn't hear Twenty-one from 4D say he was comin' in!"

Mighty Mike's face fell like a house of cards as Henderson pulled him in tow and stalked off.

A board of inquiry, Dowel thought to himself. That could mean his badge!

Mahatiel cleared the hood of car twenty-one with plenty of room to spare—effortlessly.

His powerful leg muscles propelled him and his 127-pound passenger with ease. He heard the grinding crunch of metal and glass behind him as car twenty-one swerved around the corner and plowed head-on into Mighty Mike Brown and car forty-six, thus ending abruptly his fifth chorus of "Bad Boys."

Mahatiel landed briefly, took two giant steps, and then had to leap again as car eighty-three careened into his path. He cleared it, slung Virginia over his shoulder like a sack of potatoes, and raced for the abandoned row houses and apartments directly across the street.

Barreling up Warder Street to block his way sped another police cruiser, angled just right to cut him off. Virginia moaned. "Put me down—my legs are killing me," she said as Mahatiel footraced to beat the three-hundred-horsepower engine to a designated spot he had in mind.

"Sorry," he said tersely and sped toward the buildings as he tightened his grip, his jaw set and pupils glaring purple determination.

He projected the azimuth in his mind and knew that if he made it to that point—there, just beyond that manhole cover—that at the police cruiser's present rate of speed he could beat it, though just barely, and dart through the abandoned buildings and disappear.

The darkness of the empty buildings loomed before him like a sanctuary.

Odd, he thought as he ran for his life and Virginia's, he had never, in his millennia upon millennia of existence, ever wished for darkness before.

He sped on. His hopes rose as he saw himself drawing nearer the spot. But Mahatiel was to learn that on earth, hopes can be dashed as easily and as swiftly as they come.

He watched the cruiser jump as if it had been kicked in the rear. He heard the powerful engine growl louder as if in enjoyment as the car sped toward them now at twice the previous rate of speed.

He suddenly realized that he wasn't going to make it! The driver had sped up! He'd have to leap the car to make it or be hit and crushed under its wheels!

As Mahatiel recalculated and then made his amazing leap, the quick-thinking officer had already spun the car toward the pair and was already stopped, armed, set, kneeling, and aiming dead at him.

Mahatiel made his leap high over the hood of the officer's vehicle. He instantly checked his options and knew that he could not let the man fire his weapon and possibly hit Virginia.

Just then, behind the kneeling officer and just off to his right, stood Uriel. He watched through his leap as Uriel touched the man on the crown of his head. Time seemed to slow down as he saw the officer's whole expression change drastically and his every sense became intensely heightened to the point of distraction. But the gun barrel still followed them as if it tracked by military radar.

Suddenly, Uriel touched the man's hand and lowered it as he looked directly into Mahatiel's eyes. "I know that you said you didn't need any help, but I thought that perhaps just this *one* time could not hurt," he said with a twinkle in his eye.

Mahatiel looked at his friend and smiled his thanks. He landed with a heavy thud and raced into the abandoned building, through the filthy, waterlogged basement, up a collapsing staircase, out the back door, down a manhole cover, and into the stench of the D.C. sewage system.

Uriel turned and faced officer Tony Dowel's guardian angel and said, "He is returned once again safely to your charge. See to it that he receives favor at the board of inquiry hearing . . . "

Sunel nodded once respectfully to Uriel and took his place again behind Officer Tony Dowel as the officer shook his head trying to clear it.

Uriel disappeared as silently as he had come in a blinding flash of pure light.

4
DARK MINDS . . .

WHIZZZZZZZZZZZZZZZZZZZZZT.

"Marcellus!"

"Yeah!"

"I'm done."

"You sure?"

"Yeah."

"How many rolls did you shoot?"

"Just finished wrapping up my second one—pulling the film from the camera now."

"Shoot one more."

"Aww, Marcellus, come on! I got another murder over in Southeast I gotta get to! Man, I been up all night shootin' bodies in Northeast. I took two rolls, man; that should be enough. I gotta save some for Steve's homicide. He's called me on my cell phone twice already, want'n to know—"

"Darrell! I couldn't care less! Just do your job and take the doggoned pictures! Tell Steve that I said to call Bruce and to get here pronto."

"Aw, man, you know can't nobody stand to work with Bruce. And besides that, he called off sick again today. I been doin' his job and mine too."

"That's not my problem. Get back to work. I want to catch this guy. Give me another roll. Now. I'll be in inna minute and tell you the angles that I want."

"Marcellus, all you ever think about is what you want. You never think about anybody but yourself, and what you have to do. Other people have lives too. We can't cater to you all the time. You make me sick sometimes; you know that?"

Marcellus Grimes stuck his head around the corner and grinned. "Well, if I make you sick, Darrell, you're in the right place—a hospital. Maybe I can get the doc to take a look at you, huh? And when you gonna do somethin' about that gut, man? That's why you ain't got a woman now. No woman wants a man that looks like you. They want a pretty boy," he said, rubbing his clean-shaven coffee-and-cream complexion, "a real detective who's got it all, like me."

"You get on my darn nerves, man. So you made Detective of the Year. So what? That don't mean I have to be your personal crime scene photographer."

"Shut up, you lil' detective wannabe, and get back to work."

Bill Trumball, Marcellus' partner, winced at the comments. "Man, Marcellus, why do you ride the little guy so much?"

"Aw, 'cause that peon wants to be a detective someday. Failed the test five times. He was meant to be exactly what he is—a nuthin'. Say, listen, I'm gonna run downstairs and get me a coffee. Can you, uh, finish getting these witness statements? I'll be right back."

"Say, Marcellus, get me one too while you're down there, okay?"

"Sure, Bill, no problem. Anything for my partner," Marcellus said with a sly grin and headed for the cafeteria.

Darrell Gibbons fished another roll from his pocket and reloaded the ancient motor-driven 35mm Nikon. He stepped up to the body of Ethel Mars and started shooting again.

Hmph. He wasn't waiting till Marcellus took his own sweet time to saunter into the room and survey it like it was his own private domain. He was gonna shoot this last roll and get the heck outta Dodge. That's what he was gonna do!

He knelt and got another close-up of her neck. A tiny puncture wound cried a stream of bloody tears that had dried up hours ago, the hypo dangling from her neck like a spent dart.

"Hey, Darrell! You done in there yet? 'Cause here comes the meat wagon boys."

"Yeah, yeah, almost, Bill. Just keep 'em in the hallway another minute while I get these last few shots."

"Say, hurry up, would-ja? They say they got another party to go to."

"So do I! I would've been done, if hadn't been for that bucket-headed donkey you call a partner! So don't rush me!"

"You better not let him hear you call him that!" Bill chuckled.

Darrell stepped over the body, avoiding the dried blood here and there. He noticed a green button on the floor under the bed and a matching one in the nurse's hand. *Hmph. Hadn't noticed that before.* He took a close-up of the button in her hand.

"Hey, Bill."

"Yeah."

"Did you see this green button in the victim's right hand?"

"Yeah, of course. We're detectives, Darrell—that's what we do for a livin', remember? We detect."

"Ha, ha, very funny. But did you see the matching one up under the bed, behind the left wheel?"

"Huh? Uh, no. Don't touch it—I'll be right there soon as

I finish this nurse's statement. You finished yet? The morgue boys are gettin' pretty impatient."

Darrell had one shot left and moved to a spot between the bed and the window. He had just stepped over one of Ethel's legs trying to avoid the heavy door protruding from the wall and didn't see a glistening tiny puddle of still-fresh blood. Just as his right foot touched down and he announced, "Yeah, I'm duhhh—!" it shot out from under him like he stepped on a bar of soap, and he fell backwards and down onto Ethel's lifeless body. Without thinking, his reflexes took over, and he reached up and caught hold of the bottom part of the window frame—and unfortunately the jagged piece of glass that jutted up from there like a six-inch razor.

"Ahhh!!"

"Darrell, what are you doin' in there?"

A moment later Bill came in putting away his pocket notebook, followed by the coroner. "Boy, what the—"

"I cut myself on this stupid glass! I slipped in her blood and grabbed the window to steady myself, and I cut my hand. Gimme something to wrap it with, will ya? And—hey, wait a minute. Look!"

Darrell still stood by the window. At this angle he saw something out of the window on the very narrow ledge outside. On the ledge, unseen by anyone until now, was yet another green button, identical to the one on the floor and the one found in the hand of the victim.

And Marcellus thought he was so smart.

Darrell quickly wrapped his right hand with the handkerchief Bill gave him, then said, "Bill, hold my legs!"

Suddenly Darrell was dangling out the window, reaching for something outside.

He leaned around the jagged piece of glass that had cut

him, and Bill caught his legs just in time to keep him from slipping through the window to his death five floors below.

"Bill! Gimme something to scoop it up with!" he said from outside.

"To scoop what?" Bill said, puffing.

The coroner handed him a small plastic bag, and Darrell carefully scooped up the button. Bill hauled the excited photo tech back inside. "What are you, crazy?"

"I found it! I found something you guys missed—this!" he said excitedly, holding up the clear little plastic bag and the little green button inside.

"I'll take that," Marcellus said, walking into the room, snatching the plastic bag from Darrell's hand.

"Hey!"

"Shuddup and get outta here. You're done. We don't need you anymore," he said, sipping his coffee and placing the evidence in his pocket.

"Hey, wait! *I* found that!"

"You gotta admit, Marcellus, the kid had a master eye to see that thing, 'cause we all missed it the first time through," remarked Bill.

"I ain't gotta admit nuthin'. Let a chump like this get away with thinkin' he can do detective work, and every clown in the precinct will be thinkin' they can be a detective in three easy lessons. Come on, let's go. You finish getting everybody's statements?"

"Yeah. You get my coffee?"

"Oh, uh, I forgot," lied Marcellus. "We'll pick up one on the way back to the station."

A nurse came in and bandaged Darrell's hand while the coroner gathered up the body and Bill bagged the other two buttons and then scurried off after his partner.

Marcellus stopped in the corridor outside the room and

said over his shoulder to Bill, "I really wanna get this guy. We bag this killer, and this will really put us over the top, partner."

"Us, or you?" Bill said under his breath behind Marcellus.

"Huh, what was that?"

"Nuthin, just thinking out loud, that's all."

"Should be a piece of cake with this." Marcellus pointed above the doorway to room 216. Above the now-empty door frame sat a security camera designed to cover the whole floor. Room 216 was the last room on the floor, and the camera sat just above it in the corner.

"Nope, 'fraid not," said Bill, savoring the moment.

"What do you mean, 'nope'?"

"I already checked. Camera's been out for three weeks. The security supervisor said it didn't catch a thing."

Marcellus cursed and stalked off down the hallway and around the corner to a waiting bank of elevators. Bill walked behind him, trying to hide his delight at being able to deflate his partner's sizeable ego.

"All right, listen," Marcellus said with sudden inspiration, poking Bill in the chest with his index finger.

He hated it when Marcellus did that.

Marcellus was a pretty boy. All the women loved him, until they got to know him, and all the guys hated his guts from the git-go. Handsome features, jet-black wavy hair, and a complexion the color of creamed coffee usually got him what he wanted from the local female population. But his fan club was dwindling rapidly. His ego was so big it was getting hard for him to enter a room without first turning his head sideways.

"We'll go down to the station and check the books for assaults over the past few months committed by guys over six feet. I'll bet money that our guy has a record. What we saw back there," he said, jerking his head toward Virginia's room, "the guy that did that was vicious. That kinda anger just doesn't spring up overnight. Our boy has a rap sheet a mile long, I'll bet. We'll catch this son of a—"

Ding! The elevator doors opened, and two nuns walked out on their way to visit a patient, catching Marcellus in mid-sentence.

"Biscuits! Uh, yeah, *that's* what we'll have for breakfast, Bill. Biscuits. Uh, morning, sisters," Marcellus said, smiling. Just before the elevator door closed, he leaned over to Trumball and whispered, "Bad luck to curse in front of nuns, man. The Man upstairs don't like that . . . "

Bill had no comment. This case bothered him. There was something really strange about it. He was convinced of that fact when it dawned on him that he knew the victim. Virginia Sills, it turned out, was the last case he had worked on in the Sex Crimes Unit before getting his promotion and transfer over to homicide. How weird was that? He thought about telling his partner but then decided against it. He'd probably try and take the credit for that too. No, not yet.

Hmm, you know, I never did get any leads on the perp that did that crime, cut her up like that. He made a note to check back with Mac in his old unit to see if they had come up with anything. Had the perp come back to finish the job and the nurse just got in the way?

Whew, so many what-ifs. He needed a cup of coffee—bad.

Darrell sat on fresh sheets on the bed across from Virginia's bloodstained one. He hated hospitals and couldn't wait to get out. The nurse was friendly, efficient, and caring. Still, he couldn't wait to leave. Then his thoughts turned to Marcellus. "I'm going to show him one day. I'm going to show every one of them," he said to himself.

"Show them what?" asked the nurse.

"That I do have what it takes to be a detective."

"Well, I believe you," she said as she finished bandaging Darrell's hand. "Is that too tight?"

"No, no, it's okay."

"You really should have stitches, you know," she admonished.

"No, no!" His eyes grew wide.

"I don't know what you're afraid of."

"I'm not afraid of nuthin'. I just—it's just not that bad—that's all."

"Yeah, right, if you say so," she chided.

"Doctor Gray, Doctor Gray to the ER," the loudspeaker squawked, filling the awkward silence between them.

"Do you, uh, really believe that?" Darrell asked.

"What?"

"That I can be whatever I want to be, a detective."

"Of course," she said with the most disarming smile he'd ever seen. "You can be whatever you set your mind to be if you work at it hard enough."

"Say, uh, what's your name?"

"Catherine—why?"

"Thanks, Catherine. I'm Darrell," he said, extending his good hand to shake hers. "You know, you have beautiful eyes, and you really have a way of—of helping a man to feel good about himself." He thought for a moment, then said, "And you know what?"

"What?"

"I'm gonna find that killer, and I'm gonna make detective. I don't care what it takes."

"Wow, aren't we the confident one?" she said, flashing another smile. She could tell that he liked her, and she thought he was cute and seemed to be a pretty nice guy. She didn't like how Marcellus had tried to humiliate him.

Darrell looked into her lovely hazel eyes and almost couldn't believe it when he heard himself say, "I feel like I could do anything after looking at you." Her olive skin blushed a deep red as he continued, "Uh, listen, I—I know we just met and all, but, uh, would you, um . . . go out to dinner with me sometime? I mean I understand if, uh, you, uh, said no, but I, uh . . ."

She giggled and had to admit to herself she enjoyed watching him squirm. It was refreshing. Most of the guys her age she'd met since coming to D.C. were after only one thing, and that on the very first date. And they all had the same tired line: *"Hi Baby, whut's yo name? Umph, you fine! Can I get sum uv dat?"* After a while it just made her skin crawl.

She'd even considered dating white guys for a while. Her friend Shaquita had said, "Why not? All the good black men are either locked up, married—or gay."

"No, Shaquita girl, that ain't true. There's a good black man out there somewhere. And I'm gonna find him."

Shaquita had accepted her challenge and stuck her pinky in Catherine's face.

"Bet," she had said defiantly.

Catherine hooked it with her own and said, "Okay, bet."

"How much?"

Catherine thought for a moment.

"How much!" prodded her friend.

"Wait a minute; wait a minute. I'm thinking."

"Fifty dollars."

"Fifty dollars!!" Catherine exclaimed.

Shaquita had leaned across the table in the hospital's cafeteria, her dark extensions falling unnoticed into her mashed potatoes. "You just scared 'cause you know I'm right."

"All right—it's a bet, fifty dollars. And I want my money too," said Catherine as confidently as she could.

Now here she was, looking this guy in the face. Not bad, not bad looking at all. She was twenty-three, and he looked to be about twenty-five or twenty-six, medium build, cute mustache, nice brown skin, average looking, but okay. He could stand to work out a little though, but if she thought he was worth it, she could work on that. He obviously had a good job. So far, so good.

"So if you want to sometime . . ." Darrell asked.

"Sure, I'd love to sometime," Catherine answered.

His face exploded into a smile that was contagious. "You would?"

"Yes . . ."

"Great, thanks. I mean, that's good. I look forward to that. I mean, uh, good, great!"

They exchanged numbers, and just then Darrell's cell phone violated their personal moment with its urgent ring.

"'Scuse me. Hello, Gibbons. Oh, hi, Steve. Yeah, I know. I'm sorry, man, but they gave this case to Marcellus, and you know how he is. But I'm on the way now. I should be there in thirty minutes. Okay. Okay. Bye." He ended the call.

"I'm sorry, Catherine—I gotta go. But listen, I'll call you tonight, about . . . ten?"

"Make it 9:30, and you got a deal. I work some long hours sometimes, so I try to get to bed kinda early."

"Okay, great, 9:30. Great."

"Okay, I've got to run. I'll talk with you later," she said and closed the tall supply cabinet door. She waved as she walked out of the room. *And don't disappoint me,* she thought to herself as she left.

As Catherine had closed the supply cabinet, something caught Darrell's eye that could just barely be seen under the cabinet of the room's single sink. It was a small, weather-beaten, run-over hat.

Hmph. So, a couple of green buttons weren't the only things that Marcellus had missed.

"Okay, Darrell," he said to himself, "in for a penny, in for a pound. If you do this, there is no turning back!"

He made sure no one was watching, snatched up the hat, and quickly placed it in his jacket pocket. Maybe it was something, maybe not. Maybe it belonged to the killer, or maybe it belonged to the last guy that had the room. Who knew? But there was only one way to find out.

He grabbed his photo gear and pounded his way down the hall to the elevator. Thankfully, when he got there, Marcellus and Bill were already long gone.

Later that night about 11:15, a flashlight beam danced like a mischievous firefly on the grounds behind St. Michael's Hospital. It danced around the massive air-conditioning unit, searching, looking. It played along the ground for hours, finally making its way over to a huge pile of sand behind a dumpster, and paused for long moments on two knee-deep indentations in the middle of the sandpile. Like a luminous bloodhound, it followed the indentations as they became two sandy tracks and then footprints leading off toward the street in the rear of the hospital. In following the fading trail, the flashlight stopped suddenly, and the bearer grunted in surprise and then gave a short, triumphant laugh. Immediately, there was a brilliant and blinding flash of light, followed instantly by the click and whir of a motor-driven 35mm camera.

The figure behind the flashlight bent down and examined something on the ground very closely. The figure quickly pulled a clear plastic evidence bag from his pocket, scooped up a small object, held it up before the beam to study it again. The green button glowed eerily in the grip of the powerful tungsten bulb, and Darrell smiled to himself confidently.

"I knew it! I knew it!" he whispered euphorically.

He also knew that he was removing evidence from a crime scene, which was a definite no-no. But he felt justified.

He had relayed his theory dutifully to his supervisor as soon as he'd returned from the field. It was received with less-than-expected enthusiasm. But what had happened afterwards was what at first had devastated him, then strengthened his resolve.

After talking to his supervisor, Lt. Lawrence Stewart, Darrell hurried to the gym for his workout. The gym was under renovation. Self-conscious about his body, Darrell headed to his favorite spot to work on his sit-ups.

Just past the free weights and out of sight of anyone, behind a huge pile of old lockers, was a small six-by-six-foot area where he did his sit-ups and push-ups. The pile had been there for months, yet to be taken to the dumpster.

It was here, while he lay exhausted from his personal "battle of the bulge," that he had heard someone come in and walk over to the free weights and begin a workout.

Moments later someone else came in.

"Hey, Lawrence. What's going on?"

"Marcellus! Just the man I needed to see." Lawrence grinned. "Mannn, do I have a laugh for you."

"Yeah, what is it? I could use a good laugh," said Marcellus, starting to do his warm-ups.

Darrell lay there on his back out of sight, fuming, as he listened to their conversation.

His supervisor had gone behind his back and told Marcellus!

The two had had a huge laugh about the whole thing. Marcellus had said, "Any fool would know that nobody could make a jump like that and live. Stupid little—no, wait. You know what, Lawrence? Go ahead and let that little failure do his own investigation," he said mockingly. "Go ahead, so that the whole department can find out what a real idiot he is—if they don't know already."

Darrell lay there for an hour, furious, angry, outraged, and hurt that his supervisor and friend would betray his confidence so readily.

Finally their workout was done, and there was one last burst of laughter as the two walked off toward the showers.

He made some inquiries later and found out that Lawrence and Marcellus had actually gone to Roosevelt together and had been friends ever since graduating from the local high school.

He would prove them wrong—all of them.

He took several more shots of the sandpile, the indentations, the footprints, and then of the broken hospital window five floors up.

He stared at the window. "I don't know who you are, or how in the world you made that jump," he said quietly, almost reverently, "but whoever you are, I'm coming to get you, 'cause you are gonna help me make detective."

Pitt stood docilely before the shimmering image of the TV screen. The streaked and smeared window of the electronics store reflected his huge and filthy image back to him. It was a typical image for one of the thousands of homeless in the muggy city.

He swayed slightly, as if seasick—a slow ballet of imbalance. Whether it was from the strength of the vodka clutched tightly to his chest, or from the overwhelming heat

—magnified tenfold by the overcoat he wore—an observer would be hard-pressed to say.

A poor excuse for a breeze attempted to push the stifling night heat off the deserted streets of Washington, D.C. It succeeded only in pushing a tattered piece of paper several feet along the deserted sidewalk. Failing in its attempt to cool the suffocating city, the breeze fled the sweltering heat of D.C. as if in fear for its life.

"And finally, to recap the local news, police are looking for two people, a man and a woman, wanted for questioning in a bizarre murder that took place in St. Michael's Hospital early this morning. The two were observed racing from the scene just before the body of nurse Ethel Mars was found. The woman being sought was actually a patient in the hospital at the time of the murder.

"Crime Stoppers is offering a reward for any information that leads to a conviction in the case of Nurse Mars and earnestly appeals to the public for help in solving this gruesome crime. The man is reported to be well over six feet tall. Police released this composite drawing of the male suspect . . ."

Arthur J. Pitt, filthy, unshaven, and unbathed for at least six weeks now, stood well over six feet tall himself, and on the mean streets was given a wide berth by ordinary people and other homeless alike. He was a man not easily intimidated. But as he stared at the composite of the brown giant, he felt a slight stirring of recognition of the man and a slow boil of conflicting emotions inside. He felt fear, anger, loathing—though he knew he had never seen the man before. These all tumbled deep down within him like a snowball rumbling downhill, gaining speed and force.

He took a swig from the brown bag he held, and a gush of the clear and heady liquid spilled its way unnoticed down his chin, watering his matted and unkempt beard.

There was something else too, something he couldn't quite

put his finger on. He shrugged it off and continued to watch and listen to the muffled broadcast through the store window.

If it was something important, then he would remember. His voices would tell him—they always did. They took care of him.

They told him things, things that no one else knew. Secret things.

Sometimes . . . they also told him things to do.

He frowned briefly at a disturbing memory.

Sometimes they told him bad things to do, and he couldn't help himself. They were things that no one should be made to do, but he had no choice.

The grocery clerk . . . the waitress at the Four Seasons . . . the cabdriver on Florida Avenue . . . the girl last month in the alley behind the old *Evening Star* building . . .

It was the price they demanded for helping him. They said they enjoyed watching him.

He . . . he could feel them laughing and relishing the awful things he did, as if they lived vicariously through him. They may have enjoyed the things he did, but he didn't. They made him do those things.

"Liar," said a voice so near he felt the breath of it on the back of his neck . . .

He looked around him, frightened, and seeing no one, he moaned softly and then said, "Who is that?"

"You know who it is . . ." the gravelly voice said again.

It was true. He did know. But he did not want to admit it, to himself . . . or to them.

"Admit it," the voice said in a repulsively sweet manner. *"You enjoy it as much as we do."*

"No! You're wrong! I—I'm not listening to you!" he said, trying to cover his ears with his hands.

"You can't stop us that way, Arthur. It's too late." Here it chittered

in a peal of laughter so irritating and high-pitched that it seemed enough to shatter glass. *"It's much too late for that,"* it continued. *"We're already inside!"*

This last announcement was followed by another more frightening peal of laughter that terrified Arthur J. Pitt to his soul. "Shut up! Shut up! I won't listen to you anymore! You're the Devil! Leave me alone!"

"Silence! Quiet, before you cause a scene. We have another little assignment for you."

Pitt groaned.

"Silence, I said! This should be easy for you. You could say that it's some . . . unfinished business. Stop whimpering, fool, and watch the screen. There! See her? Remember her?" the voice said slowly.

His face became expressionless as he watched the rest of the news. He stood frozen in front of the Hitz Electronics store as he watched the muted images.

No one else could be seen on the solemn streets. Washington, D.C., had become a bad place to be out alone at night. No one walked the streets at this hour but the cops, the criminals . . .

And the insane . . .

He stood and watched the screen as instructed. The next image that hit the screen bolted him to the ground, and he strained to hear the lilting staged voice of the Channel 4 News announcer as it droned on. *"The female, Virginia Sills, disappeared from her hospital room where the murder took place and is also sought by the police for questioning in the bizarre death of St. Michael's nurse Ethel Mars. Here is a recent photo of Ms. Sills."*

Pitt dropped his soggy, whiskey-soaked bag and the bottle it held. Its valued contents, worth its weight in gold, shattered on the deserted sidewalk like pieces of a broken dream, splashing his run-over leather shoes and pant leg and anointing them with warm vodka.

"Remember her?" his voices repeated.

"Y—Yes . . ." Pitt said slowly. "She was the one that I—that you . . . the one that—" Pitt stammered.

"The one we told you to rape and kill, Arthur. But you didn't. Did you? You failed. You failed us! Because you failed us, We will have to leave you, Arthur—alone. All alone. What will you do, Arthur?" it teased, *"when we leave you alone? All alone . . ."*

"Please," he said in a childlike voice.

"What will you do, Arthur? Because you know no one loves you."

"Please," he said still pleading, louder this time.

"No one loves you but us. What will you do?"

"Please don't."

"No one cares for you."

"I—I can't . . ." he whined.

"No one wants you, Arthur . . ."

"Stop, please stop!"

"No one can stand you, Arthur . . ."

"Please!"

"No one can bear to be near you, Arthur, but —us!"

"Why do you do this to me?" Arthur buried his head into garbage-smeared hands and sobbed.

"Everyone's left you, Arthur."

"Why, oh why, oh God, why, oh Jesus, why?"

"Don't say that Name! I told you, don't ever say that name!"

"Okay, okay, okay. I'm sorry; I'm sorry; I—I won't do it again. I'm sorry—it was an accident. I won't, I'm sorry . . . sorry . . ."

"That's better. See, no one else loves you. Not even . . . Him. No one *loves you. Everyone's left you, Arthur. Your family left you. Your friends have left you. Your* wife *left you.* We *are the only ones you have left."*

"Yes, yes, you're right."

"We are the only ones, Arthur. Because we love you, Arthur. You believe that, don't you?"

"Yes . . . yes, I do."

"Good, now you'll do what we say, then, won't you?"

"Yes . . ." came the hollow reply.

"Good, then."

"What do you want me . . . to do?" Pitt said obediently.

"See the girl?"

"Yes . . ."

"Kill her. It's important that you find her and kill her—for us. If you love us, Arthur, you'll do this for Us. For us, Arthur."

"Okay . . . You don't like him, do you?"

"Who, Arthur?"

"You know who, the brown giant. He frightens you, doesn't he?"

"Don't ever ask us questions again! Just do what we say. And Arthur . . ."

"Yes?"

"Kill him too. Very important. Kill him too—for us."

Pitt continued to stare at the image on the screen. He had stabbed her in the chest and head several times. He was amazed that she was still alive. He learned now that her name was Virginia Sills, and that she was a new paralegal working her way through school and attended the prestigious Georgetown School of Law. She had been a hardworking young lady who had been on the honor roll of her high school, Duke Ellington School of the Arts.

Afterwards followed a litany of people who were shocked by the attack and still others who refused to believe that she could have had anything to do with the death of the nurse.

An exasperated James D. Wilkerson, chief of police, was peppered with questions about the inability of police to locate a veritable giant, who should stick out like a sore thumb, and a formally comatose woman, who still had to be incredibly weak from being bedridden for six weeks.

Why hadn't the police been able to find them? Was this indicative of the police department's inability to handle high-profile cases?

And, a follow-up question, please: If the police were indeed unable to handle and swiftly close such a high-profile case, how could the public possibly have confidence in their ability to handle the smaller everyday crimes?

How were the killers able to get away, with an officer on duty right in the hospital? Did they really believe that the patient was involved in the murder? Had the police consulted with the FBI? Was there an FBI agent assigned to the case? Would he be in charge of the case? There were allegations of corruption made last week regarding the department. Would this current dragnet over the city and the citywide manhunt interfere with that investigation? No? Well, would that investigation affect the use of manpower by tying down other officers that should be involved in the search? What could he tell the residents of the District to assure them that they or their loved ones wouldn't be the next victims of this crazed killer? Was it true that the new addition to his house was paid for by a local businessman?

Exasperated even further, the chief of police left the blare of the lights abruptly. Muttering that he had no more time for questions, he stalked off, his patience at an end.

An officer in the Office of Public Affairs stepped in front of the gaggle of bright lights and hungry reporters to inform them that they would be briefed again as soon as there were any substantial new leads or information. A fact sheet was distributed of current leads the department was investigating.

Finally they showed a tearful mother and stoic-looking father who came on and appealed for the release of their daughter. This was followed by another appeal to the hordes of press that trampled their lawn like African locusts.

"We're just a typical, hardworking, African-American family. Therefore, we hope that you'll understand when I say that we're not used to this kind of attention and publicity. Please respect our privacy and extreme concern during this trying time. Any questions you have, please direct them to our family attorney. Thank you."

One could see that Robert D. Sills's once proud shoulders were now stooped under a burden that many viewing parents were glad that they did not have to bear. An additional burden for Robert Sills was the fact that the last memory he had of his daughter was of her shouting at him in anger from the other end of the phone, telling him that she was going to live life on her own terms.

Nearby, Virginia's mother, also named Virginia, a woman in her forties and strikingly attractive, looked haggard and worn after her six-week ordeal beside her comatose daughter's bedside, and now this.

The family lawyer appeared looking appropriately concerned and displayed a large photo of the missing young woman and appealed for the public's help in finding her. The image of Virginia in happier days filled the screen.

Pitt reached out and touched the glass window tenderly as if it had been her face. He must find her and finish what his voices had told him to do. His voices would help him.

He suddenly felt them moving deep down inside of him. His entire mood changed in an instant, and he giggled devilishly. He felt better now—much better.

He liked it when he felt them move inside. It reassured him of their presence, and that they were not going to leave him.

He felt comforted. They would never leave him, as long as he did exactly what they told him to do.

For a brief moment he allowed himself to reflect back on

the night of the rape. There had been an odd occurrence that night, one that he would never forget.

There had been a lightning strike in the alley moments after the rape, not more than ten feet away from him. It alarmed him so much he thought that God was trying to strike him dead for what he had done to the girl.

His eyes had exploded with light, and it took him several moments to get his sight back. When he did, he couldn't believe his eyes.

For a brief moment he actually saw his voices in that brief flash of lightning, and he did not like what he saw. He saw an unearthly thing, dressed in rags, looking—no, peering at him, turning its malformed head this way and that, as if trying to determine whether Pitt could indeed see him or not. Pitt couldn't help but react with revulsion as the thing moved closer, crouching low for a better look.

It reacted with surprise at his reaction, although not altogether displeased.

"It can see us! The chalice, it can see us!"

Pitt looked beyond it to a group of about fifteen creatures standing around something or someone lying on the ground. Several more loathsome and shadowy things crawled around the fallen Virginia, sniffing and licking the air around her as if savoring the aroma of her pain and torment.

"Leave him! And come help us. It is the effects of the lightning. They will wear off soon enough, and he will soon forget. Quickly! We must finish this before help arrives!" The figure who spoke seemed in charge.

The creature in front of him turned in seeming compliance, then paused and looked over its humped shoulder back at him. It stole a glance at its leader, Slean, who was once again preoccupied with the pummeling of something on the ground.

The misshapen thing turned a depraved grin on Pitt, and as it did so, the multitude of pustules around its eyes and mouth started to burst and stream little murky yellow jets of repulsive and putrid-smelling liquid down its repugnant and revolting face.

Even Pitt found it nauseating and disgusting. He felt his stomach begin to heave, and he fought for control of it. He found himself backing away as the creature seemed fascinated with him, and stealing another glance at its leader here and there, it eased its way up to Arthur, continuing to turn his head this way and that. Pitt was visibly shaken, and he looked around him. He was trapped in a corner of the alley, and there was no way out, except past this . . . thing.

This must be a dream of some kind, he told himself, *a nightmare.*

Meanwhile, the creature kept turning its massive, malformed head from one side to the other, examining Pitt's reaction. It noted with deep interest and even deeper satisfaction Pitt's repugnance to its many infection-filled pustules.

To Pitt it seemed the thing derived tangible pleasure from his revulsion.

It started playing with the pustules on its face like some depraved pimpled-faced kid. It threatened him with a squirt from one of the many fetid filled lumps of skin.

Arthur J. Pitt, trembling with revulsion, found himself backed as far into the corner of the trash-strewn alley as he could go. He had tried keeping a ten-foot cushion of distance between him and his painstakingly slow stalker. The creature, hunched and bent over, almost crawling on all fours, would raise up every few seconds and sniff and then lick the air euphorically as he backed the frightened rapist into the corner. Pitt watched his cushion of space shrink from ten feet to six feet, six feet to four, four to three, three to two . . .

The thing raised up on its haunches, sniffing and licking

again. Pitt watched the long, gray, scum-covered tongue carefully, cringing every time it came near him, though for now the creature seemed content to just lick the air around him.

It seemed to be milking the fear right out of him, and then, like a drug, inhaling and licking it from the very air and enjoying it immensely.

It stopped and looked at him, greedily.

It smiled.

The massive wart-filled head was hairless, except for a single strand, trapped in a lump of putrid flesh ripe for bursting. The huge head was low to the ground now, as if its sheer weight kept the creature from raising it too often.

It seemed to be pondering something, whether to continue this slow and delightful nursing process, or to quickly put an end to it before he was missed.

It lunged at Arthur suddenly and squeezed one of the large pustules on its malformed face, bursting it violently. It grinned and tittered evilly at Pitt's terrified recoil.

Pitt flung himself backward with nowhere to go. Quickly he raised his arm to shield himself and turned his head at the last second.

Too late.

He felt the warm viscous liquid strike his left cheek and slowly run down under his chin. It seemed to have a life of its own as it slowly ran down his neck. It had the feel of a thousand maggots trying to dig into his beard and under his skin.

The six-foot-six-inch rapist screamed like a six-year-old child as he tried to run, wiping his neck desperately with his filthy sleeve.

He tripped over a rusty paint can and fell heavily to the pavement, the wind knocked out of him. Pitt almost lost consciousness and lay there for a moment.

"Shree! You maggot! I told you, leave him alone! You prolong the effects by the agitation of his fears!"

The thing shrank back at the reprimand. "But I was just feeding. It's sooo delicious! Hard to resist. I could not hel—"

"Silence! Your greed will be the ruin of you yet! Get over here and—"

Pitt must have lost consciousness for a few seconds, because when he awoke, he was alone except for the girl who lay dying in her own blood. He figured that he must have had a seizure or something and passed out.

It was a dream. It had all been a dream. Except, that is, for her—she hadn't been a dream.

He had heard a car approaching and had hurried away from the scene.

That must have been when the police found her, he thought to himself. As he stood now, remembering the events of almost two months ago, he absentmindedly scratched his matted and food-flecked beard. His hand fell casually to his throat and began absentmindedly scratching the huge pustule that had been growing there for weeks . . .

Marcellus Grimes believed in doing whatever it took to get ahead. Whatever it took. If it meant he had to break a few eggs, a few hearts, or a few heads, it didn't matter.

Results—that's what mattered.

That's why when Mac, in the Sex Crimes Unit, sent over a file for his old partner Bill Trumball marked urgent and confidential, he decided to take a look. He made sure no one was looking when he slipped it up under his jacket and headed to the men's room.

Well, now, let's just see what ole Bill is up to.

He opened the file in the stall, and the first thing that struck his eye was a mug shot of one Pitt, Arthur J.

As he continued to read, he discovered that Trumball had been holding back on him.

When Trumball was in SCU, he had been the detective assigned to investigate the rape of a certain paralegal named Virginia Sills—the same Virginia Sills who was now missing. Once Trumball had left SCU, they had still continued to work the case and came up with a suspect who had been seen in the area, this Pitt character.

As Marcellus read Pitt's rap sheet, he became more and more convinced that this was their man. The guy was big, about six foot six. He weighed 260 to 280 pounds. The guy had been living on the streets for the past few years, had a series of assault charges, and was wanted for questioning in a dozen more. He was noted as a Chapter 35 and extremely dangerous.

Marcellus looked at the mug shot again. Scruffy-looking character, no more so, though, than all the other homeless in D.C., he thought.

Except for the eyes. There was something kinda strange about the eyes.

No matter—he'd have this case wrapped up now in no time. He finished reading the file and the special note that Mac had included for Bill:

> *We've been so shorthanded since you left that we haven't been able to follow up our leads on this guy. We know he likes to hang out in S.W. around Half Street. We alerted officers that patrol that area to be on the lookout for him, but so far, nothing.*
>
> *Bill, this guy is dangerous. Don't try taking him down by yourself.*
>
> *He migrated down here from Jersey. I've got a buddy on the force*

up there and I put in a call to him to see if he has anything. I'll let you know as soon as I have anything more.

Mac

Marcellus noted with interest another piece of information that Mac had included about the girl, Virginia Sills. The information made him raise his eyebrows in surprise. But, no matter—it was this Pitt he was after. The girl was ancillary.

That's it, then, Marcellus thought to himself. *That's my guy.* The guy was close to the height of the suspect, had a ton of priors, was the same joker who probably assaulted the girl in the first place. Yeah, this had to be him.

In thirty seconds he had all the loose ends tied up in his mind.

He obviously had found out the girl was still alive and had come back to finish out his sick fantasy, but Ethel Mars got in the way, so he killed her. With all the screaming and commotion going on, he panicked, took the girl, and maybe has her in some out-of-the-way place, planning to finish the job. Or maybe he took her as insurance just in case the police got too close.

Piece of cake.

He had a snitch that lived in Southwest who should know where this joker could be found.

He should have this case solved by morning, and no one would be the wiser as to how he did it.

He stood up, whistling to himself, and flushed the toilet so as not to raise suspicions. He slipped the file back up under his suit jacket and walked out of the stall . . . and into his partner, Bill Trumball.

"Hey, Marcellus."

"Oh! Bill! Hi, whut'zup, partner? Uh, good to see you—How's it going?"

"All right," said Bill, washing his hands. "Is that you funkin' up the bathroom like that?" Bill chided.

"Me? Naw, naw, man. You know me," Marcellus said, smiling. "My stuff don't stink, cuz I'm too cool," he added, slipping out of the men's room and heading quickly down the stairs to his car . . .

Ten minutes later, Mac Kolan of SCU stuck his head in the office and dropped by to see his old friend.

"Hey, Bill."

"Mac! Hey, how's it going, partner? How are things back at the ranch?" Bill said, smiling broadly. The two of them had been through a lot of scrapes together, from Vietnam to the streets of D.C., and there was a genuine bond between them.

"Okay, but missing you like crazy, man. I'm the only one that does any real work down there now." He grinned, then turned serious. "Say, did Marcellus give you that file on Pitt?"

"On who?"

"Pitt, Arthur J. You know—the suspect in that rape case you asked me about, the one you were working on."

"No," said Bill, the smile suddenly gone from his face.

"He didn't give it to you?"

"No," said Bill through tight lips. "When did you give it to him?"

"Not twenty minutes ago."

"No wonder he was in such a hurry to get out of the men's room. That no-good—"

"You mean he didn't give it to you? I marked it urgent and confidential."

"That don't mean a thing in the world to that toadstool, other than 'you better look in it and see what it is—now.'" Bill was incensed.

"I'm sorry, Bill."

"It's not your fault, Mac. Fill me in; tell me what you've got."

"Well, what I dropped by to tell you is that I heard back from a buddy of mine who works homicide in the Jersey PD. This boy is dangerous—a real nutcase. They've been looking for this guy, Pitt, for quite a while. He's wanted for questioning in a number of ritual murders up there, gruesome stuff, including a cop killing."

"A cop killing?"

"Yeah. Seems the guy used to be a hunter before he went nuts. Carries this huge knife around he used to use to skin deer, some monster of a thing he ordered through mail order. He killed one officer and skinned the guy's partner alive with it. Guy's crippled for life—can't show his face anywhere."

"Sick," gasped Bill.

"Yeah, it's no wonder everyone at the hospital was so amazed that the rape victim's still alive. He must've been scared off before he could finish. And by the way, he's got a thing for wearing his overcoat all the time. Never takes it off, not even in summer. My buddy says this guy stinks to high heaven. He's also been classified as a Chapter 35, a Sexual Psychopath."

"Come with me, Mac," Bill said suddenly.

"Where we going?" said Mac, following him out the door.

"To see Captain Hanley, my boss."

Just then another thought struck Mac. On the way down the hall to Capt. Hanley's office, Mac stopped his friend and pulled him by the arm to the side of the busy hallway.

"What is it?" Bill said, puzzled.

Mac ran his hand through his thinning hair and said, "Well, I guess since you didn't get the file, then there's no way for you to know this either."

"Know what?" Bill said impatiently.

"She's pregnant."

"What? The girl? You're kidding."

"No. The hospital does follow-up tests on all rape victims—you know, to make sure there's no STDs or whatever. Only this time, there turned out to be a big 'whatever'—pregnancy. And, uh, there's one more thing . . ."

"There's more? What's that?"

"She was taken before they could tell her, so she doesn't know."

"But how do they know—could it be by a boyfriend or, or—"

"'Fraid not. By all accounts she was a virgin, saving herself for marriage, and that's confirmed by the amount of damage that was done. She's now six weeks pregnant by that animal that raped her."

"Oh, no . . ."

"Seems you have two victims to search for now. I just hope that you find them in time."

They had started down the hallway again, when Mac's face turned up as if he had just eaten a sour pickle. Bill glanced back to see why his friend was lagging behind.

"Now what's eat'n you?"

"There is one other thing that may not be related," he said slowly, as if reluctant to bring it out.

Bill threw his hands up in exasperation as they stopped in front of a well-worn door with faded black letters, which read, "Capt. Hanley, Chief of Detectives, Homicide Div."

"Mac! You know I hate it when you do that—give me stuff piecemeal! Come on, man, spill it—all of it."

"Well, maybe it's nothing but . . . you know the doctor? The one that worked on the girl in the emergency room and saved her life?"

"Yeah?" said Bill impatiently, like a little boy waiting to go to the bathroom.

"He's missing."

"Yeah, so? Maybe he's on vacation or something."

"Nah, he went missing the day they saved the girl's life, and no one's seen him since. His best friend and senior staff doctor, umm, Doctor . . . Doctor . . . Doctor Hardison—that's it. Yeah, he died of cancer three weeks later, and this guy never showed up for the funeral. Hasn't been back to his apartment in weeks now, says his landlord. His mother's filled out a missing persons report, but so far, nothing."

"Hmph. Strange."

"That's what I thought."

"What's his name?"

"Uhh, Jefferies. Yeah, Dr. William Jefferies."

5

THAT WHICH IS DONE IN THE DARK . . .

DARRELL GIBBONS had followed the sandy footprints until they faded away to nothing in the sweeping lawn that encircled the front of St. Michael's Hospital complex. The word *complex* seemed very appropriate to Darrell—he felt the tangled maze of driveways and tall buildings were purposely arrayed in a haphazard pattern designed to confuse.

He went back to the sandpile and proceeded to rope it off, along with the walkway that ran in front of it, using a roll of yellow police tape he had in his bag. He wanted to make sure no one trampled this area in the morning when construction resumed.

Darrell knelt on one knee and examined the surrounding area meticulously. He pulled a macro lens from his camera bag and switched it out for the normal one. He then took several close-ups of the sandy print before him. He noted the unusual tread of the shoe. He had three good footprints heading around the corner of the building toward the front. They faded off into nothingness after that.

Thanks to the early morning rain that day, the sandy tracks held together with some consistency, he noted. He then set down his shoulder bag and pulled several items from it and placed them in a specific order on the ground.

The lab had turned up no significant prints from the room, but they did recover one small piece of latex from one corner of the broken window. And of course he still had the hat.

The latex was the same kind that was used in rubber gloves, the *same* kind of gloves used by St. Michael's staff.

Darrell opened a small box and set it down on the ground.

For the past three years, in his desire to become a detective, he had performed a brain drain on anyone in Forensics who would talk to him. He felt that he knew almost as much now as they did, especially in the area of evidence collection and evidence integrity.

He prepared to perform the very sensitive task of getting a cast of the faint sandy footprint. Sweating profusely, after twenty minutes he had a reasonable facsimile that he was satisfied with. But it was the results from the next forensic item he used that made him gasp with excitement.

There was a sharp *pop* as he pulled on his latex gloves and they snapped into place snugly on his hands. He then put on the surgical mask that came with the kit. He stood up and began slowly spraying the surrounding area he had roped off with Luminol. After a few seconds, he turned on his portable black light. The ground glowed strangely under the purple light.

There on the ground were several drops of blood that glowed an eerie green, leading from the sandpile, around the corner, and toward the front of the building where they abruptly stopped. *Probably wrapped it quickly, or put his hand in his pocket,* Darrell surmised.

He lifted some of the blood samples to take back to the lab for DNA analysis. He'd submit them on the q.t. along with the hat.

He walked what he imagined to be the steps of the killer. He knew for sure that the killer had walked around to the front of the building, but which way he went from there was anybody's guess.

Soon he found himself at St. Michael's main entrance. Had the killer caught a cab from here?

He walked around the front entrance, looking at the ground. The automatic doors opened and closed several times as he walked back and forth, the electric eye watching him.

An alert security guard wearing a dark blue uniform with a gold badge approached him from inside the lobby.

"Can I help you, sir?" the tall muscular figure said with his hand casually but noticeably near his gun.

Darrell noted that the officer wore the stripes of a sergeant. The shoulder patch said Region Wide Security Services.

Darrell sized him up as ex-military probably, and more alert than most that sat behind a lobby desk. He flashed his badge, and the officer visibly relaxed.

"Man, what are you doin' out here this time of night? Thought you guys had finished up everything for the day."

Darrell engaged him in conversation and asked how long he'd been on duty. Sergeant Tommy Fuell told him that he had been on duty all day. He was doing a double shift because he needed the money to finish up a project for his church. Tommy was a pastor, and this happened to be his last week on the job. He was going back to the Howard School of Divinity to get his degree.

After some small talk, Darrell asked him what he'd seen around the hospital that day, especially anything unusual around the time of the murder.

"Well—" Tommy took off his uniform cap and scratched his head—"I told the other officers everything I remembered. There was really nothing unusual, though. Nobody suspicious—at least not in the lobby."

"What do you mean, 'at least not in the lobby'?" said Darrell, his curiosity piqued.

"Well, I tried to tell the other officers, but they didn't seem particularly interested, because it was outside the lobby and it didn't fit the description of the suspect they were looking for. I believe one officer's words to me were 'too short.'"

"Tell me what happened."

"Well, maybe ten minutes before the hospital went crazy with alarms and cops and stuff, there was this guy. . . ."

"What about him?" asked Gibbons, urging him on.

"Well, there was this guy who was standing out here, looking kinda strange and seeming kinda upset. In fact, if you really wanna know the truth, he looked like he was kinda upset with himself."

"Describe him," said Darrell, pulling out his pad and pen.

"Well, he was about your height, five foot seven. Maybe 150 to 160 pounds."

"What was he wearing?"

"Well, he wore an overcoat over his scrubs."

"His scrubs—he was a doctor?"

Tommy's hands went out from his sides. "I think so, but I dunno. That was the odd thing. Because he seemed kinda familiar one moment, like maybe I had seen him somewhere before, ya know? But, I just couldn't place him. And he was fiddlin' with his surgical mask, so I couldn't see his face or what he looked like. But he was definitely wearing hospital scrubs under his overcoat."

"You sure it was a man?"

"Oh yeah, I was sure of that. Oh! And he wore those

special shoes that they've started wearing in the ER over the past few months. They're casual and comfortable like tennis shoes, but have kinda special rubber soles that maintain their grip through blood, guts, and whatever else can hit the floor during an operation, you know?"

"Where was he, and what was he doing?"

"He was walking over to the parking garage across the driveway, and another doctor, one who drops by from time to time, approached him and spoke, like he knew the guy. But the guy in the mask just kept his head down, brushed past him, and kept talking—no, fussing to himself the whole time. And then just walked away."

"I appreciate this, and you've been very helpful. Just a few more questions, and I'll let you get back to your desk. Could you tell me where they were standing when they passed each other and if there was anything else unusual that can help us identify this man?"

"Well, they brushed past each other. In fact, they bumped into each other about right here, where we're standing."

Darrell's eyebrow went up, and he looked at the ground at his feet as he said, "Anything else?"

"Umm, yeah, maybe. Maybe nothing at all, but this guy kept his right hand jammed in his coat pocket the whole while he was in my sight. And his coat . . ."

"Yeah, what is it? Go ahead—no clue is too small."

"Well . . . his coat . . ."

"What about his coat?"

"Well, it looked to be brand-new, but from what I could tell, it didn't seem to have a single button on it."

Darrell's heart began to beat faster.

"Tommy, I really appreciate the help, as I said. You've been great. Just one more thing."

"Sure."

"You didn't happened to see what direction this guy came from, did you?"

"Yeah, same direction you did, from around the back of the hospital. I watched him all the way. Because I wondered why in the world someone in scrubs would be coming from back there, where the construction was. But just then, all heck broke loose, and I had to scramble upstairs."

Darrell Gibbons knelt down and pulled the small spray bottle from his pocket and began to carefully spray around where the two men were standing.

"What are you doing?" asked the security guard.

"Playing a hunch, Tommy—playing a hunch." He made sure the caustic liquid didn't touch him and watched as within seconds a single drop of blood glowed faint and ghostly green under his handheld black light.

"Is that what I think it is?" queried Tommy.

"Sure is."

"But there's nothing unusual about finding blood in front of a hospital."

"There is when the ER is around on the other side of the building," he said, suddenly discovering another drop, "and there's definitely something unusual about it when they lead away from the hospital."

Darrell queried Tommy Fuell about the identity of the doctor who had bumped into the mysterious figure, and found out that it was a visiting specialist whose name the security officer didn't know.

Darrell followed the sporadic blood drops across the deserted driveway into the hospital's parking garage. Apparently the killer's hand had begun to bleed profusely and possibly dripped inside the coat, seeping through the pocket, then down the inside lining to the ground.

He almost lost the sparse trail amidst the transmission

fluid, antifreeze, and oil stains. He was almost out of Luminol when he picked up the trail again. He followed it carefully and ended up at the area of the parking garage reserved for physicians. He followed it farther and found that the blood trail stopped dead in one of the parking spaces. Darrell looked up to see whose name graced this particular spot. On the wall ahead of him was a faded but still clearly legible name: Dr. William Jefferies.

Darrell's camera flashed as he captured both the trail and name.

"Gotcha," he said under his breath.

The stench of the sewage system was stifling. The 193-year-old system was one of the oldest in the country. Being inside of it was like trying to breathe through a blanket, a blanket smeared with human feces.

The musk of sludge and human waste that had flowed through these conduits since 1810 made Virginia retch repeatedly. Finally they emerged into a system of huge concrete pipes that led them to the city's McMillan Waste Treatment Plant and its adjacent reservoir. Once there, they slid quietly into the water at a far corner of the reservoir, out of sight of prying eyes, and quickly rinsed off the suffocating stench.

Mahatiel managed to find an enclosed area of huge collectors that had once held massive amounts of sand as part of D.C.'s slow-sand water filtration system. These large abandoned structures overlooked the entire reservoir. It was the perfect vantage point to see anyone coming, even from a great distance away. He had used his sizeable strength to bend the grating that sealed this area so they could squeeze through. After bending it back into shape, he felt that the rear was somewhat secure.

They both collapsed to the trash-strewn floor of the silo-type structure.

They'd passed an army of rats on the way in. *Thank God there are none here,* thought the exhausted woman.

It had been quite a morning for Virginia. She lay on the floor, her chest heaving. Mahatiel sat with his back against the wall of their temporary refuge. He looked out the open end of a huge pipe on the other side of the silo that looked out over the quiet beauty of the still waters of the reservoir. Off in the distance he could see a helicopter scanning an ever-widening area in the direction from which they had come. Above them the silo went straight up for 150 feet into open blue sky.

Finally, after she had caught her breath, Virginia started to dress with the clothes Mahatiel had given her. He discreetly turned his back. Once done, she lay down. Feeling sorry for her, he fished around in his pocket for something and found it.

"Here, eat this," he said.

It looked like a small, light, round biscuit of some type, and she eyed it suspiciously.

"What is it?"

"Eat it; it won't hurt you. It will give you strength."

"What is it?" she repeated again.

"Manna."

"Manna? What's that?"

"Just take it, Virginia," he said, tossing it to her and fishing out another for himself.

It fell on her stomach, and she picked it up gingerly, like a child seeing her first croissant, unsure of whether she wanted to eat it or not. Her stomach won out, and after testing the tip of the little round thing with her tongue, she found herself devouring the surprisingly sweet morsel, wanting more.

"Hmph. That was good." She suddenly felt strengthened. She sat up, looked at him, and asked for another.

"All right, my last one," he said, tossing her another. She ate it ravenously.

"This will help us to go on for a few days."

"Where did you get these?"

"A friend," he said and thought of Uriel.

She pondered him for a moment before she spoke. She then said, "What's going to happen to me? And why did that man try to kill me? I mean, why? And now we've got the police after us. What are we going to do?"

He paused and thought for a moment before he answered. How could he say this so she would understand? How could he possibly convey to her the answers that she needed without conveying to her the extreme danger that she was facing?

He couldn't tell her. He would have to show her.

He sat forward suddenly and touched both her temples at once with his index fingers. His touch was as light as the touch of a butterfly, yet she fainted dead away.

She awoke to find herself in total darkness. With a sharp intake of breath, she felt fear begin to rise within. The panic she had fought all morning endeavored to make itself known. She fought it just as she sensed a presence behind her and at the same time heard a deep, powerful voice say, "Don't be frightened . . ."

She spun quickly to face the speaker, and there was Mahatiel, in all of his angelic splendor, wings spread out like those of a giant eagle, making soft whispers of motion in the air. His armor shone and glistened like sunlight shimmering on the water. She suddenly remembered the hospital and what had happened six weeks earlier. She took a couple of steps back, aghast.

"So I wasn't dreaming after all. That really happened! You really are an angel!"

"I brought you here to answer some of your questions. But I felt that it would be much easier to *show* you, Virginia, than to tell you." He moved his hand from left to right as if he were moving aside an invisible curtain.

Suddenly she saw in front of her something that she could only liken to a gigantic screen of some type.

"Many eons ago," Mahatiel began, "God created the heavens and the earth."

On the screen she watched in stunned silence as creation's story unfolded right before her eyes. She saw a form on the screen, huge, manlike, standing in the blackest dark she'd ever seen. It looked like outer space, only there were no stars. It was entirely pitch-black.

Instinctively, she knew that this figure was God. She saw no facial features, just pure glory in a manlike shape. Behind Him, almost as if they were reflections in a mirror, she saw two more forms exactly like the first.

"Virginia, what I am about to show you, no human being has ever seen before," Mahatiel's voice intoned behind her, deep and comforting as he continued. "I'm going to show you what transpired from the time that God created the earth. In the time *before* the creation of man, millennia before Adam and Eve were placed in their position as governing factors over the earth—"

"Governing factors?"

Ignoring her interruption, he continued as if pressed for time. "I will reveal to you why and how a warm, vibrant, and beautiful earth became, without form and void, and how darkness was upon the face of the earth, and it became a waste and barren thing . . ."

"Wait, wait!" said Virginia. "Why are you showing all of this to me?"

"Watch and see," his deep voice boomed.

In front of her, on the screen, she saw the three figures create mass before her very eyes—something from nothing. It was astounding. She saw matter appear in the hand of the first figure. The second and third seemed to look on with approval. They didn't say a word, but she could feel, as if it were a tangible thing, how pleased they were. In her mind she assigned them names she remembered from Sunday school.

The first and preeminent figure she silently named God the Father. The figure to His right she named God the Son. And the figure to His left, the Holy Spirit.

She watched as a tiny subatomic particle in the palm of His hand seemed to spin and grow and revolve and expand into a perfect sphere. And then another, and another, and another, and another, until the Father's hands were full of planets. Behind Him, the figure that she named the Son did the same, only in His hands instead of planets, there were stars, in clusters and galaxies, by the millions. Together, at the same instant in perfect tandem, they tossed these elements up into the dark. It was then that the third figure, the Holy Spirit, launched Himself upward, and at the moment He made contact with these elements, there was a massive explosion and whirlwind that flung the earth and other planets and the stars into space all around her as far as the eye could see! For suddenly she was not observing these vivid events on a screen, but she was actually there, in space several feet away, feeling the wind of the Holy Spirit on her skin and face and rustling her clothes. She looked down, terrified, and saw that she stood on absolutely nothing as easily and firmly as if it were a concrete floor!

"Don't be frightened," said Mahatiel's strong and soothing voice behind her. "Watch."

And she quietly swallowed, her heart in her throat, and focused again on the activity in front of her.

She watched as the trio in perfect tandem, again like one person, grew trees and plants, created streams, rivers, and waterfalls, and formed birds, antelope, lambs, tigers, and other animals she'd never seen before and placed them on the planets.

She saw then a staggering number of light beings that she knew must be angels gathered around the trio. They were innumerable. There were so many that they filled space! There were angels of every kind, some with wings and some without. Some had two wings, some four, and some six. Some had two eyes, and some had eyes over every square inch of their bodies!

She saw them assigned over the various planets.

"Virginia, watch and see," she heard Mahatiel's voice turn decidedly cold and abrupt.

She heard an audible gasp en masse from the assembled angels and turned in the direction of wonder that echoed all around her. Far back in the crowd, down one of the many aisles, she saw a lone figure approaching.

She saw an angel unlike any other. He was awe inspiring. All the angelic beings held their own particular splendor, but this one was amazing.

"Who is that?" she whispered reverently, unable to move her eyes from him.

"That," said Mahatiel pointedly, "is the Morning Star."

"Oh," she said quietly, too embarrassed to admit that she still didn't know any more than she did in the beginning.

She watched as all the other angels made way and bowed to him. Rows upon rows, ranks, legions, leagues, and divisions a million phalanxes deep—all bowed to him, like waves in a glittering sea . . .

"That," said Mahatiel, "is Lucifer . . ."

"Oh my G—" She caught herself, cutting a quick eye at Mahatiel, remembering his obvious disapproval of a previous irreverent outburst.

"Goodness," she said.

The tall and imposing figure strode in the direction of the Three who were now seated on three magnificent thrones on a resplendent raised dais of gold and pearl. Confidence like she'd never known radiated from this huge and towering creature. He was as immense and muscular as he was exquisite.

She squinted suddenly as he turned at the end of the row and ascended the steps approaching the throne, and the glory emanating from the throne of God struck him. A barely perceptible smile trembled at the corner of his lips at the sudden awe that escaped from the mouths of the innumerable crowd of angels.

"He . . . he did that on purpose, didn't he!" said Virginia with dawning realization.

"Yes," came Mahatiel's matter-of-fact reply.

He was dazzling. Miniature razor-sharp shafts of light seem to burst from him in a veritable rainbow of colors so pure and powerful that they stunned and strained the senses to their limit. It was frighteningly strange. It was as if her very senses were stretched to their maximum to perceive all the colors that assaulted them. And it was not just her eyes that teetered on the very edge of exploding, but her very skin seemed to crawl with the feel of each color. They each affected her flesh, her body in a different way. She shivered when the shafts of blue struck her optic nerve, sending chills throughout her nervous system. The bright shafts of deep bloodred left her feeling hot flashes well beyond her young years. The yellows left her nauseous, and the purples pulled her with a dominating and mesmerizing force. The greens left her feeling light-headed, dizzy, and euphoric. He was a kaleidoscopic wonder with each purposeful stride he made toward the throne. He was a living rainbow of dominance, assurance, and power. All of this flowed and exploded from a one-piece tunic that covered him from his throat down to his bare feet, and over this was a vibrant and stunning robe of red and royal blue.

"What are those shafts of light? They're hurting my eyes. It's like trying to look inside of a thousand-watt diamond! Where are they coming from?" Virginia said, raising her arm in front of her eyes for protection. It was painful and yet hypnotic. She could not seem to tear her eyes away, no matter how excruciating.

"His clothes . . ." responded Mahatiel.

"His clothes?"

"Yes."

"On earth you take cotton, wool, nylon, and other materials and weave them into garments, do you not?"

"Yeah, so what does that have to do with—"

"The Holy One did the same for the one who was the anointed cherub. It is written: 'Every precious stone was thy covering, the sardis, topaz, and the diamond, the beryl, the onyx, and the jasper, the sapphire, the emerald, and the carbuncle, and gold . . .'"

"I—I remember that from Sunday school! But I thought that meant that they were a patchwork of stones just stuck on his clothes. Like with glue or something. But this . . . this is like nothing I ever imagined!" she said, mesmerized.

Mahatiel smiled at her naïveté. "The same way that humans weave cotton and wool into cloth and then garments, the Holy One processes precious stones into clothlike material, and then creates garments."

"What?" Virginia exploded. "Weave emeralds, onyx, beryl, diamonds, and . . . *gold* and make them into a flexible clothlike garment! That's impossible!"

"Nothing is impossible with God, Virginia. He *is* God, after all. Where do you think man after his fall obtained the concept of clothes in the first place?" he said, turning to look at her briefly.

"But do you know how much that process would be worth on earth? Billions—no, trillions—no zillions!"

He smiled again at her juvenile excitement. He could see dollar signs in her eyes.

"Virginia, remember why you are here." His voice took on the tone of a college counselor tearing a student's eyes away from the electives, back to the required course at hand.

"I know, I know; *watch and seeeee,*" she said, imitating Mahatiel's deep baritone voice.

He turned to watch the unfolding scene before them, then added quietly, with humor, "What is it that they say on earth? 'Imitation is the highest form of flattery'?" He smiled.

She realized in that moment that this was the first time she'd ever seen him smile. It was somehow comforting, consoling, and appealing to her soul.

6 TRIBUTE . . .

LUCIFER BOWED STIFFLY, the curt bow of one of rank and supreme importance.

Virginia could not understand what they were saying.

"What are they saying? What are they talkin' about?" she whispered to Mahatiel.

"He is asking that he be given the earth as his own. He is reminding the Godhead how loyal he has been in his position as the anointed cherub," Mahatiel replied with irony.

"*Anointed cherub*, what's that?"

"The guardian of the very throne of God."

"Ohhhh," she said reverently. She watched as the Godhead briefly discussed his request. Then she felt it—a ripple of something so minute between them as to be almost imperceptible. But she felt it nonetheless.

Mistrust.

"But, if they didn't trust him, why—"

"Shhhhh," Mahatiel interrupted. "Watch and see . . ."

The Father nodded His head in agreement, and Lucifer

followed with another curt bow, and turned swiftly with a sweep of his fine robes and a final burst of brilliance.

Then millions of years seemed to pass before her eyes in a single moment. The scene settled on a particular epoch of time, and she watched, fascinated, as if it were a movie. In fact, she said so. "This . . . this is like a movie."

"Only this is real, Virginia," he reminded her.

"But what does all this have to do with me? You said you were going to answer my questions, and I mean . . . Don't get me wrong now; this is fascinating. And it has answered a number of questions about God and the Bible that I've had since elementary school. But I'm no theologian or anything. Why show all of this to me?"

"Because all of this is about *you*, Virginia. As a human being, it is all about *you*. You, like every other human being on the planet, hold more sway over the earth and your life than you have ever realized. This whole thing is about you. Watch, because more will be revealed to you."

She sighed, like a kid who's had too much ice cream.

"Okay, I guess it's like a friend of mine once said: 'Did you want what you got, when you got what you wanted . . .' Okay, I asked for this, so let's keep going."

She looked at the screen and saw, "You!" she exclaimed excitedly. "That's you!"

Mahatiel stood motionless while on the screen she saw him, these eons in the past, darting back and forth between heaven and Earth, Venus, Mars, and Jupiter, the moon, and other planets. There were other angels with him that seemed to be assisting him, helping him.

She watched as he visited each planet and the angelic hosts over those planets. The planets teemed with angelic life. Each planet had a ruling authority that resided in a resplendent palace. Mahatiel went to each planet's palace in turn. She watched as each angelic being greeted him with warmth and respect, like old friends. Mahatiel gathered something from each angelic leader, a tribute of some type. In addition, there seemed to be varying degrees of authority among them. The rulers over the larger planets seemed to command more respect and had more angels under them. But everywhere, Mahatiel was greeted as an old friend, and with dignity and reverence for his office and his duties.

The head of each host, before speeding him on his way, gave him something that, by the way they conveyed it to Mahatiel, seemed to be with great veneration and of great value.

At every planet he landed and entered the grand hall in the palace and conversed with the angels. Upon leaving, they knelt and passed to him a large globe of power, a globe that seemed to throb with energy, life, and color. Everyone on the planet, it seemed, contributed to the orb, and then on the appointed day, it was brought and given to Mahatiel with much ceremony. Mahatiel would never touch or receive it personally, as if not to taint it. He would turn to his two assistants, who carried a large solid-gold box borne between them. The host of each planet would in turn gently place the orb in the box. Each time, Mahatiel would lift his hands to the heavens and glorify God. The lid would be closed, and Mahatiel and his two assistants would take flight to the next planet, and the process would be repeated again and again, graciously and with much celebration. At every planet, that is, except for one.

Earth.

Virginia watched closely as Mahatiel arrived at the rich and lush planet that looked nothing like the one she knew as her home. There were no polar ice caps. The entire planet was a lush green. There were no islands or continents. There was only one huge, massive landmass that spread well over half the planet and stretched from what today is the North Pole down across the equator to the South Pole. It was unbelievable!

The whole planet was a tropical paradise. She saw angels soaring two abreast through the open blue skies, relishing in the freedom of flight. They were swooping down in tight formations over a vast, clear blue sea unlike anything she'd ever seen or could imagine.

She watched as on the screen she saw Mahatiel and his two assistants, carrying the large gold engraved box between them with its precious cargo, make the journey to earth. She cast a glance at Mahatiel beside her as he was obviously reliving this scene in his mind even as he watched it unfold before him on the screen. She observed and felt him stiffen and become tense as though steeling himself as he watched. She soon saw why the memory was so troubling to him.

She became absorbed in the images as she watched Mahatiel and his companions sail like eagles over the sweeping paradise toward the North Pole and Lucifer's residence, an expansive castle.

She gasped.

It was huge! Its spires reached miles, not feet, up to the very heavens. It was as grand as it was ominous.

Mahatiel read her thoughts.

"It's six hundred forty-six miles high and six hundred forty-six miles wide on all four sides, and the foundations plummet six hundred forty-six miles deep," he said without taking his eyes from the screen. "And, at the time of my arrival," he said, nodding toward the image of himself on the screen, "he was still building . . ."

"Good Lord," she said, her eyes growing wide with wonder. "You think he was trying to compensate for something?" she said aloud half to herself.

"What?"

"Uh, nothing," she said quickly. "Bad joke."

"Hmph," said the angel, engrossed in the next scene.

She watched as Mahatiel approached the monstrous castle. *The North Pole!* she thought to herself. *And not a drop of snow or ice in sight! This is unbelievable! Nobody would believe this! The place looks like Hawaii on a summer's day!*

"Say, how come—"she started.

"You'll see" was Mahatiel's abrupt response.

"Well, what's in the box that's so—"

"Watch," he said curtly.

Okay, so much for questions and popcorn during the movie.

The massive dark stone castle loomed larger and larger as they drew nearer until the three angels with their precious cargo looked like three white specks with a gold snuffbox between them.

Hothiel, his senior assistant, flew abreast to him and within earshot. He looked at Mahatiel and said, "I don't like this, Mahatiel. It's larger now than when we were here last. Is he building a dwelling, or a shrine to himself?"

"I know, but hold your tongue. For we—" He paused in midsentence, for as they drew even nearer to the castle, they picked up what could only be described as a military escort—Lucifer's angels, elite guards by the looks of them. There were sixteen altogether, four that took flying positions in the front, four below them, and four on each side. They did not say a word. They wore dark brown apparel and stern looks as they boxed the three angels in. Hothiel looked at Mahatiel with a look of concern and irritation, but as instructed, he held his tongue.

Mahatiel shared his friend's uneasiness, especially as he noted that their escorts held staffs in their hands, and somehow he felt they knew how to use them.

About twenty furlongs out, the large, regal, gold and

diamond-crusted doorway, the size and height of a giant redwood tree, towered before them.

As they drew even closer to the castle, their escort suddenly tightened its perimeter, and there was a jostling of feathers as they maneuvered the trio abruptly to the left and away from the entrance.

"Where are they taking us?" said Hothiel in obvious irritation.

"I think," said Mahatiel pensively, "they're taking us to the rear entrance."

"The rear entrance!" Hothiel said angrily. "Why, that's an insult of the vilest kind! The Master shall hear of this!" he continued, enraged.

Mahatiel held his hand up for silence and studied the activities on the ground beneath them as he responded quietly, "I believe that is exactly what our friend Lucifer wants."

Hothiel's jaw tightened, and he was silent the rest of the way.

Mahatiel looked over his shoulder at Uriel, the third member of their team. Their eyes met, and Uriel gave him a curt nod. Yes, he had seen the activity below them too.

Their escort took them on a wide swath around the mammoth structure, and Mahatiel found the scene very disturbing. On the other planets as he flew over their vast fields, he saw angels at work and play. They were building, expanding, talking, and laughing, their white robes billowing in the wind as they chased one another in the heavens, tagging and teasing one another with their wingtips.

In contrast, here he found aerial maneuvers, but not play. He found marching ranks of angels many rows deep below them, but no joy. And everyone was working—hard at work.

Doing what? And so far, in his traverse over Earth's surface, he had not seen one single smile.

Suddenly the scene changed to a room deep inside the formidable fortress. Virginia immediately recognized the tall imposing figure, his back to them, bent and stooped over what appeared to be a worktable of some type.

It was a large room, dark except for two candles at either end of the worktable. On the four walls were shelves with all manner of plants and roots, vials, powders, herbs, potions, and strange devices. The shadows danced and flickered among the shelves and vials, like animated and mischievous things.

There was a pounding at the door that echoed throughout the large room.

"What is it? I told you I was not to be disturbed!"

"They are here for the Tribute, sire."

"Is all in readiness?"

"Oh, yes, sire. The others have been briefed and are well prepared. They know exactly what to do."

Lucifer sat up and started wiping his hand on a nearby cloth. "Good," he said with a note of finality. He carefully draped the cloth over his project. His body and shoulders were so massive that Virginia couldn't see around him to see what he was working on.

He rose stiffly, laughed with an air of self-satisfaction, opened the door, and left. She heard him double lock the door from the other side, then try the door several times to make sure it was secure.

What could he be working on that was so secret?

Virginia was pondering this question as she stared at the cloth covering the table. She jumped suddenly when she saw the rag slowly move, apparently of its own accord.

Curiosity crawled up her back and took a front-row seat on her shoulder and badgered her until she almost couldn't think of anything else. After a few seconds, which seemed like centuries, she spoke. "Well, since you're not going to volunteer the information, I have to ask. What is under that cloth?"

Mahatiel turned to look at her sternly and said through tight lips, "Only the worst blight to ever strike mankind, Virginia. The unthinkable," he said sadly.

Lucifer's custom-made boots pounded their way down the ornate hall of his grand castle, largest in the entire kingdom of God, second only to that of heaven itself. He walked regally up the steps from his secret chambers to the upper floors and the greeting hall, the place where he welcomed visitors. And there had been many of those in the last few lunar cycles.

He checked his hands carefully. Mustn't leave even a trace of what he was working on anywhere on his hands. He stopped suddenly on the stairs and looked at his left hand. There, near the first finger, on the back of his hand near the first knuckle, was a black spot.

Pure dark.

Quickly he pulled a kerchief from his pocket, one he kept there for just such occasions. He rubbed vigorously to remove the evidence of his doings. The spot did not smear onto the cloth, but transferred neatly, perfectly. He examined his hand closely, turning it this way and that to the light flowing through the stained glass-windows of the hall.

He saw it then. Just where the spot had been, there was a discoloration of his skin. His heart leaped with surprise and excitement! It had worked! His latest experiment had worked, and he hadn't even known it! If it weren't for this annoying interruption of His messengers, he would even now, no doubt, be rejoicing in his laboratory.

He was nearly at the top of the steps and smiling broadly to himself. *Excellent!*

He brought his hand close to his face and eyed the light

spot carefully. There was no doubt; it was definitely deterioration of the skin.

Abruptly and without warning, he heard footsteps approaching down the long corridor toward him—and voices.

"No! I will not wait here patiently any longer. Where is he? This is the second time in as many months that we have arrived for the Tribute and have had to wait."

He immediately recognized Mahatiel's voice, though he had to admit that he'd never heard it raised in anger before.

He heard Azael, his assistant, continue to try to stall, as he had been instructed. It was rather amusing.

"Where is he? Where is your leader—"

"Oh, you mean the Master?" said Azael, playing dumb.

There was abrupt silence, and Lucifer's smile faded at Mahatiel's next comment.

"No. We have one Master, the Holy One, and you would do well to never forget that, nor to get the two of them confused. Now, for the last time—where is your leader, and where is the Tribute that is due? For months it has been late, and last month's was of some strange quality I have never seen before. It was not well received by the Master. I have been extremely patient with your leader, but my time of patience has come to an end!"

Mahatiel was furious, Hothiel noted with unbridled appreciation. Usually it was he that was the impatient one. It was he who was quickly offended at the multitude of such slights. It did him good to see that Mahatiel had a limit to his patience. For Hothiel, such items had crossed his own threshold of tolerance eons ago. He studied Azael thoughtfully. The angel's eyes grew wide with surprise; he knew that he had pushed this official courier of the throne far enough. He represented the Very God of Glory. To rancor the one who received the Tribute was to challenge the rule of the throne of God Himself! One took his very existence and life into his own hands with such insolence!

Azael was visibly uncomfortable and wished for a hole to crawl into. *Where is the Master,* Azael thought to himself, and *why is he leaving* me *to deal with these three? The Master is playing with fire, literally, in playing this cat-and-mouse game with the Tribute of the almighty God!*

Lucifer's smile disappeared instantly. A strained and diplomatic one forced its way across his lips as he emerged from the staircase and addressed his troublesome guests, much to the visible relief of his senior aide.

"Well, welcome, honored guests," he said with oily charm. "Azael, you may leave." He dismissed the aide with a wave of his right hand. He was the epitome of deceitful charm. He carefully hid his left hand from sight.

Hothiel stepped forward, barely controlling his anger. "Where is the Master's Tribute!"

Mahatiel placed a restraining hand upon his assistant's chest, easing him back a step. He understood the young angel's anger. He too was angry, but he could not allow such a blatant breach of protocol. Ill-mannered or not, Lucifer was still the anointed cherub, for now, and could be addressed with such a direct rebuke only by the Lord Himself or one authorized to do so.

"Who is this winged dog who wishes to speak in the council of its elders?" Lucifer mocked.

Hothiel bristled.

"Mahatiel," Lucifer continued, "if your pets cannot control themselves, then I shall have to have them restrained, so that we may discuss our business in . . . peace. Perhaps you would allow me the pleasure of restraining them—personally," he said with a strange smile and deep meaning.

Hothiel's wings snapped open powerfully to full length,

every feather straining with fury at such a base insult. Like Uriel, he too was dressed in a gold breastplate engraved with the name of God inscribed in bold letters. Beneath this was a three-inch-wide belt of gold. All of this was over a brilliant white robelike garment with pants underneath. His long, shoulder-length hair was the color of sand, tied back by a gold headband. His skin was the color of tanned gold normally, but now it turned a reddish tan with his rage. His eyes flashed white, the literal color of lightning, in his exasperation.

"Uriel, take Hothiel and wait for me in the courtyard." Mahatiel's voice was strong, controlled, and insistent. With much effort, Uriel got Hothiel to comply. "Take the adytum with you."

Uriel's eyes queried him.

But Mahatiel repeated his command. "Take the adytum with you. I'll call for it when I'm ready."

Uriel's wings fell, in synch with his countenance.

Lucifer fought hard not to smile behind Mahatiel's back. *So predictable,* he thought to himself. *So predictable* . . .

Now both angels gripped the handles of the gold Tribute box and launched themselves several feet into the air. For long moments, the only sound heard was the sweep of their sullen wings as they flew down the long hallway and then exited to the courtyard beyond.

Mahatiel turned to face the creature who was his equal in height and authority. Now began the game of protocol and tête-à-tête.

"What are you doing, Lucifer? What kind of game are you playing?"

Lucifer strolled casually to a very large and ornate chair, resplendent with precious stones dug from the earth and brought from all over the planet to celebrate his palace and leadership. They were contributions from his servants, his angels, which required only a little coaxing and intimidation on his part. This chair was a duplicate of the one sitting in his lavish throne room. He had duplicates like this strewn all over his mammoth castle. He felt that in his own way they symbolized his authority, the fact that he ruled every square inch of the earth.

"My dear Mahatiel, whatever are you talking about?" he said, crossing his legs and studying the fingernails of his right hand as nonchalantly as possible.

Mahatiel studied him for a moment. They were of equal height, thirteen feet tall, and of equal build and stature. They were both as strong as a dozen bulls, with the massively well-built physique of ruling angels.

But Lucifer, the Morning Star, had a much greater anointing. He was still the anointed cherub, even though he had requested and received this position as a ruler of worlds. He held a throne and dominion. He combined two positions into one, unprecedented in kingdom history. But being the very guardian of the throne and glory of God, to trade that for this, unprecedented though it was, still seemed, in his mind, a step down. Why?

Lucifer had changed since he had first been appointed the anointed cherub. He had always had an air of superiority. That was just Lucifer, and one just accepted it as part of his personality. Some angels held their own suspicion when he had first requested and then been set in place as a ruling angel, a throne as it was termed. And in addition to that, he requested to be designated an Indisputable Angel of Dominion. As a throne angel, he held sway over the Earth and ruled it and all the angels assigned there. But as an Angel of Dominion, all the angels that were throne angels in their own right in this solar system and among the nine planets answered to him, and he to the Lord God.

Again, many questioned whether his position change was a step down, or more a move of equal influence. But what a change had come over him in the last millennia of ruling . . .

Lucifer shifted uneasily under Mahatiel's steady gaze and probing questions. Mahatiel noticed now that even his physical features had started to change, imperceptibly at first, but now more and more.

Mahatiel studied Lucifer's features as the huge angel continued to try to appear calm and unmoved and toy with his fingers—of his right hand.

Why was he keeping his left hand hidden from sight?

Lucifer wore a beige formfitting tunic and breeks, a pantlike garment that clung to him like a second skin. They tapered down into the top of his boots. Mahatiel's eyes flared briefly. The boots appeared to be made of animal skin. He wore from his shoulders a black robe that flowed like dark water. He had a habit of wrapping himself in it whenever he talked to anyone at length, as if it gave him comfort to enshroud himself in its dark folds. The tunic, stretched over his massive, powerful chest, rose and fell rhythmically as he breathed deeply. The deep V-shaped collar dove to a peak and exposed the tops of his mammoth pectoral muscles. This was designed to impress, intimidate, and draw attention to his phenomenal strength.

His face was devoid of hair, for angels did not grow beards or mustaches. The facial features were beautiful, yet entirely masculine. The eyes were deep-set and brooding, the brows elegant and smoothly arched. The nose was curved and sharp. The jawline, powerful and set, conveyed resolve and determination. The broad forehead betrayed deep intelligence. The hair was the color of spun gold, though Mahatiel noticed that it seemed slightly darker now for some reason. It was held in place by a beautiful ruby-encrusted crown. Lucifer was nothing if not opulent.

"Are you planning to attend to the business at hand, or are you just going to stand there and stare at me all day?" said Lucifer, turning his nails this way and that, pretending to study them. He still kept his left hand neatly tucked out of sight within the many folds of his dark robe.

"Where are your ruling garments, your white garb?" asked Mahatiel. "I know you still have your glorious garment of the Stones of Fire. I know you cherish—no, worship—that with a love that rivals any I've ever seen. But where are your white ruling garments?"

The Morning Star didn't answer.

"Why don't your angels wear the garments of the kingdom anymore?" Mahatiel continued.

"Is there a rule against wearing garments of one's own design?" asked Lucifer.

"No . . ."

"Well, then, perhaps there should be," Lucifer noted curtly. "But since there isn't, then I will do what I want."

"You know that I will have to report this."

"Report what you like."

"Where is the Tribute?" Mahatiel asked, businesslike.

Strong sunlight fell through the windows on the back of Lucifer as he rose without answering and headed toward the stairs leading back down to his laboratory.

"Lucifer, where is the Tribute?" Mahatiel asked again, louder this time.

Lucifer kept walking as if oblivious to there being anyone else in the room.

"Lucifer! In the name of the Lord God of heaven, where is the Tribute?" Mahatiel shouted, using his full authority as a representative of the kingdom.

Lucifer froze in his tracks. Anointed cherub or not, when the name was invoked, the power of it demanded immediate response and obedience. He struggled to regain his composure. This was an unexpected development. He had anticipated a more mild-mannered response from Mahatiel.

But Mahatiel had had enough. He knew when he was being toyed with, and when it came to the Tribute, that would not be tolerated.

"I . . . have no Tribute to give this month," said Lucifer.

Mahatiel was stunned and speechless. For a moment there was total, absolute silence between them. This was unprecedented and absolutely unheard of! He was flabbergasted!

"No Tribute! That is unthinkable!"

Lucifer had played his hand. His die was cast. This was a little bit ahead of his timetable, but he was confident that everything was still well in hand. Azael had been given his orders; he knew what to do.

Lucifer headed down the stairs. Mahatiel followed him, then stopped at the head of the stairs. "Lucifer! What have you done! Do you realize what you are doing?"

Lucifer continued down the stone stairs without looking back.

Mahatiel watched Lucifer's hulking figure grow smaller as the black-robed angel rapidly descended the steps into the dark bowels of the castle. Finally he heard the deep voice waft an answer back up to him from the underground depths.

"Why should I give to Him what rightfully belongs to me?" And with that, he was gone, swallowed up into darkness.

Mahatiel called several times, but there was no response—only his own voice called back to him as it echoed off of the thirteen-foot-thick walls.

What is he doing? What has come over him?

In a moment, Mahatiel decided to use the Name to force

Lucifer to pay the Tribute due. The penalty was severe to those who chose to use the Name lightly, but the Holy One would surely understand in such an instance as this.

He started down the granite steps after Lucifer, when suddenly he heard a loud cry from outside. He glanced down into the blackness once more, torn between his duty and the obvious disturbance out of doors.

The matter was settled for him when he heard Hothiel call his name, loudly.

He grunted in frustration, stretched his wings full length, and launched himself into the air and quickly down the hall like a golden arrow.

He had never missed a Tribute before, not since the Holy One had appointed him! What would he say? How would the Holy One react? How would He receive him? Would He receive him—or would He blame him? He had much to ponder.

He was still deliberating these things within himself when he burst out into the courtyard into the middle of a melee that took his breath away.

Mahatiel couldn't believe his eyes! Hothiel and Uriel were under attack! Angels, of the same type that had so rudely escorted them here, were attacking his two assistants with their staves! They were trying to steal the Tribute!

The two angels were trying to hold off their attackers bare-handed, and were the worse for it.

One of Lucifer's angels swooped down low. The angel swept past Uriel, who was fighting off several escorts, and grabbed one of the golden handles of the adytum and tried to make off with it. But the box was much heavier than he thought. Hothiel spun away from the two angels he was fighting and struck the thief with his fist just below the eye. The escort let go and withdrew. But Hothiel paid for his courage by being pummeled in the back by several staves.

Mahatiel leaped into the fray. He and his assistants were unarmed. This was a Tribute-gathering mission, not an armed expedition. Mahatiel saw that they were all beyond reasoning. Apparently whatever had poisoned Lucifer's mind and heart had affected these too.

"In the Name cease!" The escorts were caught by surprise at the invocation of the Name. They immediately fell back as if hit by a physical blow. Frightened, they quickly dispersed and disappeared from sight.

Mahatiel quickly saw to his comrades. Hothiel was badly bruised, and Uriel's shoulder was separated, possibly broken.

Mahatiel was furious. To steal the Tribute, and to attack the emissaries of the Holy One! This was tantamount to war! Lucifer must be mad to think that he could get away with such treachery. *Could his servants have acted alone, without Lucifer's knowledge?* he pondered.

No was his next immediate thought. He remembered how tightly regimented their every move had been since arriving on the planet, and the massive marching maneuvers that he and Uriel had noticed as they flew over. No, every single movement on the planet was carefully controlled and orchestrated. This was a planned attack. And they had better remove themselves before Lucifer's minions returned with reinforcements.

He and Hothiel grabbed the golden handles of the adytum, and with Uriel as scout, they took to the air cautiously and flew swiftly to the Sides of the North, toward heaven. Unknown to them was the fact that small contingents of angels from Mars and Venus moved without delay to intercept them, on Lucifer's orders.

Lucifer had returned to his laboratory and continued his experiment as he awaited Azael's report.

Azael paced back and forth in the main hall, terrified of reporting to his master. He would be furious. They had failed. He knew that Lucifer would inquire about the box. "Did you get the box?" he would say.

He remembered Lucifer's charge to them that morning before the Tribute gatherers were scheduled to arrive: "You must get the box," Lucifer had said. "All of this is for naught if we do not get the box. Mahatiel is predictable—protocol demands that at a perceived disagreement, others of lower rank may not be present. He will undoubtedly then send the two with the adytum outside, and when he does, that is your time to strike—and swiftly! There can be no mistakes, Azael! Or there will be judgment to pay! Can I trust you in this? Of course I can, for you know what will happen to you if you fail. Don't you?"

Azael nodded enthusiastically.

"Well, you're wrong, my winged friend. You only think you do. You have no idea of how I will make you suffer."

"Soon we will launch an attack against the Holy One Himself," Lucifer continued. "I have already spoken with a number of others, and we have at least one-third of the angels with us—all those who rule among the nine planets. The others will join us too, no doubt, once they see the might of our armies. Our attack must be swift and merciless."

"We here, and the angelic rulers of Venus, Pluto, Mars, and the rest of the nine planets, are with you, but tell us, how can you hope to overcome the the almighty God of the universe?" asked Archiel, a throne angel.

"A valid question," Lucifer had said, smiling. "I told every one of you and the nine dominions you represent that if you followed me, we would rule all the heavens. Would I begin such a venture without a plan? Would not a fool begin such a venture without first having a resource—a weapon of such fury so as to even out the balance of power? To launch an attack without first having such a weapon would be to invite certain destruction—and I assure you, I have ambitions of grand leadership, not of noble suicide. Hearken to me, my faithful minions and future rulers of galaxies! I am developing a weapon that will guarantee our total and absolute victory!"

"Are you sure, Lucifer?" Samael, another throne angel, had asked. "We take our very lives into our own hands being here today, joining you in this." His eyes showed his concern.

"Am I sure?" Lucifer had snapped, seizing him with his eyes. "I will tell you how sure I am! You will see me ascend from here, from this very spot—to there!" he had said, pointing up into the heavens. "I will ascend into heaven! I will exalt my throne above the stars of God! I will sit also upon the Mount of the Congregation in the Sides of the North! I will ascend above the heights of the clouds! I will be like the Most High," he said, clenching his fists, "and destroy Him!" The onlooking crowd of secretly gathered angels oooed and ahhhed with wonder.

"And it begins, here—today! That is why we must not fail. That is why we will not fail! First the Tribute, and then we invade heaven itself! To your posts! We will rule all of heaven, my brothers, and the God who made it!"

The hordes of core leaders in the room had rocked the castle with their roars of approval.

And now, in the crucial first part of their plan, Azael had failed.

What will I say? What will I say? Azael asked himself. He took a deep breath, gathered his courage, and headed uncertainly down the steps to the chamber of his master's deepest and darkest secrets, where he knew his master would be eagerly waiting for news of the day's events.

The door to his master's laboratory was ajar. He peered

in first. He saw his master's shadow lying on the floor, stretched long and flickering across the cold stone in the prancing candlelight.

Azael swallowed hard and gently eased open the large oaken door. The door swung open slowly, silently sweeping the stone floor. The master seemed so intent in his work that Azael thought twice about disturbing him.

Bent over his worktable again, Lucifer seemed enthralled in his latest experiment, oblivious to anything else. Azael held his breath. He purposely did not make a single sound. He forcibly controlled his breathing to keep himself calm. He opened his mouth to speak, then stopped.

The master is busy, hard at work. Perhaps I shouldn't disturb him. Uh, perhaps it would be better if I came back later, when, uh, the master was less busy. Yes, that sounds like a good idea. The master always hate being interrupted in the middle of his work.

Azael had just convinced himself that this was the best course of action and was starting to gently close the door when Lucifer stiffened and said, "Is that you, Azael?" His voice was seductively smooth and deceitfully calm.

Azael froze in midmotion like a deer caught in the open. "Uhh . . . yes, Master."

Lucifer straightened up slowly, without turning around. He began cleaning his hand with a cloth, speaking slowly and deliberately. "Let's see . . . you come skulking into my laboratory without knocking. You usually come bounding down the stairs, your footsteps heralding your presence leagues before your normal greeting does. However, this time you come walking so quietly that even a neurotic mouse would have a hard time hearing you. That could mean only one thing."

He suddenly stopped wiping his hands.

"You've failed."

Silence.

"Isn't that so, Azael?" Lucifer turned suddenly, facing him with deep and piercing dark eyes.

Azael swallowed deeply. "Master, I—we—there were extenuat—"

Lucifer rushed him suddenly, until they were nose to nose. "You know how I feel about failure! Don't you."

He was in trouble, and he knew it. Lucifer was biting his words, an indication that he was totally incensed.

"What happened?" The words were not a question, but an interrogation.

Azael explained in detail, exactly what had happened.

Lucifer's jaw tightened visibly. Controlled fury pumped through his veins, and Azael could swear that he felt waves of anger radiating from the enraged ruler, like heat from a roaring fire.

"And finally, sire, he invoked the Name, and we had to withdraw."

Lucifer raised an eyebrow. The stakes had just gone up again.

The Name, Lucifer thought to himself. *Hmph, Mahatiel is cleverer than I thought.*

He stared at Azael for a long moment. He despised the creature for his dismal failure.

If you had slit Mahatiel's throat, he would have been unable to use the Name . . .

Azael wilted under his master's piercing gaze. What was he thinking? He had never failed his master like this before. What would his master do to him? He was prepared for almost anything, except for what his master did next.

Lucifer smiled and put his arm around him. "Of course, I understand," oozed Lucifer with a sweetness that chilled Azael down to the bone.

"In fact," he said, guiding the angel over to his worktable,

"I have an experiment that I need your help with. You do want to help me and make up for your horrendous failure, don't you?"

There was just the slightest hint of a threat implied, a bone-chilling evil behind his words, a subtle caveat that warned powerfully against declining his offer.

"Of course," Azael said in a hoarse whisper.

"Good," said his master slowly. "Here," coaxed Lucifer, nudging the frightened but nonetheless curious angel closer to his worktable. "Come, come closer. Bend down here near the table so that you can get a good look, and tell me what you think."

Azael leaned closer until his nose was just inches from the mysterious faded brown cloth on his master's worktable.

"This, my faithful and most valued servant, is my latest experiment. I call it Muth. This will give me the power to rule the universe. This will give me the power to have the throne of heaven and God Himself at my feet!" said Lucifer, his voice slowly rising in crescendo. Lucifer's eyes grew wide with excitement. Azael's did too, swept up in the moment, his excitement building, not knowing what to expect next.

Lucifer paused for a moment, as if in thought, then mused aloud, almost to himself, "But I need to know first if it will work."

Just as his master said this, Azael choked back a gasp.

The faded brown cloth—it had moved! Something stirred beneath its frayed edges.

Quickly, before Azael could back away, Lucifer snatched the rumpled cloth away and leaped back several feet with all the swiftness of a panther avoiding the spring of a trap. The speed of the move surprised Azael, and in spite of himself, he felt a sudden nervousness that he couldn't explain.

Lucifer's eyes were wide and flashed dark blue with wonder and excitement. Azael noted in the next brief moments that he lived that he had never seen his master's eyes, or any angel's eyes, flash that color before. He turned his head back to look at the small gelatin-like thing on the table. It moved and undulated before him. It was shiny and was as black as the darkness of space itself.

Something within him warned him to move away. But . . . but it was so mesmerizing in an odd sort of way that he couldn't pull himself away. *Hmph. Surely, this is no threat . . .*

He stood up, and, looking at his master, he pointed a finger at the shapeless, undulating, small mass of dark matter and said, "Master, what is this?"

Lucifer watched as his creation latched itself onto Azael's extended finger and spread rapidly up the surprised angel's arm. Azael screamed in fear, pain, and abject terror.

"Master!" he screamed, "What is this?"

Lucifer watched the creature feed. He was fascinated and entranced, like a proud father watching his child's first steps.

Azael felt the thing entrench itself into his very bones. The thing seemed to draw the very life from him, sucking on it, feeding on it. He felt parts of his inner being burst inside of him as this thing sucked so much life force from him that his very bones began to crack and cave in on themselves from the pressure.

"Remove this—" he gasped, and suddenly realized he couldn't breathe. "What—what—" he stammered, realizing that he was losing coherent thought. His mind then seized up with terror as he watched the blackness spread rapidly over the tall frame of his once powerful body that now turned brown and shriveled rapidly, like a fruit left out too long in the noonday sun. He watched the blackness spread up his body and felt it enter his throat. He struggled to get away, but the tide of sweeping devastation was so rapid that within seconds he found himself being consumed alive where he stood.

He fell up against the worktable and tried to steady himself with his right arm, watching in horror as the shriveled limb snapped like a dry twig. He collapsed onto the table, face-first. His mind was frozen with unbearable terror, his eyes locked helplessly on Lucifer as he screamed in pain and kept repeating, "Master—what is this? Master, what is this? Master, what is thisss?"

The last scream was so loud that even Lucifer had to cover his ears. Finally, the last screaming question was choked off in a throat suddenly gone silent, and eyes that were a revolting murky gray stared sightlessly at him.

Lucifer looked at the lifeless form. The question still echoed around the hollow chamber and up and down the subterranean halls. Finally he whispered an answer, as if in reverence of the disquieting and frightening display: "This . . . is Death."

The dark, carnivorous energy force latched itself onto Azael's finger and consumed him. The consciousness of the entity was solely focused on one thing: consuming and devouring whatever it touched. It was a primordial urge that moved it, drove it to consume. It penetrated the skin cells of the angel. Like a shark following the scent of its intended victim, it dove into the cell structure of Azael, hungrily seeking for his life source.

It vigorously penetrated and swam its way through the cell structure of this creature, down to the bones in the hand, up the wrist to the arm, up the arm to the shoulder, from the shoulder to the throat, from the throat and neck, finally to the head.

Here it paused for a moment.

Yes, there was life force here, but it was not the source. It must have the source of this creature's life. That was its reason for existence, that was its reason for being, that was its dark purpose and dream. Thus, it vigorously devoured the brain, swiftly and efficiently, and then quickly moved on.

It continued down the spine to the feet, up the feet to the ankles, from the ankles to the legs, and up the legs to the groin. It ate its way from the groin to the stomach, and from the stomach to the lungs. All the while that it furiously ate its way through the creature's body, the creature writhed in pain. In its wake, the entity left total devastation. The creature's skin shriveled horribly and turned brown, and then black, stiff, and brittle. As the entity ate its way viciously like a rampant piranha, it noted in passing that the creature fell up against a table and the right arm snapped under the weight. Just as the creature gasped its last and lay paralyzed across the table, the entity finally located what it had been searching for. It reached the core of the creature's body. It reached the source of life and energy.

It had reached its heart.

This was what it was animated for and drawn forth from the blackness of nonexistence for. This is what the Morning Star told it that it must do.

At last.

It attacked the lamp of life with all the tenacity of a great white shark. Finally, the light in Azael's eyes went out . . .

Lucifer stared at the body in the sudden silence for several long moments. Even he was taken aback by the rapid success of his . . . experiment.

He smiled and started to laugh. The frightening sound

echoed off the walls and filled the entire lower level with its self-satisfying and unsettling noise.

Lucifer started to pace back and forth in glee, hands clasped together like a child opening his very first gift.

"Excellent! Excellent! It works better than I could have ever conceived! Once I extract it from the body, then I shall be able to use it at my whim! All who oppose me will . . . will . . ."

He paused and sought for a word to convey his thought. He could not find one. *Hmph.* He would just have to invent one.

All who oppose me will . . . will . . .

Finally it struck him like a thunderbolt.

All who oppose me will die!

He would use his new creation to attack the kingdom and the very throne itself!

There had been a prohibition on angels experimenting with creating new forms of life. And he knew that full well. But after all, he had done nothing wrong. He had not broken any laws, for there had never been a prohibition regarding creating forms of nonlife! There had been no written or verbal prohibition against creating something that was never really alive in the truest sense! There was no prohibition against his sole creation! Nor was there a defense against it.

Death—it fed on the very life force and emptied it, *drained* it!

His eyes grew wide with the pleasure and wonder of his next thought.

To attack the very throne of the Creator Himself! To launch this entity at the very God of heaven! To watch death drain the very life from the Life-giver Himself!

He's a God who lives forever! So be it! thought Lucifer mockingly.

Then my perfect creation shall drain Him of life—forever! The Triune God shall be three emancipated drying husks, drained of all energy, all vitality, all power, all strength, all thought—except for one: the thought that it was I, Lucifer, who did this to Them . . .

"Marvelous!" he said aloud. Of course it was! Look at what he had already accomplished, unnoticed and unhindered!

He was unaware that his plans may have gone unhindered, but they did not go unnoticed.

Lucifer continued to relish in his self-proclaimed genius.

Now his true genius would be seen and recognized by the universe!

"I will ascend into heaven, not just when I am summoned like some mere servant—no! I will go when I wish! Indeed, now I will exalt my throne above the very stars of God!

"I will sit also upon the mount of the congregation in the Sides of the North, the gathering place of all the angels of God, where He rules and instructs and receives their unfettered praise, adoration, and worship!

"I will ascend above the heights of the clouds!" he exulted, then paused as a thought struck him that made his eyes narrow with avarice and lust for power.

"I will be like the Most High." He savored the thought like a fine wine and rolled it across the palate of his mind. He relished the strong taste of his own pride and consumed it like a drug. He repeated these phrases to himself over again and again and again. Then, "I knew if I was patient that all would be mine!" he said aloud with unbridled arrogance and delight.

"Hmmmmm," he said, and paused again. "After I extract my precious pet"—here he smiled coldly, and began to pace again—"I must design a delivery system, a way of getting it into the heart of the Kingdom and into the throne room itself before the Holy One has a chance to react."

Finally, at last, after years of planning in secret, the war had begun.

The entity enjoyed itself immensely. It devoured the life force in Azael and searched for more.

There was none. Only one was found in this body.

The entity Death found that now it was not limited to the mere diminutive form it found itself in when the master, Lucifer, had actualized it. It found now that it had an entire body at its disposal.

It went back to the brain. It activated, prodded, and manipulated the pieces that were left.

It had a body now. It could move of its own accord now. Surely the master would be pleased, and it could feed as the master promised it that it would, on all forms of life, including, as the master had promised, a Life Force that would last forever. Such a force would be worth consuming. The master had promised it thus—and it must be so. It smiled its satisfaction . . .

Lucifer heard a crackling behind him. Shocked, he turned quickly and stared at the body of Azael. It still lay across the table where it had fallen, but the milky gray eyes were still open, and he felt for some reason that they were no longer sightless. They actually had been following him as he had paced back and forth across the room.

He was taken aback as, without warning, the head, with an odd creaking sound, tilted at a bizarre angle as if studying him—and it was.

A chill suddenly went up Lucifer's spine.

It was looking at him. And it was smiling.

Aghast, Lucifer took a step back.

Suddenly the body moved, and a horrified Lucifer leaped backwards in alarm, in spite of himself.

"What are your orders, Master?" came the deep, throaty

reply to his gasp. "What are your orders, Master?" the thing said again as it nonchalantly picked up its severed arm and somehow reattached it.

"My orders?" he said cautiously, and then had a dawning realization.

He'd done it! He had done it! He no longer had need of a *means* to deliver his greatest weapon! The weapon could deliver itself! He no longer had a mere *entity* to do his bidding.

Now he had his very own angel of death!

His eyes narrowed with cunning as he planned his next move.

Virginia had become so engrossed in the unfolding scenes before her that for a moment she had forgotten where she was. The scenes mesmerized and enthralled her. She had lost herself completely in them. She glanced to her left at Mahatiel, and he too was totally absorbed. She was completely unaware of how much time had passed while she stood mesmerized. It could have been minutes, or it could have been hours. She had no way of knowing. Somehow, here—wherever "here" was—in this realm, there was no sense of the passage of time. "So death is—"

"An enemy, Virginia. Have you not read in your Bible: 'And the last enemy which shall be destroyed is death'? And again, after the summation of all things, 'And death and hell were cast into the lake of fire'?"

"No . . ."

"Oh, that's right. I forgot. You don't read your Bible," he remarked pointedly.

"All right, all right, point well taken. It's just all the 'thees' and 'thous.' They, uh, you know, slow me down. Nobody talks like that today."

"That's no excuse, Virginia, and you know it. Your mother gave you a Modern English Bible. And it is still in the top of the closet behind your collection of winter pajamas that she also gave you, the ones you did not like."

"No comment."

"Do you know why I have been instructed to show all of this to you, Virginia?" Mahatiel stood so still and immobile that at first she questioned whether the query came from him or some other unseen presence in the room.

"Uh, uh, no," she said hesitantly.

"Because the Lord wanted you to realize that you and all humans play a momentous role in the course of events. You live in one of many realms, Virginia, realms as vast as the seas and oceans of earth." He turned and stared directly into her eyes, and his voice seemed to echo not just in her ears but also in her mind and the very pit of her soul as he said, "Why is it, Virginia, that you wish to believe only in that which you can see? Why is it that you wish to believe that which it is easy to perceive? Because you live in one realm, you choose to believe that there cannot be another."

"But I believe in God," she protested.

"I know you do, Virginia, but that is not enough."

"Not enough?"

"That's right, Virginia, not enough. It is written: 'Thou believest that there is one God; thou doest well: the devils also believe, and tremble.' You believe in God, Virginia, and that's good, but not enough. Satan, his demons, and his fallen angels alike believe that there is a God, and what's more, knowing His power, they tremble at the thought of Him."

"What do you want from me?" she said.

"It is not enough for you to know about Him, Virginia, but you must come to know Him, personally, through His Son . . ."

"Is that even possible?"

"Of course it is. That is why He sent His Son, Virginia, and that is why the Son willingly came."

"How? How do I do that?"

"You remember what your mother taught you, and what you learned in Sunday school, do you not?"

"You mean about asking the Lord to come into my heart and forgive me of my sins and stuff?"

"Yes, Virginia, and to become your personal Savior."

"But I thought that because I went to church and because my mother was a Sunday school teacher and—"

"Virginia, it is a personal step of individual acceptance and faith. Simply because your mother was a member of the church, or even if your father had been a pastor, it would have made no difference in your salvation. God has sons and daughters, not grandchildren. Again, it is personal. You must receive His Son as your personal Savior."

"But I thought He was the Savior of the world."

"He is, for everyone in the world who will receive Him. Soap is a product that is available to the world for cleansing, but it is only those who apply the soap to themselves personally who are cleansed . . ."

"Oh . . ."

"And what's more, Virginia . . ." Here Mahatiel paused as he considered how to tell her what he knew he must. But was now really the time?

She searched his face with her eyes. "What is it— You're holding back something, aren't you? What is it?"

"Virginia . . ."

"What is it?" she asked anxiously.

He turned and looked at the screen. He suddenly turned philosophical as he pondered all that had happened to them and all that still lay ahead . . .

"Oh, humans, how insignificant you are in the scheme of

things, and yet"—here he paused, and his voice took on a wistful tone—"how grand you are . . . Oh Lord, 'what is man that thou art mindful of him? and the son of man that thou visitest him? For thou hast made him a little lower than the angels, and hast crowned him with glory and honor.'" His tone was that of one who pitied another.

He turned and looked at her. "Virginia, the minions of the Evil One were responsible for what happened to you, but God has decided that what they meant for evil, He will turn to good, for both you and the world. They sought to ruin your life, but what was the worst day in your life will give way to the most joyful."

Then his face turned sad somewhat as he said to her, "When you are told the fullness of what has happened to you, you will weep bitter tears, and Satan's minions will rejoice."

"I don't understand . . ."

"But," he continued, "when the fullness of God's wisdom is revealed to you, you will rejoice, and all of Satan's kingdom will mourn and weep because of you . . . "

"I—I don't understand," she repeated, more puzzled than ever. "What are you saying?"

He smiled sympathetically and looked back at the screen and the next stunning scene that emerged. It stirred deep emotions within him that he sought to hide.

Ever curious, Virginia started to continue her questions to Mahatiel when she glanced at the screen again and did a double take. Her question died quickly, drowned in a sea of wonder.

On the screen she saw Mahatiel, Hothiel, and Uriel racing back to the throne room of heaven with the adytum. As they passed through the vast reaches of space, she gasped at the speeds at which they were traveling.

"Just how fast were you going?" she whispered, her eyes fixed on the screen.

"We travel at twin rates of speed, that of thought and light. Light is the slower of the two speeds. It is akin to the path traveled by lightning."

"Excuse me?"

"At the speed of light and thought there are expanded wave patterns, and light and thought variables. Lightning is the physical manifestation of the controlled—"

"Never mind, never mind. The next time I ask you a dumb question like that, just tell me, 'Watch and see; watch and see.'"

He smiled. He was beginning to understand her sense of humor.

As rapidly as they were moving, Virginia noted with concern that she saw streaks of light moving from several planets on what appeared to be an intercept course. She gasped as her fears were realized when a contingent of angels dressed like Lucifer's guard surrounded the three angels and demanded that the Tribute be surrendered, or else . . .

"Surrender the Tribute—now!" screamed a throne angel with several hundred armed angels behind him.

Mahatiel pulled up short. "Archiel! Are you mad? Has this madness infected you too? We were friends once . . . "

Archiel hesitated. He had the look of someone determined to do wrong but embarrassed at having been caught in the act. Behind him one of his lieutenants leaned forward and whispered, "Remember what the master said: 'No mercy.'"

Suddenly a cold glared spread across Archiel's face. Compassion drained from it as swiftly as the wind. He looked at Mahatiel and said,

"The old alliances are dead. You are either with us or against us. You either serve Lucifer, our new sovereign, or perish with the old God and all His ways."

It was Mahatiel's face that turned cold then as he responded, "I would rather perish with His Word in my heart than Lucifer's treacherous, evil name on my lips."

Archiel recoiled as if struck, then roared in anger, "Then perish!" He leaped forward and attacked with his two-hundred strong-cohort.

Archiel attacked Mahatiel with his staff. Mahatiel raised his arm to block the blow as Hothiel and Uriel braced themselves as best they could for the onslaught. The staff broke over the angel's upraised arm with a loud snap. Above them then there was the loud and mournful sound of a horn.

Ba-rooo, Ba-rooo!

The sound had never been heard before. For the first time, it was the sound of angel being led in battle against angel as Michael charged the renegade angels with eight hundred of the kingdom's personal guard, Michael's own contingent of war angels. They surged forward, shouting their battle cry. Eight hundred swords raised high, and eight hundred voices raised as one as they charged, uttering their maxim, "Yes, Lord!"

It was here, unlike before, that Mahatiel began to give her a running commentary about what was taking place on the screen. She watched as dozens of contingents of brown-garbed angels armed with staves blocked their way as she listened.

"Lucifer was the first one to introduce violence into the universe and creation. He felt that he should keep all of the Tribute for himself. He fought ferociously to get it, and we were willing to give our lives to prevent that. It was the most powerful and valuable thing in the universe that we had to give to our God."

Good, well, since he was talking, maybe now I can get some of my many questions answered.

"It is still the most powerful thing that we can give to our God," Mahatiel continued.

"Lucifer became insanely jealous after man was created, and this ability to give Tribute was passed on by the Most High God to man also. Lucifer fought to steal the Tribute from us then, and fights yet now to steal that Tribute from man. For it is from this Tribute that Lucifer has derived his courage and uses it to augment his limited power. His greed for it knows no bounds. Like an addict of the basest sort, he craves to have it in one form or another.

"In its purest form, it is rare and most powerful. In its derived or diluted form, it is not as potent, but it still feeds and nourishes his ego, nonetheless. The quality of that given by mankind is the most sought after and esteemed for its strength, its potency, and its power.

"Those humans who have sampled its essence have found it more addictive than any substance known to mankind, more than all the drugs of this world combined. It is something that they will kill for, even enslave a whole people and race for. Lucifer for centuries has sought to keep the whole human race enslaved so that he could milk this precious homage from them one precious drop at a time."

"What exactly is the Tribute?"

Mahatiel turned and fixed her with somber eyes and said, "Your worship and your praise . . ."

"Worship?" she said incredulously. "Are you kidding? All this was over that little ten minutes' worth of singing we used to do in church every Sunday before the message? That's what all this is about? Why, that's why I stopped going to church in the first place, because that stuff was so boring. What could anybody possibly want with that?"

Mahatiel stopped the screen. He stared at her, and his eyes flashed purple. She could tell he was displeased.

He took a deep breath, then sighed audibly. His features softened somewhat, and then he spoke with the tone and patience of a parent instructing an impudent child.

"This may come as a surprise to you, Virginia, but the Eternal finds that kind of heartless worship just as boring as you do."

"He does?"

"Yes, He does."

"But I don't understand. You just said that—"

"That's not worship, Virginia. There's no power in that."

"But that's what it said on the church program—'Worship Songs.'"

Mahatiel shook his head. "Virginia, have you not read in your Bible where the Lord hath said regarding the heavenly Father: 'They that worship him must worship him in spirit and in truth'?"

"Uhhh, I think so."

Mahatiel raised an eyebrow. "When is the last time you read your Bible, Virginia?"

"I, uh—" She squirmed like a worm on a hot plate.

"How often do you read your Bible?"

She blushed. She couldn't even remember the last time she had read her Bible! *Has it really been that long?*

"You don't know, do you? Virginia, this is why the people of God perish so quickly. This is one of the reasons Satan's minions are after you, to reach you before you have a chance to absorb the truth of His Word and the protection it affords. Virginia, haven't you heard that God hath said, 'My people are destroyed for lack of knowledge'? It is the lack of knowledge of His Word. The lack of knowledge of the grand truths that can only be found there, and in no other place, in no other book . . ."

"Perish," she corrected, trying to use what little Bible knowledge she thought she had.

"What?"

"You said 'destroyed.' But it's *perish*. That's at least one Bible verse I know. It says, 'My people perish for lack of knowledge.'"

Mahatiel dropped his head and smiled.

"What's wrong?" she queried.

"You, who haven't picked up a Bible in ten years other than to dust under it, are endeavoring to correct me in its content?" He continued patiently, "Who told you that?"

"I dunno; I heard someone say that it's in the Bible, somewhere, and I remembered it."

He shook his head again. "Virginia, you have proven my point. If your life depended upon your knowledge of that Scripture alone, you would be dead right now. And do you know what? It does."

She was taken aback. "What does?"

"Your life depends upon your knowledge of His Word."

"Why—what's the big deal? I mean, it's only one little Scripture."

"Virginia, the God of the universe has said: 'The Words . . . are spirit, and they are life.' His Word is your covenant. You must know it for your own protection and the protection of those you love!"

"What's a covenant?"

Mahatiel threw up his hands.

Virginia looked at him in surprise. "I don't understand. Wh—?"

"Wait, this is too much to expect you to learn so soon, and I digress. I apologize. I shall teach you, one step at a time. But first let us continue with the importance of true worship. The rest will come in time."

"Oh, okay."

"True worship is from the heart, Virginia. It is not worship simply because it is labeled that way in a program. Genuine worship and praise come from the heart and have the power to change the course of nations and the very lives, hearts, and minds of those who touch the true essence of it. Do you understand?"

"Kind of . . ." she said, still puzzled.

"I'll give you an example. Remember the time you were a little girl and your friend Lauren was hit by a car?"

"Yes—all too well."

"You attended her wake. You stared at her little nine-year-old body lying stiff and cold in the casket. Remember how it terrified you?"

Her face clouded over with the reflection. "Yes, it was horrible. She looked like a cold wax mannequin—a wax version of herself." Even here, Virginia's body trembled inadvertently at the memory.

"Do you recall what Lauren's father did at the wake?"

She stared off into the distance, and her voice became quiet. "He was a very tall white man with jet-black hair and real deep-set eyes. He knew we were best friends and always treated me nice. But he used to scare me because he was always so quiet. But Lauren had said he became that way after her mother died. After that, Lauren was all he had left. When he walked up to the casket, he broke down and cried, and somehow I felt her death was my fault. I felt so guilty for just being alive, and I just knew that he must've felt that way too, that her death was my fault."

"And did he?"

"No. They—they started the service, and he came over to my momma and me. I stood there terrified, and he—he said to my mother, 'I'm sorry that my little girl had to die, but I'm so glad that your little girl didn't.' Then he patted me on my head, kissed my mom on the cheek, and slowly walked out. Nobody ever saw him again, from that day to this," she said wistfully. Then coming to herself, she looked at Mahatiel, puzzled. "But what does that have to do with this?"

"Do you remember what happened to you next?"

"Nnnoo—," she said slowly, thinking.

"Think hard."

"I am, I am," she snapped quickly. *What is he trying to get at?*

"I'll tell you what I'm getting at in just a moment, but first—think!"

"Oh! I hate it when you do that!" she protested.

"Think!" he insisted.

"All right, all right, this isn't easy for me, you know. Umm, okay! They started to sing this song, and . . ."

"Annnd," he encouraged.

"And I started thinking about what he had said, that he was sorry that it had happened to his little girl but was glad that it had not happened to me. Then, it dawned on me—that could've been me up there, right beside her. Then my mother would've been crying for me. It really struck me—hard."

"Then . . . ?"

"Come on, where are we going with this?"

"What happened next?"

"What are we doing going over all of this again—"

"You're embarrassed by what happened next, aren't you?" It was a gentle and knowing accusation, not a question.

"I—how did you know?"

"I'm an angel, Virginia. There's not much I don't know. Besides that, in heaven it's already been recorded."

"It has?" she gasped, amazed.

"Continue."

"Okay, okay. The choir started to sing some slow song—'Thank You, Lord,' I think it was—but I just couldn't get what he had said out of my mind: 'I'm glad it wasn't your daughter.' The more I thought about it, the more I realized that it could just as well have been me up there, if my uncle hadn't just happened by at that time, saw what was happening, and had just enough time to snatch me out of the way of that truck. And I suddenly started to thank the Lord that He was watching over me and had protected me. And it's funny, and I've never told anyone this before, but the more I thanked Him for saving my life, the better I felt! I mean, I could feel this deep and genuine gratitude. I realized I could've been crushed under those wheels like she was. And there was this . . . this . . . something, inside—deep inside my heart that just kind of released, and I didn't feel as miserable anymore. And there was this real presence of joy and forgiveness. I still missed my friend and felt the loss, but I didn't feel guilty for being alive anymore."

She paused for a moment in deep thought. "In fact, I felt like He heard me, like He really heard me."

"He did, Virginia. And that—what you did from your heart, your earnest gratitude that you expressed to Him for sparing your life—that is the essence of worship! That cannot be done from merely singing a song on a program simply because it is on the program. But you sing it because you realize He is genuinely worthy of your worship and praise. And whether it is done in the sanctity of a church or in the privacy of your own home, it is well received by Him as long as it is done sincerely—from the heart.

"Virginia, every time, or rather, the few times you've gone to church since then, you've felt it. You would sit in church and cry and didn't know why. You would start weeping sometimes, and no matter how hard you tried, you couldn't stop. That was Him, tugging at your heart, wanting to fellowship with you again. He was wanting to continue with you what the two of you had started when you were nine years old. Virginia, most people say that God never speaks to them, and that because things are so bad in the world, He couldn't possibly exist. He does exist, and you have seen that for yourself today, haven't you?"

"Yes . . ."

"I have permission to share another divine secret with you, Virginia, and I want you to hear me very clearly. It will help save your life if you take heed. And if not, then not even I can help you."

"Okay . . ." she said slowly.

"Some say God never speaks. They are wrong, Virginia. He is speaking all the time. The Word of God hath said in the book of Job, 'For God speaketh once, yea twice, yet man perceiveth it not' and the Word of the Almighty says He does this so that He may keep 'back his [the individual's] soul from the pit, and his life from perishing by the sword.'

"God is warning, alerting, guiding, helping all the time. The problem is not that God is not speaking, Virginia. The problem is that no one is listening."

"Huh? What do you mean?"

"The Lord Jesus Christ, Son of the Most High God, revealed a divine truth to His disciples, and they in turn recorded it so that it could be revealed to you, to mankind. The Lord said: 'The Words . . . are spirit, and they are life.' The Great God of the universe, the Holy One, is a spirit, and the Son of the Highest has said that they that worship Him must worship Him in spirit and in truth."

"Yeah, so?"

"So, Virginia, that is how He speaks to you personally, through His Spirit and His truth. His Word is truth."

"Okay, and . . . ? I don't get it."

Mahatiel kept his patience and decided to try another tack.

"Have you ever done something, gone somewhere, or

participated in some type of activity and the end result was less than satisfying, or just downright negative?"

"Yeah. So, who hasn't—so?"

"Have you ever had a conversation with someone afterwards about that situation or activity and said to them, 'Something told me not to go there, or do that, or go that way, or told me to wait till a better time,' or something to that effect?"

Her eyes grew wide with the very beginnings of comprehension. "Yeah! You mean—?"

"By ratio, Virginia, how many times would you say that has happened. A few times?"

"No. To be quite honest, lots! But I just thought it was—you know, me."

"It was you, Virginia. It was God speaking to the innermost part of you. It was God speaking to your heart, your inner man, your spirit, warning you. And what did you choose to do in most cases?"

"I went ahead and did what *I* wanted to do anyway," she said quietly.

"And who suffered for it, Virginia?"

Her eyes looked for a place to hide but couldn't find one. "I did," she said, childlike.

"And one more thing. Who got the blame for what happened to you?"

She suddenly felt very small and uncomfortable. She remembered saying many times to her girlfriends after just such incidents, "Why did God let this happen to me?" *Good Lord, is it really that simple?*

"But what about when little babies die, and people like my friend Lauren, and good people, and—"

"Whoa, Virginia. One thing at a time. One point at a time. Let's finish with you. Part of the reason you felt so guilty regarding Lauren's death is because you were the one who convinced her to go outside and play that day when she really didn't want to. Am I not correct?"

Virginia's head fell to her chest. How did he keep managing to know so much about her?

Lauren had said that she didn't want to go outside to play that day; she wanted to stay in the house and play. But Virginia had persisted. "But why, Lauren?" she had whined.

"'Cuz!"

"'Cuz what?"

"'Cuz I don't wanna!"

"But why not?"

"I dunno! I just feel—I just don't wanna!" Lauren must have felt exasperated at not being able to articulate the depths of her heart.

Virginia recalled that for a brief instant she had looked into her friend's eyes and saw something there, some inner concern perhaps. But she had dismissed it; her young mind at the time was too concerned with having its own way.

She had continued until she got her way, and the results had been disastrous. *Children can be so selfish,* she thought.

"Yes, you are correct," she answered Mahatiel's question.

"Virginia, God speaks to you by His Spirit," Mahatiel said, holding up his left hand, "and by His Word," he said, holding up his right hand. "The Son of the Most High said that the Spirit and the Word agree. So when you bring the two together"—he clapped his hands together and held them there—"then you have His Word and His Spirit sensitizing your spirit and increasing your ability to hear Him distinctly and follow His directions and will for your life."

"You make it all sound so easy."

"Virginia, that's why the Son of the Highest came. It is not as hard as most people think, nor as difficult as the world makes it out to be. That is why His Word was given."

"Well, what I'm going through now is not so easy! And why did He let all of this happen to me anyway?" she said, and then burst into tears.

Gently he said, "Haven't you been listening to anything I've been saying to you, Virginia?"

"Yesss," she said in between sobs, "but that was years ago." She then wiped her tears on her sleeve.

"No, Virginia. That was just weeks ago. *Six* weeks, to be exact."

She looked up, shocked. "What do you mean?"

"Remember what I said to you in the hospital when I was trying to get you to go back into your body?"

"Ye-yeah," she said, trying to remember exactly what he'd said.

"Let me refresh your memory. You were acting rather stubborn at the time and pestering me with questions, at a time when actions, not words, were the order of the day."

"Ohh, yes, I remember now. You said you had tried to warn me that morning."

"Yes, we did. The Spirit of God Himself, in fact, to be specific."

Her face twisted into a pretty puzzle. "But I don't remember seeing an angel or vision. And I certainly don't remember seeing God appear in my room. I would certainly have remembered that!"

"He didn't have to, Virginia, and neither did we. Do you recall the first thing that came to your mind when you decided to work late that night?"

She responded without even thinking about it.

"Yeah, something told me not to work late that night, but to wait until the next night, and I—oh."

She was astonished.

"Oh, my Go-gosh!" she caught herself. "You mean—?"

"Yes, Virginia. The Word of the Most High God says that He speaks in a still, small voice. That was not some*thing* that warned you not to stay and work late that night, Virginia. That was Some*one*—the heavenly Father . . ."

"But—but," she stammered, "how can I know if it's God every time?"

"Read and study His Word, Virginia, because, as it is written: 'The Word and the Spirit agree.' He will never tell you to do anything wrong or anything that is contrary to His nature or His Word. You will find, Virginia, that in this world, it is not enough to believe *in* God, but you also must believe *Him*."

"But . . . I always thought the Bible was . . . uh . . . you know, kind of . . . um," she hesitated and considered her next words carefully. How could she say this? The last thing she wanted to do was make Mahatiel mad. How could she say that she thought the Bible was, was—

"Outdated and old-fashioned?" said Mahatiel, finishing her sentence for her.

Virginia looked up, exasperated with herself, and groaned in frustration. "Arrgh! I keep forgetting that you can read my mind! I wish you wouldn't do that!" she protested, shaking her head.

"And I wish you wouldn't be so gullible as to believe every piece of satanic propaganda that spews out of the mouths of dark things," he said firmly.

She dropped her head, pouting slightly.

"Satan says it, and you believe it. God says it, and you require a sign."

Here Mahatiel threw up his hands and imitated someone praying, in a high-pitched and whining voice, "Sho' me a sign, Lawd! Sho' me a sign!"

She laughed in spite of herself. She had to admit that he

did look funny, while at the same time she could remember hearing both her mother and others pray that way.

"Satan and his minions tell Christians, 'You need to ask for a sign before you can trust and believe that the Bible is true. You shouldn't spend too much time reading the Bible; other people won't understand. The Bible was written so long ago, could it possibly be relevant to what's occurring today? Did God really mean what He said? Is the Bible really the Word of God?'

"This is the same strategy he used on Adam and Eve in the Garden. 'Yea, hath God said?' And after eons of years he still finds listening ears, even among God's people. It would indeed be humorous," he said quietly, "if it were not so sad.

"In this realm, if you have a preeminent agreement of binding force between two or more parties, to make sure it is preserved for posterity, what do you do?"

As a paralegal, she instantly knew the answer. "Well, it's recorded, of course, on paper."

"Why?"

"So that both parties can review the document and refer to it if necessary. They are each required to have a copy."

"What is such a document called?"

"Well, it's called a contract."

"How is it, then, that you do not understand, Virginia? The Bible is not a book of fairy tales. It is God's contract with mankind. The Son of the Highest was the legal representative between God and man. He was the representing attorney for the human race, and He ratified the contract in His own blood. You cannot give any higher attestation to the legitimacy of a document than that."

She had never before viewed the Bible as a binding legal document between God and man.

"Yes, Virginia, as it is written, 'He has promised, and shall He not do it?'"

Her eyes popped wide open as if on titanium springs as a revelation hit her spirit like a cannon. "So the Old Testament is an example of God's contract and the results for those that kept His covenant/contract and those that didn't."

"Yes," he encouraged.

"And the New Testament is His contract with us *TODAY*."

"Now you've got it!" He smiled, genuinely pleased that at last she was beginning to understand.

"Wow . . ." she said, trying to absorb it all. "This is amazing! It's . . . it's starting to make sense. I see why now the old folks always encouraged us to read the Bible."

Mahatiel smiled.

"Say, look, I've got more questions, but I want to see what happens here," she said, pointing to the screen. "I want to see the war when Satan got kicked out of heaven and the creation of man and when God said, 'Let there be light' and the serpent and all of that."

He smiled. Now she was like a child at Christmas.

"Okay," he said. "You know, of course, the creation of man took place after the fall of Lucifer, who became Satan. The Holy One destroyed everything that Satan had anything to do with—the nine planets, the surface of the earth, the moon. And then He began again and decided to create man and give him dominion of the planet that Lucifer, or Satan, had sought to abuse. He said, 'Let there be light,' and brought forth the land from beneath the waters—"

"Matt," she whined like a little kid. "Don't *tell* me; use the screen, and go back and show me. All of it. I wanna see everything!"

"All right," he said. "Let's begin just past where we left off and move forward from there."

The scene started with Satan beginning to launch his assault on heaven, then—

Suddenly, everything froze in place around her. She turned to Mahatiel with a quizzical look, saying, "You can't stop it here. Not now—it was just getting interesting."

"Virginia! We must go back! They have found us."

"Who, the police?"

"No—worse." With that, he took her by her hand. Instantly they were back to the material world and running once again for their lives.

"Who's after us?" said Virginia as she stumbled over refuse and a broken metal chair.

"Dark things" was his tight-lipped reply.

From one abandoned, ivy-covered collector to another crept Arthur Pitt, his inner voices lashing him on.

"Find them; they must be here. It is the only place not searched by the police."

In the distance and just out of sight, darting here and there behind trees, cars, and whatever cover he could find, yet another dim figure could be seen.

Marcellus Grimes strove to keep Pitt within sight without being seen himself. He had trailed the derelict all the way from Southwest D.C. to near the reservoir. Pitt was easy to spot, wearing the huge, grubby blue overcoat that had apparently been his constant companion day in and day out—for years.

The guy had to be sweating like a pig. It was eighty-two degrees today!

He had parked his car around the corner and decided to follow the rest of the way on foot. He knew that the girl had to be somewhere nearby. Pitt had probably stashed her near here after kidnapping her from the hospital, which was only a few blocks away.

Clever son of a gun, Marcellus thought to himself. He watched Pitt suddenly crouch down low to the ground and pause, as if looking for something—no, sniffing! He was like a dog, a bloodhound on a hunt! He watched the man then act as if he were talking to someone.

"This guy really *is* a nutcase," Marcellus said to himself.

A little clarion started going off in the detective's gut, and the thought came to mind, *Wait—call for backup. Don't try to take this guy alone.* Marcellus turned the idea over in his mind several times and then discarded it like an overripe fruit.

"Nah, come on, Marcellus, you can handle this guy. You don't need any backup. You got all the backup you'll ever need right here," he said, pulling his 9mm from its hidden holster.

He ducked behind an old beat-up Ford Fairlane as Pitt looked around as if to make sure no one was watching, then suddenly darted around the corner to his left and disappeared from sight.

Marcellus darted after him just as quickly so as not to lose his prey. "If this guy gives me any trouble," he told himself, "I'll pop him one, right between the eyes. With the kind of record he's got, they'll probably give me a medal. And I'll get Detective of the Month again on the biggest high-profile case that has hit D.C. in the past ten years. And a fat bonus check to go with it!"

There were no houses on this side of North Capitol Street starting at Channing. They had been torn down over eighty years ago to make room for the expansion of the McMillan Waste Treatment Plant. Efficiency, however, had made the large slow-sand collectors that took up this entire block unnecessary, and now they stood like tall concrete silos, empty and forgotten for two full blocks trailing off into the darkness.

Marcellus checked his watch. The luminous dial glowed 11:10 p.m. He cursed. Too late to make the eleven o'clock news, he'd have to settle for the arrest making the *Morning News* on Channel 4 at 5:00 a.m.

He quickly ran to the spot where Pitt had rounded the corner and crouched low, scanning the darkness.

Channing Street emptied into North Capitol and had one lone working streetlight on the west side of the street. The two others stood useless and dark. The nearest of the two had a globe and shaft missing, obviously in for repair. Only the base remained, wearing an orange safety cone askew like a dunce cap.

On the east side stood modest homes dating back to the early 1920s, bathed in the warm glow of tungsten streetlights. But the west side stood vacant of pavement or houses and was eerily dark with its single working light. The two sides of the street faced each other like opposing worlds—one light, one dark.

A black chain-link fence ran the entire length of the west side of the street. Its barbed wire top was a hostile greeting to trespassers and interlopers. Behind the fence stood a huge grass-covered berm that also ran the length of the street, behind which, unseen, lay the two long, dark rows of deserted slow-sand collectors, each nearly three stories high.

He paused to let his eyes adjust from the brightness of North Capitol Street to the hovering shadows of Channing. He bolted from the shadows to the west side of the street.

Pitt was up ahead, somewhere along the fence, he surmised, and he couldn't afford to lose him.

Pitt, obedient and oblivious, plodded on at the urging of his voices. He was trusting that, as promised, they would give him another chance at satiating his appetite with the girl. He eagerly obeyed them.

Suddenly, behind him he heard a bottle rattle across the empty sidewalk on the opposite side of the street. Hastily, like an animal on the hunt, he crouched, turned, and leapt into the shadows, interrogating his voices, "What was that?"

"Someone is hunting us."

"Who-who is it?" he asked them.

"Someone who thinks they are clever—but they are not more clever than us."

Marcellus cursed his clumsy feet and stood perfectly still behind the old warped maple tree, which he prayed would hide him from the eyes that he could feel scanning the darkness, looking for him.

Stray cat, Marcellus prayed. *Think stray cat.* He hoped that somehow Pitt would believe that the noise was indeed caused by one of the many felines that proliferated the D.C. streets in summer.

Pitt darted from his shadowy refuge and through a hole in the fence. The huge derelict moved with all the speed and agility of a monkey. Quickly he scrambled up the tall grass of the berm, staying low. He slipped silently through the knee-high growth to the top and lay there, facing the direction he had come from. He slowed his breathing, lying as still as a dead man, watching the opening in the fence below.

While he lay there, he smelled something. It was something in the wind—something faint in the distance—a scent, a human scent, a female scent. She was close after all.

Like a bloodhound on the trail of a fox, Marcellus crept quietly along the dark side of Channing Street and almost passed by the hole in the fence. Perhaps it would have been better if he had, because the events that followed changed his life forever—what few moments of life he had left . . .

Marcellus checked his weapon as he spied the trail of bent grass leading up the berm into even deeper darkness. Fully loaded, he was ready. He ducked through the hole in the fence and then off to his left and decided to make a parallel thrust up the hill. He knew better than to follow in the direct steps of a suspect and end up walking face-first into a trap or ambush.

He started quickly and silently up the hill. Seconds later he cursed his three-hundred-dollar dress shoes. They had all the traction of a wet bar of soap in a bathtub, and he fell repeatedly trying to scramble his way quietly to the top.

He was nearly there finally when he fell the last time with a yelp of pain as he landed on his left wrist. Curse words burst from his lips in muffled tones, and he rolled over onto his back to cradle the wrist, which felt badly twisted. He laid his gun down and tried to gingerly test his ability to flex his wrist. He glanced at the hilltop only a couple of feet away and cursed Pitt under his breath for being such a pain.

Suddenly he smelled something, something incredibly foul. It smelled like—

In midthought, a huge hand suddenly reached over the berm top and grabbed Marcellus' injured wrist and snatched it taut. It snapped loudly like a plastic piece in an Erector set.

The detective screamed in pain as the hairy overcoated arm jerked him suddenly to the top, wrenching the wrist as he heard a voice whisper sadistically in the darkness, "Here, let us give you a hand."

"You're under arrest, you psycho son—" and Marcellus peppered Pitt with a string of obscenities as he strained with his free hand to reach his weapon, which lay just inches from his desperate fingertips.

"Don't you know it's not nice to use the Lord's name in vain?" said Pitt, flashing a huge grin, "even though *we* do . . ."

Then, there was a flash of a different kind, and a huge hunting knife pinioned the detective's injured hand to the ground. In an instant, the huge man had leaped onto the back of the detective, stuffed a filthy rag from his pocket into the struggling man's mouth, and rode him like a bucking bronco.

The extra two hundred fifty pounds bore on the man's hand with excruciating pain, the sole support for their combined weight. As Pitt sat astride the frantic policeman, the knife tore its way through sinew. The detective's body slid down several inches in the cool grass until the knife caught itself on a single bone in the knuckle of his hand.

The volcanic pain was horrendous and caused tears to well instantly in his eyes. But at that same instant he felt his fingertips graze his weapon. In desperation he snatched up the gun with his good hand and tried to roll over and throw the grinning maniac off his back for a clear shot.

The six-foot-plus madman rode the policeman's back like a champion rider and instantly grabbed his gun hand. "Oh, we'll have none of that," he said, laughing, and a horrible deep multitude of two hundred voices erupted simultaneously from Pitt's throat.

"He is ours! He is ours! Another soul for hell's flames and the master's delight!"

Marcellus' eyes grew wide with fright. He had never seen or heard anything like this in his twenty-three-year career.

"Now . . . do you want to live, Detective?"

Marcellus didn't answer, but continued to struggle vainly.

"I said, do you want to live, Detective?"

Marcellus was helpless, and he knew it. He had no choice but to cooperate.

His hand was killing him. He didn't stand a chance like this. For the moment, he had to do what this psycho wanted. But when he got the upper hand on this guy, he didn't care if he was in cuffs. He was going to kill him.

He nodded that he wanted to live and would cooperate.

"That's good, Detective, very good. We'll remove the cloth and let you live, if you tell us what we want to know."

He felt as if he would pass out. He would be willing to agree to anything at this point, so he nodded.

The cloth came out of his mouth, and a string of threats and vile obscenities flowed out with it.

Pitt laughed. "Ahhh, I love it! A man that speaks our language!"

Marcellus tried to move his gun hand again. He couldn't budge it—not an inch. Pitt's grip had it locked down tight. He may as well have had his gun hand in a cast. "Get off me, you crazy—"

Pitt bounced on the detective once, causing the knife to shift slightly in the impaled limb. Even the minutest movement caused thunderous pain. Marcellus screamed and looked up at his blood-soaked wrist and arm. "Okay! Okay! Okay! I'll tell you! I'll tell you anything you wanna know! Just don't kill me and just—don't—move! Please!"

"Goooood, that's better. Nice policeman. Now, tell me what you know about the girl—everything."

He was surprised at the request, but in between screams and curses and the obligatory "I'm going to get you" and "You'll never get away with this," he told Pitt everything he knew—even about the information he'd read about the girl in the file.

"Thank you, Detective. You've been most cooperative," said Pitt as he suddenly thrust the filthy cloth back in Marcellus' mouth.

"Shame I don't have the girl like you thought. Big mistake on your part. It's also a shame you won't live long enough to regret it."

Marcellus screamed through the cloth as what felt like the strength of a hundred men gripped his gun hand and bent it back on himself. He felt a finger squeeze into the trigger guard immediately over the top of his own, and when the barrel was against his temple—it squeezed the trigger.

Pitt rose, his face and overcoat covered with blood and matter. He breathed deeply and inhaled the scent of blood that hung in the air, like a lion after a victorious hunt and kill.

"Good! Good!" said his voices. *"You have done well! Now find the girl and the other one! Quickly! Before they escape! They are near here—we can smell them! We can smell their flesh!"*

Pitt howled a bloodcurdling scream that could be heard for miles and broke into a run after them.

"What was *that?*" Virginia asked as they burst out into the fresh night air.

How much time they had spent in that trance or whatever it was, watching those scenes unfold, she didn't know. But it must have been at least several hours, though it did not seem that long.

"A host," ejected Mahatiel abruptly as he cleared a tall chain-link fence and then helped Virginia over.

"A . . . host?" she said breathlessly.

"Yes, a human host. When demonic spirits are able to take over a human being completely, they live there and open the human for entrance by other evil spirits. They then regard that human as their property and their host or their chalice. If humans are not available, then they will take over the body of an animal."

"Oh . . . " she uttered in comprehension. Then, "Oh, I—Ohhhh!" she shrieked as she fell down the slippery grass embankment and tumbled uncontrollably toward the street far below. "I . . . can't . . . st-stop!" she managed to scream.

Mahatiel was after her like a shot. He caught the woman as she tumbled head over heels just before she hit the concrete sidewalk. His feet slid out from under him on the slippery slope, but he still managed to hold on firmly to Virginia. She clung to him as her head seemed to spin around and around for several moments.

"Thank you. I'll . . . I'll be okay as soon as my head . . . stops spinning. And to think I used to love this when I was a kid."

"Come, we don't have much time." Mahatiel stood her quickly to her feet and guided her down the last several feet to the sidewalk.

He looked up and down North Capitol Street. "What is that cross street, there in the distance?" he said, pointing to his left.

"Uh, I think, I think that's Michigan Avenue," she mumbled, still dizzy, trying to focus her eyes.

He saw a taxi approaching in the distance and hailed it. The old yellow cab pulled up to the curb in a gray cloud of smoke, and the two exhausted fugitives piled in.

"*Ware tooo?*" said the driver in heavily accented English.

"Let's go to my apartment. I can take a hot shower and change clothes and get some food, because I'm starving." Virginia mumbled.

"I don't think that would be such a good idea," said Mahatiel firmly.

"6826 Riverdale Road, Lanham, Maryland, please."

"*Yase mam,*" said the driver, tooling into the far left lane of North Capitol and making a sharp U-turn.

"Virginia."

Silence.

"Virginia."

She looked out the window and pretended not to hear him.

"Virginia!" Mahatiel uttered in a fierce whisper.

"What?" she said irritably.

Mahatiel leaned forward and spoke so only she could hear. "We cannot go back to your apartment. The police will be there."

"You don't know that for sure," she argued.

"Yes I do," retorted Mahatiel. "There are three squad cars sitting in front of your apartment building as we speak. One is leaving, but the other two will remain—all night."

"How do you know that?"

"Trust me, I know."

She sighed deeply, then whispered, "Well, let's go to my mother's. She's staying in a nearby hotel."

"No, Virginia, they will be watching there too."

"Well, do you have any more of those 'manny' thingees?"

"It's called manna," he corrected.

"Manny, manna, whatever it is, I'm hungry again."

He looked at her with a look of surprise. "One person can go several days on just one manna tab alone, usually."

"Well, I hope you have a better idea, because I'm tired, I'm hungry, I'm dirty, I'm thirsty. And I've got to use the bathroom really bad."

Mahatiel flushed at this last comment, and Bashir Mahlab, the driver who pretended not to be listening, smiled and chanced a glance in the mirror.

He had his suspicions about the couple in his cab. The man must be a basketball player. He played for the Wizards, didn't he?

The woman was pretty except for all the dirt, filth, and a scar near her scalp. Yes, he should get a good tip tonight.

Maybe if he were friendly, he could get a bigger one. Americans, he noted, always like to talk about themselves—their jobs, what they do, what they have accomplished, how they were never appreciated by their husbands or their wives or their bosses or their friends or their families or their cats or their dogs.

"Say . . . uhh, yoo arr, arr ehhh, dat baskeetball playur, yes? Uhh, Shaak, eh?"

"No, I am not," Mahatiel said politely.

"Shoor! I saw yoo game against dee Kneeks! Goood game! I t'ought yoo bee breking dee basket on duh lass shot! Very powerful!"

"No, it was not me that you are thinking of. I am sorry."

The driver made a right turn onto Michigan Avenue and was planning on driving the long way to Lanham. *This should be a good fare tonight,* he thought to himself.

Virginia turned to Mahatiel and said, "Oh, Shaq, don't be shy. Why don't you go ahead and give the man an autograph?"

Mahatiel shot her a look which convinced her that her joke was not in the least bit funny.

"How did you do that?"

"Do what?" he asked.

"How did you do that thing with your eyes?" She leaned forward and whispered the rest. "They turned dark green! They seem to change with your moods. Are all angels' eyes like that? They turn purple when you're determined, white or dark green when you're mad, golden when you're pleased . . ."

"Shhh, not here—not now," he said, casting a glance at Bashir, who seemed oblivious.

Bashir sat ramrod straight, eyes straight ahead, profoundly disappointed that they were whispering.

"And we are not going to your apartment. It is too dangerous," Mahatiel whispered tersely.

Suddenly, and without warning, in the front passenger-side seat sat Uriel, invisible to everyone but Mahatiel.

Uriel smiled at the look of surprise on his friend's face. "Look inside the coat that was given you."

Virginia noticed that Mahatiel's eyes shifted from her suddenly as if he were listening to something.

"The coat—check inside of it," Uriel urged, then vanished just as silently as he had come.

In all the excitement he had forgotten that he still had on the trench coat that someone had thrown to him when he made his rather unexpected entrance in the restaurant weeks earlier. He checked all the pockets and found nothing as Virginia eyed him suspiciously. He checked again and noticed a small compact lump that he had never paid any attention to before.

He checked very carefully again on the inside of the coat. On the left side, he found a hidden pocket, and deep inside the hidden pocket, he found a wallet. Inside the wallet he found a stack of bills.

He pulled the wallet out and showed it to Virginia, and her jaw dropped. He asked, "Is this enough for us to get a hotel room somewhere?"

"Where did you get that kind of money?" she gasped, looking at the mix of hundreds, fifties, and twenties. "Of course that's enough!" she said, taking the stack from him and counting it.

In the front seat, Bashir was grinning from ear to ear.

"Oh, look dare, see? Dis is dee Cat'olic Univerrsatee. Look at dee beautifull buildings. And look! Over dare to dee left. See it? Dee uh, Shrine of dee Immaculate Conception."

Mahatiel suddenly sat forward and touched Bashir on his right shoulder and said, "Are you a believer?"

Bashir looked over his shoulder and smiled. *Ahh, day must*

bee Christians, people of the Book, he thought. "I believe dat dare is God, yes."

Mahatiel knew the moment that he touched him that the man was not a believer, however. There was no life flow within him. He sat back, disappointed.

Bashir kept his smile in place. *What did I say wrong? Ha! I will not deny Allah and his one true prophet, not even for all the American dollars in the world!*

They had been driving for only a few minutes, not nearly long enough in the mind of Bashir. So he was greatly disappointed when Mahatiel looked out of the window and shouted suddenly, "**STOP HERE!**"

There was something about the commanding tone of the man's voice that made Bashir stop on a dime right in the middle of the street, nearly causing an accident.

"Whut tis rong?!" shouted the surprised driver.

"We will get out here."

"Herrre in dee middul of dee street?? It is not safe!"

"Thank you for your concern," said Mahatiel, exiting the cab with Virginia in tow, "but we are getting out here."

"Bot, bot, you kan't!" he stammered in broken English.

Mahatiel turned around impatiently and snatched a bill from the fan of bills in Virginia's hand. "Here."

"Do you realize what you just did?" Virginia protested as Mahatiel guided her through the sparse traffic and across the street. "You just threw him a hundred dollar bill for a twenty-dollar fare! And that's with a tip!"

Bashir sped off gleefully in a cloud of oily smoke before the big stranger could change his mind. Americans may be infidels and crazy, but he had to admit that they were also tremendously generous.

"Why are we stopping here?" Virginia queried as they

walked up the long, steep driveway to the even steeper stone steps in front of them.

Mahatiel took her by the arm and said, "Come, we will find shelter and food here."

"Here? Are you kidding? Are you sure?" she said, breathing heavily. But still she struggled to move up the wide stone steps as her body, after hours of running, hiding, little food, and no water, began to shut down.

Mahatiel sensed something was wrong before Virginia did. She had taken to calling him Matt for short, saying his name was too long and needed to be shortened. "Matt . . . ?" she said before she passed out.

"Yes, Virginia?" he said tenderly, trying to get her up to the top step.

"I don't feel so . . . good."

She fainted dead away, and there he stood, with Virginia collapsed in his arms in front of the huge wooden doors of the Shrine of the Immaculate Conception.

Rev. Monsignor Barnaby Miles crossed himself and rose from the ornate altar and prepared to turn in. As official caretaker of the Shrine, he liked to turn in late after everyone else had gone for the day. He was usually the last to leave, even after the janitor. He liked having this quiet time alone with his own thoughts and the presence of God.

He felt it was his duty to inspect the resplendent structure to make sure that all was in readiness for the next day. For though the Shrine of the Immaculate Conception was a popular tourist attraction, it was after all still a church, and it held services every Sunday. So he always made sure that the gorgeous building was ready for both the tourist and the faithful alike.

He glanced at his watch—11:58 p.m., he noted. Two minutes to midnight.

He stifled a sneeze, and the muffled noise reverberated throughout the gigantic structure like a pistol shot. As the fifty-three-year-old priest dabbed his nose before leaving, he noted with humor that a whispered thought in this cathedral could be heard as clearly as a shout anywhere else.

That's why it startled him greatly when he rose from the altar and found a gigantic man behind him who was holding an unconscious woman in his arms. "Who—who are you and how did you get in here?"

"I am sorry to startle you, but this woman needs help."

"Quickly, lay her down here on the nearest pew, and I'll go call an ambulance. St. Michael's is just up the street, and—"

"No," said the massive black man. His voice rolled around the cathedral like thunder around the throne room of God.

Father Barnaby was caught in midstride as he headed toward the anteroom and the telephone there. He froze in midstep. His heart skipped a beat in spite of himself at the abrupt and loud command that reverberated off the cathedral's majestic walls. He turned slowly and watched as the man rose gradually, and his eyes locked on the girl who lay quietly on the red-cushioned pew. "Wait—I know who you are," said the priest, his eyes widening with realization.

"You're the two that the police have been looking for all day. Turn yourself in, my son, and I'm sure the police will deal fairly with you."

"We have done nothing wrong," said the man, looking at him. The giant then walked up to him. The priest found himself taken aback, and fear gripped him. *These are the two who killed that nurse earlier today, and now they are here—in the church! Oh Mary, full of grace, help me!*

"Fear not, William Barnaby. I will not harm you. Have you anything here to eat?"

Father William Michael Barnaby trembled with excitement and fear in spite of himself, in spite of the words of assurance from this human giant, and in spite of a sense of peace he felt emanating from the man. "Food—uh, yes, a sandwich or two in a small refrigerator in my study. But how did you know my name, my real name? No one but my bishop—"

"Would you get them for us now, please? The woman needs something to eat," Mahatiel said with a strong note of concern as he looked back at her sleeping form lying peacefully on the huge pew.

"She is in mortal danger, and I cannot leave her side."

"Of course," the priest said, acting as if he believed the man. He left and then returned a short while later with two tuna sandwiches in two neat ziplock sandwich bags. "How is she?" he inquired.

"Sleeping tranquilly," said Mahatiel, sitting on the floor beside her pew.

"You must be tired too. Why don't you get some rest? I can watch her, and you can have my bed in the study. I use it when I'm tired and don't feel like walking to my apartment across the street."

"No. I cannot leave her side."

"She'll be okay with me, my son."

"You don't understand. Her life is in my hands."

"I can keep an eye on her just as well as—"

"No. You can't. She is in danger from forces you can only begin to imagine—both human and nonhuman."

"But surely no danger will come to her here in the church—"

"I am her guardian angel."

The priest's left eyebrow rose almost to his hairline. "Oh . . . I see," he said condescendingly.

"No, you don't," Mahatiel said wistfully, and gently stroked away a strand of dark hair that had fallen across Virginia's face.

"She was raped by a savage derelict six weeks ago. The demons that control the man did it on a lark, a whim—looking for something malicious and destructive to do. She just happened to be the one they set their evil sights on that day."

"Well, sometimes, my son, we don't know why God wills such things to—"

"**That was not the will of God! That was not the will of the Holy One!**" Mahatiel's eyes transfixed the priest and shot fire. Barnaby could have sworn they changed color and turned white-hot with anger.

"You worship the Holy One here in this place, and yet you don't know Him any better than that? He is neither a sadist nor a monster, and neither is His Son. That is a lie of the Evil One designed to make humans either hate their Creator or make them suppliant to Satan's will and his grossly destructive urges. It is part of the Evil One's repugnant plan to slander the Son of Heaven and the God who sent Him."

William Barnaby swallowed hard after the sudden outburst, found his voice, and started to speak. "Well . . . uh, everyone is entitled to their own opinion, my son—"

"That is not *opinion,* Priest Barnaby. That is fact. The Lord God of heaven, Jesus Christ, said, 'If you have seen *Me,* you have seen the *Father.*' Tell me, Priest, when did you ever see the Lord or any of His disciples raping, killing, or harming the people He came to help, or encouraging those who did?"

"It is said that the best theology is a simple one—merely good versus evil," answered the priest. "But, my son, you oversimplify things. You obviously have zeal and earnestly believe what you say is correct. However, God is wiser, and why He does these things—"

"Priest Barnaby, you believe. I do not believe—I know . . ."

Barnaby paused to ponder the words of this fiery young man.

"This was *not* God's will," continued the angel. "I have executed the will of the Holy One for one thousand millennia, and never was I asked to rape and pillage the innocent, nor to encourage those who did." Mahatiel turned and faced Virginia, who had slept through his outburst. "Her angel tried to warn her that day not to work late. But she insisted. She treated the warning like most of you do. She turned the thought over briefly in her mind like a piece of paper in the wind and then dismissed it. The dark things saw her leaving work late that day."

"Dark things?" queried the priest.

"Yes—you know them as demons. They followed her in their host—"

"Host?"

"Yes. Pitt, the man they possessed."

"Ohhh . . ." the priest said slowly. He had participated himself in an exorcism once, long ago. The conversation brought back dreaded memories he had long since hoped he could forget.

"The man is possessed with hundreds of spirits. A number of them attacked her angel to keep him from protecting her, while the rest used Pitt to satiate themselves vicariously with her."

"And how did you get involved?" asked the priest, trying to keep Mahatiel talking.

"I was sent to reinforce and relieve her guardian angel and to take his place, and to preserve her life—at all costs," he said, recalling the battle and the chaotic scene.

"Well," said Father Barnaby, glancing quickly at his watch, "how long have you been an angel, and uh, where do you keep your wings when you visit earth in, uh, human form, like this?

Do you see many of the saints when you're uh, 'up there'?" He was sweating.

Mahatiel suddenly stopped and turned and looked at the man, his eyes flashing purple.

The priest gasped. It wasn't his imagination—he was sure of what he'd seen this time.

Mahatiel spoke in somber tones, discerning something. "You haven't believed a single word I have said, have you?"

The priest was obviously hiding something.

Mahatiel jumped to his feet suddenly and threw the girl over his shoulder and ran for the front doors. She moaned his name once but was still too weak to move.

"I trusted you!" Mahatiel shouted. And the look of disgust the angel threw him as he rushed past struck the priest in the face like a fist.

Mahatiel skidded to a stop in front of the huge oak doors at the end of the long aisle just as he heard footsteps pounding up the stone stairs on the other side of the cathedral's enormous doors. Multicolored lights played like fairies on the walls through the high stained-glass windows, flashing from the roofs of six police cars outside.

"It's for the best, my son. The girl needs medical attention. God will help you, if you just turn yourself in. Please," the priest called to him.

Mahatiel bolted to his left and down a flight of stairs to the lower depths of the colossal church.

The police struggled briefly with the locked doors and then began pounding and demanding immediate entrance. The priest went swiftly down the long aisle to unlock the oak doors, but halfway there, something happened.

He slowed to a stop. He could feel it as he looked around the huge basilica, something strange.

He was not alone.

He turned suddenly and looked at the altar. Nothing moved, and nothing stirred. Nothing broke the stillness but the thumping of policemen hammering on the doors with their fists.

He dismissed his uneasiness as nothing and started toward the door again. Thoughts like mini-tornadoes began to swirl through his mind, however.

What if you're wrong? As wild as it seemed, suppose the man's story were true?

Bah, impossible! Absurd! An angel—in this day and age? Everyone knew that God didn't do those things any more! The bulk of that had passed away with the early disciples. Miracles and visitations were theoretically possible, but to think that here, in this geographical area, such could occur—preposterous. There was no need—

Then a Scripture invaded his thoughts that he hadn't remembered reading since seminary, over thirty-five years ago: *"Be not forgetful to entertain strangers: for thereby, some have entertained angels unawares."*

He slowed his footsteps as the pounding on the door became even more incessant. He turned suddenly and faced the gigantic painting of Christ on the majestic ceiling at the far end of the basilica above the altar. He stared for a moment into the fiery eyes of the expansive mural of Christ seated on His throne, looking stern and resolute.

Very quietly a voice spoke to his heart and arrested him with its words: *I'm sure Judas Iscariot convinced himself that he was doing the right thing too . . .*

Mahatiel found himself on the crypt level of the huge basilica in a frenzied haste to find an exit that seemed as elusive as peace of mind. He rushed through the memorial hall and its marble walls that were covered with hundreds of names. He raced past the numerous naves and chapels dedicated to Mary. Several turns later, he ended up face-to-face with a dead end. He had just turned to go back the way he had come when he heard footsteps rapidly coming his way—running!

Suddenly around the corner burst the priest, sweating and red-faced. "I'm sorry I didn't believe you. God forgive me—this way!"

The priest made three quick turns and led them to a small out-of-the-way and hidden corridor and a door, over which hung a dilapidated exit sign. "We don't use this exit much anymore, but you can use it to get to the street. God be with you, my son." He pushed open the ancient door with a horrendous screech.

"He always is, and thank you."

With that, Mahatiel disappeared with Virginia, still unconscious over his shoulder, into the suddenly cool and brisk night air. He emerged from the rear of the basilica near a gravel driveway. He started down the drive, the sharp rocks crunching quietly beneath him, as he heard frustrated voices say, "Let's try going around the back! This guy Pitt is crazy, so watch yourselves! Bill, you come with me! The rest of you stay here and try to get inside! For all we know, the priest could be dead already."

"Captain Hanley!" called another voice.

"Yeah, what is it?" yelled the first.

"Paul's on the way with a crowbar."

"Okay, good, we gotta get in here, but I want to do as little damage as possible. Bill, you come with me, and let's see if we can find a way in round back."

Bill Trumball and Captain Hanley raced down the long curved driveway and then toward the back of the massive building. They ran up the gravel driveway, weapons drawn, and Bill yelled out that he saw something. Hanley froze, and then both men suddenly rushed toward the ancient and pockmarked rear door that stood ajar near the driveway. They paused outside the door and then looked at each other. Captain Hanley nodded at Bill Trumball and then covered Bill as the detective burst through the door, gun drawn, and rushed inside.

Mahatiel watched the two detectives rush inside the door he had just emerged from. Swiftly, but silently, he slipped from his hiding place in the shrubbery with Virginia still unconscious in his arms. With a quick glance over his shoulder, he raced up Harewood Road and away from the Shrine of the Immaculate Conception.

It was nearly a mile to the next cross street, Taylor, but it looked, from this distance, more like ten.

Mahatiel was exhausted. His legs felt as if they had been running for hours. He ducked out of sight at the stabbing headlights of an approaching car. He was relieved as it went by and he saw that it was not a police car.

His muscles had begun to ache mercilessly after the events of the day. He felt discouraged. This assignment had been more trying than he had ever anticipated.

He had spent six weeks in a homeless shelter as a black man and had experienced every negative thing he could imagine, from being harassed by cruel and mischievous teenagers and his fellow homeless, to being chased by stray dogs as homeless and as furtive as he.

He had encountered bias and prejudice and insults from many sources, even his own kind. In the underbelly of the city's depressed areas, drugs, hopelessness, and fear swam the waters of these pools of misery like sharks looking for survivors after a shipwreck. He felt deeply what it was like to be a black man in this day and age, and it was not easy. He felt that without the power of God, it would be impossible.

In the meantime he had kept moving, constantly trying to stay away from the prying eyes of both human and demon alike. He was trying to stay out of sight until just the right moment to rescue Virginia. And the moment had come, and he was glad that he had been there, but he had missed saving the life of Ethel Mars by only seconds. He was being hunted by the police as a murder suspect, the demon-filled Pitt was dogging their trail, and he was extremely concerned that the doctor, Jefferies, also under the control of dark things now, could show up suddenly out of nowhere and turn an already unpredictable situation into an explosive one.

His wound had stopped bleeding and was healing, but it still pained him periodically, and the constant running they had been doing had not helped any at all.

Maybe Uriel had been right. As much as he hated to admit it, he did need help.

He moved off of Harewood Road into a small park, and with Virginia cradled in his lap, he sank down onto a small wooden bench and began to pray. But the prayer quickly turned to a torrent of tears. "Lord," he sobbed, "I repent for my stubbornness, saying I did not need or want any help. I do need help. My Lord, I can't . . ." Here he broke and wailed silently to himself in uncontrollable sobs. He could not find the right words anymore.

"Please, please help me . . . I don't wish Virginia's life to end, here—like this. I will give my very life to prevent that. And that You well know, but—but I cannot do this alone any more. I need Your help." He cradled Virginia to his chest and felt something for her that he had never experienced quite so deeply before.

Compassion.

It appeared that at last he had learned the two most valuable lessons that the Lord had been trying to teach him for centuries. First, his job as an angel could not merely be one of robotic obedience. But, like the Father and the Son, the care he showed to humanity should have its roots in genuine love and compassion for the sons and daughters of God that he was assigned to protect. And second, he could not successfully fulfill the mission and purpose of his call alone.

There were no thunderclaps or booming voices from heaven in answer to his prayer. He was in human form now and had to function under the rules of this dispensation as long as he maintained a human body. It was a dispensation that was required to trust the Holy One and take Him at His Word. It was a dispensation of grace and faith.

"And as You have declared and decreed, I ask these things in the Name of the Son, the Lamb of God, the Lord Jesus Christ. And I know that You have heard me, because You have said that You would hear all those of this dispensation who pray in the Name, through the covenant of Your Word. So, sign or no, thank You." The gentle giant rose slowly and struggled momentarily with Virginia, as fatigue, like a subtle temptress, tugged at his exhausted arms and legs. He strove forward, trusting that he had been heard and that true help was on the way . . .

A quarter mile later, Mahatiel stood swaying from exhaustion at the corner of Harewood Road and Taylor. Nothing moved in either direction.

Harewood Road dead-ended into a garden apartment complex, and even that seemed dim and deserted this time of night. There were no cabs to be seen, and traffic on the deserted streets was as scarce as hope in the eyes of a condemned man or food in a starving country.

Food. Why did he have to mention that to himself? He was ravenous. Even the manna's considerable energy had been used up by the strain of all that he had to endure today.

He struggled across the street to the other side of Taylor. Behind him and unseen, two red-white-and-blue Metropolitan Police cars accelerated up Harewood Road toward Taylor.

Mahatiel reached the far corner and slowly turned around, shifting Virginia in his aching arms as he contemplated which way to go. He suddenly saw the approaching police cars in the distance and could hear their growling engines like two metallic animals closing in on their prey.

What would he do?

Suddenly behind him he heard an elderly voice say, "I told my grandson you'd be out here dis time. Y'all come're."

He turned slowly and stumbled, almost dropping Virginia. Behind him stood an old, surprisingly tall black woman. She appeared to be in her late sixties or seventies, easily weighed two hundred pounds, and wore a multicolored housecoat. She stood beckoning him toward the front of the apartment building that he found himself standing in front of.

"Come on, come on, don't just stand there. Da Lord showed you to me. Told me you'd be coming. Look just like He showed you to me too. Lookin' like two rag dolls—all worn out." She flashed a warm big-toothed grin that was the most welcome and comforting sight he'd seen all day.

As best he could, he hurried into the apartment building and up the first flight of stairs and into a modest but pleasantly furnished apartment. Outside, the two police cars, after seeing no one at the corner, proceeded down Taylor Road, lights flashing.

"Billy! Bring dat food out we been keep'n warm." She turned and looked at Mahatiel. "The Lord told me you'd be comin'. Showed me in a vision last night dat you'd be here today and to be ready for you. Look at cha', lookin' so tired. Come, sit down, rest cha' self. You gon' be here awhile."

Mahatiel silently thanked the Lord and suddenly remembered the Scripture, *"Before you call, I will answer . . ."*

"Here, take dis plate. Food's good; I cooked it myself. No, give her here to me and you just sit down and eat. No, no, I ain't takin' no for an answer. Um gon' put her to bed, and after you eat, din you goin' ta bed too! G'on, g'on, eat now, before it git cold. You ain't too big now for big Mama Melbourne ta spank," she said, smiling. Surprisingly strong, she picked up Virginia and carried her into the other room. "What's yo' name, son?"

"My name is Mahatiel."

"Muh-Hata-who?"

"It's okay. Please, just call me Matt."

"Okay, cause dat sho' is a mouthful. What a black man doing with a name like dat?"

"It's a long story—perhaps some other time."

"Oh. None of my business, huh?" She smiled. "I can take a hint. Okay, let me put dis child down here on a bed." She placed the still unconscious Virginia in the bedroom directly in front of them and left the door open so that Mahatiel could see her.

When she returned, Mahatiel was busily wolfing down the sweet potatoes, potato salad, greens, and fried chicken. To Mahatiel it tasted every bit as good as the manna he had eaten earlier. He scooted to the edge of the couch that he was sitting on. The plate of steaming food and a large glass of fresh lemonade sat in front of him on a low cocktail table that Mama Melbourne had cleared off for him.

It was a small but cozy three-bedroom apartment decorated with simple but clean furnishings. Virginia lay quietly in one bedroom with brown and rustic-looking décor. The other bedroom had posters of Batman, Superman, Spiderman, and other superheroes and football stars, and Mahatiel figured that must be her grandson's room.

The door to the third bedroom was closed.

He looked around the apartment as he ate and noted the landscape paintings on the wall. There were also several pictures of the Lord that graced her front room, some of them very lifelike. All of them depicted the Lord doing something, either talking with children, healing the sick, or, in one case, at the tomb of Lazarus, raising him from the dead. Mahatiel had actually been there that day and had to admit that he liked that painting the best.

He noted a large-screen TV in the corner, about thirty-two inches. She saw him looking at it with some interest. It seemed out of place with the other extremely moderate furnishings.

"You like it? Gotta watch my shows, now. Can't miss my shows!" she remarked with that huge genuine grin that he was really starting to like. It was the kind of grin that when you saw it, you just couldn't resist it. You had to grin back.

"Befo' I wuz saved, my shows use ta be da soaps, you know. But now, I love them preachin' and teachin' programs with da Word. I got's ta git my Word!" She laughed good-naturedly. "And I told the Lord, it's just me and my grandson now, so I don't need much, but I at least would like a real good TV set ta watch my shows on! And da Lord, He's so good; He sent me one!"

She looked up toward the ceiling and with deep and genuine affection that Mahatiel could feel, she began to worship and say, "Thank You, Jesus. Thank You, Lord, for Your sweet goodness to me and Billy. Thank You. Not just for what You do, Lord, but even more so for who You are . . ."

As an angel, even in human form, he couldn't resist, and didn't try to. He jumped to his feet and joined in a deep and genuine heartfelt appreciation to his Creator.

Whenever genuine praise and worship to the Holy One went forth, it drew a prompt and automatic response from the angels of God. As he worshiped along with Mama Melbourne, the Father and Son, he remembered the Scripture, "Let the Lord be magnified, which hath pleasure in the prosperity of His servant." He thanked the Father and the Son for Their goodness to him and Virginia.

A few moments later, he and the big, jovial black grandmother were both wiping away wet tracks from the corners of their eyes and smiling rather sheepishly.

"He *is* truly worthy," Mahatiel said, and sat back down to finish his meal.

"He sho' is," said Mama Melbourne with another big grin. "Like dey say at my church, 'Da Lord is good, *alllll* da time!'" She rose, went into the kitchen, and returned with a huge pitcher of lemonade and refilled his empty glass.

She had just placed some fresh napkins by his ravaged-looking plate when she said something that caught him off guard and disturbed him: "And after you finish eat'n, you can go on in n'ere and see your friend," she said, nodding her head toward the closed bedroom door.

"Friend?" he said in midbite, chicken leg in hand.

"Yeah, been here since six o'clock wait'n on y'all."

Mahatiel looked suspiciously at the large blue door and then quickly at Virginia lying in the other room.

"Leastwise he said he was a friend of yours . . ."

Mahatiel's eyes locked on the blue door as he dropped the chicken leg on his plate and rose slowly from the couch. "Mama Melbourne," he said, staring at the door.

"Yeah, baby, what is it?" she said with a note of concern in her voice.

"That woman in there, Virginia—her life must be protected at all costs. I was sent and assigned to protect her. If anything happens to me, promise me that you will guard her life with your own."

"I will, baby. But why—"

He snapped his head in her direction and his eyes flashed deep purple. "Promise me!"

"I will, baby, I will," she gasped and sat back in her chair in awe.

He turned his attention back to the bedroom door. "She was raped, Mama Melbourne."

"Oh my Lord, no . . ." Her hand flew to her mouth in shock.

"She is also pregnant, but does not know it yet."

"Dear Lord . . . by da rapist?"

"Yes."

"But how could anything good come of—"

"Remember. Nothing is impossible with God."

"Yes, you right. Fo' give me, Lord. What Satan did in evil, You can always make it turn out fo' good. Serves him right too," she said in indignation at the thought. She despised Satan and his minions' constant attempts to milk the misery of man for their personal pleasure.

"And there is also something else that she doesn't know—that every demon spirit in hell wants to see her dead . . . "

"Lord above!" Her eyes grew wide with wonder and shock at each new revelation.

"The reason they want her dead is because they suspect what I know—that what they meant for evil, the great God of heaven, as you have said, is indeed preparing to change into the ultimate good—for you, your nation, and your people. God has decreed that the child, born of this demon-inspired rape, will be a godly man, and eventually become the first African-American president of the United States of America. I'm sure I don't need to tell you the grand good that will come from such an earthshaking event."

"Oh my Lawd! Look at the goodness of Jesus!"

"I'm also sure that I don't need to tell you that every force of hell and evil men will do anything possible to prevent such a thing from happening. Do you understand now why her life has to be protected at all costs?"

"Yes, baby, yes, I do. Mama know sumpthin' about spiritual warfare and using da name of Jesus too, so don't you worry!" she said with a new grit and determination that gave Mahatiel a strong sense of comfort.

"If something should happen to me, you won't have to fend for her alone—help will be sent to you. But in the meantime, guard her with every ounce of your soul and strength."

"Yes, suh, I sho' will. Is dat man in the next room your enemy, one of dem dare demons?" she said, pointing.

"I don't know, Mama Melbourne," he said as he approached the door and placed his hand on the doorknob.

"But I'm about to find out," he said, and slowly opened the solemn blue door . . .

7 DARK WAYS . . .

"WHAT'S HE DOING?" said a whispered voice.

"Shhh! He's getting in touch with Mom's spirit," answered the second one, also whispering.

"Well, it sure is taking a long time!"

"Shhhh! You can't rush things like this."

"Shoot, for seventy-five dollars an hour I can! We've been here twenty minutes, and all he's done is mutter and mumble up under his breath."

"Shhh! Floyd, he gave us the special. For a personal session like this, it's usually two hundred dollars!"

"What?"

"Someone's coming through to me. I-I see a woman, an older woman, wearing . . . wearing a green print dress."

"It's Momma! I knew it!"

"Oh, good Lord, puh-leez . . . !"

"Floyd!"

"I'm . . . I'm getting a name. Ma— Ma— . . ."

"Mabel Rogers! Mabel Rogers! It's her! It's her—it's Momma; I told you!"

"Aww, Floe, all he did was say one syllable, and you jumped on it like a chicken on a bug and told him your momma's name!"

"Shut up, Floyd!"

"Oh. I see we have an unbeliever among us," said a smoother-than-oil voice.

"Sorry, don't pay him no mind. Please, continue. My aunt Lola told us you helped her to speak to her dead husband, so we came so that you could help us."

"Us?" her husband muttered under his breath.

Floe Corey shot her husband a look that meant no dinner if you don't shut up, and he quickly adjusted his attitude.

The medium, dressed in a green silk shirt, an expensive pair of black slacks, and an even more expensive pair of black shoes, said to the middle-aged couple in front of him, "Come with me. I want to show you something."

"And how much is this gonna cost me?" Floyd Corey grumbled as he rose with his portly wife from the small round séance table where they were sitting.

He led them through a set of curtains and then several yards down a dark hallway covered on both sides with black drapes. He abruptly stopped and turned to his right. He held open a door for them and quietly ushered them inside.

Floyd felt uneasy, but before he could say anything, his wife darted through the opening, no questions asked, and he felt obligated to follow her through. She seemed to trust this guy so much that she'd probably follow him into hell and back, Floyd thought to himself.

The medium, Marcus Sebastian Talbert, smiled to himself as if at an inside joke. He closed the door behind them, locked it, and then walked past the suspicious blue-collar worker to get in front of the couple again and lead the way.

They were immediately surrounded by more black drapes

that hung like dark rain from the high ceiling. Suddenly, the couple realized that they were on a stage, and they emerged into an auditorium that was huge and echoed their footsteps like cannon shots as Marcus led them to the middle of the platform. The portly couple stood mesmerized and more than a bit self-conscious as they stood in the warm yellow glow of lights situated high above them.

Floe clutched her pocketbook to her bosom as if it would provide some protection from the mysteries of this canyon-sized place.

Marcus turned in midstage on his heels like a dancer, looked at the surprised couple, and with a majestic and flamboyant sweep of his arms said, "So, what do you think?"

Floe was the first to speak, while Floyd wandered slowly around in a circle gawking at his surroundings like a country bumpkin on his first trip to the big city.

"What—what is this place?" Floe said in a reverent whisper.

"This," said Marcus, "is my new auditorium and studio. Back there," he said, pointing a magnificently manicured nail to the back of the huge theaterlike room, shrouded in distant dark, "back there is all the equipment, technology, and cameras I need to take my message of hope and inspiration around the world."

He had always wanted to help others, ever since he was a young man. As a child, he had brought home every stray cat he'd found in the neighborhood and nursed it back to health. There was something so rewarding in that, something wholesome in helping others. His mother, who was religious, always wanted to channel his efforts into and through the local church. But he had always felt drawn elsewhere. Unlike his mother, he felt there were many ways to God, and he had found his own unique way. And besides that, he'd found his way to be the most lucrative.

He turned and faced the couple again. He suddenly took a step toward Floe June Corey and took her left hand and kissed it. "I wanted to thank you, Mrs. Corey," he said with the most soothing voice and mesmerizing dark green eyes, "because it's people like you that make all of this possible. You make it possible for me to take my gift around the world." His lips slowly spread into a syrupy grin that would have made Satan proud.

Floe Corey, unused to such attention, blushed and put her hand over his, patted it, and said, "Oh, it's nothing, I'm just so glad to help, because I knew when my aunt Lola told me how you had helped her, I knew you were the man I needed to talk to."

He then turned his attention to Mr. Corey, and Floe reluctantly let his soft hands slip from hers. "So, what do you think, Floyd? Mind if I call you Floyd? I wanted you to see this so that you would know that this is no fly-by-night thing that your wife has gotten you into. A major network has contracted with us to do daily broadcasts and a special show once on the weekends. We want to help and reach as many people as possible, giving them the opportunity to speak with their departed loved ones."

Floyd continued to look around, visibly impressed, but still suspicious.

"Think of it. There are no restrictions on the other side by things like time or space. So those that have crossed over are able to see and hear and be aware of things that we could not even dream of. Imagine having access to that kind of help from the other side. Find out whether your boss plans on giving you that raise or not, and if so—when? Find out what's going to happen in your future. Who will your son marry? Find out whether you approve or not, and if not, do something about it."

Floyd stopped walking and looked at him with a quizzical look. *Do something about it?*

"What's the stock market going to do? How's your company going to do? Are there rough times ahead? Wouldn't you like to know how to avoid a calamity before it happens? Ever had a relative die, then another—and you know they say death comes in threes. Wouldn't you like to know if it was going to be you that was next or someone else? And if it was you, wouldn't you like to do something about it? Pass it on to someone else rather than you? Hmm?"

Floyd was starting to sweat. He usually did when he thought a lot. He took off his gray suit jacket, tossed it over his arm, and wiped his face with a handkerchief.

"All right," he said, looking at the handkerchief and folding it. "We just came in here to get a quick séance, a quick reading done. But I have to admit that you do have a serious operation here. And I work in sales—that's how I make my living. So yeah, I would like to know what's gonna happen and maybe have some things, uh, changed, so that things would, uh, go a little smoother, shall we say. So how much is this gonna cost me?" He looked Michael directly in the eye.

Michael knew he had him and smiled broadly, spreading his hands as he walked slowly up to Floyd Corey. "That's the beauty of it, Floyd! It costs hardly anything—when you compare it to the awesome benefit you receive. Listen," he said, placing his arm around Floyd's shoulder and walking with him. "You'll have access to either myself or one of my personally trained staff members. These are people that I have personally introduced to their spirit guides, who will in turn guide you into a better life. Access twenty-four hours a day, including weekends. People you can trust. People you can ask questions about anything, anything at all, and their spirit guides will provide the answers for you."

"Suppose . . . suppose I have a situation that I need, uh, changed. You said that my spirit guides can, uh, help with that?"

"Most certainly they can. They can arrange for circumstances, situations, and even people to be, oh, shall we say, removed from being a problem to you . . ."

"Okay, so how much is all this gonna cost me?"

"Well, that's the beauty of it, Floyd. We've made it affordable for everyone. Instead of paying some huge fee ranging in the thousands of dollars, we've eliminated all of that."

"You have?"

"Yes."

"Well, how do you—"

"All we ask for is your support in a small membership fee of only one hundred dollars a month, and everything we discussed can be yours. You'll make ten times that in your first month with the new success that you'll enjoy in your business. How much would it be worth to you to know your competitor's next move or to have an idea that will earn you a promotion to VP of sales for your company?"

"Priceless . . ." said Floyd, his eyes glazing over with the thought of it.

"Yes, it would, wouldn't it! So—"

BANG!

A five-thousand-dollar studio light crashed to the floor in the back of the darkened auditorium. The glass fragments exploded across the floor and lay there in the darkness, twinkling like a thousand stars in the sky of some distant galaxy.

The loud and sudden noise came without warning. Everyone, including Talbert, jumped with surprise. "Who is it? Who's there . . ." said Marcus, his voice suddenly gone cold and demanding.

A strange and distant voice called back to him. "I need to talk to you—Now."

Marcus walked slowly forward to the edge of the stage, shielding his eyes from the bright light, trying to see into the darkness.

Floe went to her husband's side and clung to him, feeling suddenly a little unnerved and slightly embarrassed for feeling so.

"I can't see you—what's your name, and what do you want? How did you get in here?"

"I came to see you about seven weeks ago. You introduced me to my spirit guide. I need his help. I need another séance, and I need it now. My name is Will—Will Jefferies."

Marcus Sebastian Talbert quickly dismissed the curious couple, and with a brief handshake and a small brochure on how to become Psychic Coalition International members, he sent them on their way, promising to get back to them later that night.

Will Jefferies stayed in the shadows of the huge auditorium, watching until the couple left, ushered out by their polite but hurried host. Will carried with him a large, heavy brown sack.

Talbert returned to center stage pretending to search his memory for that name.

"Jefferies . . . hmmm, do I know you?" he said, but Talbert remembered him well. He had never seen such a dramatic session before. The young black man had been ripe for the plucking. He had found that when people are suffering their most devastating or traumatic events, that was the best time to introduce them to their spirit guides.

Talbert had an intimate relationship with his own spirit guide that he strove to help others emulate. Talbert's own guide had commended him for his help and cooperation for leading so many people to a new level of enlightenment. But he, in turn, had voiced the fact that he was only too glad to help, though the huge sums of money paid by some to talk with their dead relatives didn't hurt any, either.

His spirit guide was George Washington. Always cordial, regal, stately, and ever the gentleman, he appeared in Talbert's visions or actually sometimes in person, wearing the uniform of a Revolutionary soldier with a gold sword at his side. He was always helpful, patient, and courteous with Talbert, no matter how numerous or childish the psychic's questions might be. He personally assigned the various spirit guides to each of the psychic's customers.

Now, here was a returning customer, a young man he had helped a number of weeks ago. He was eager to help the man make contact with his personal spirit guide again. And the third returning session fee would be nothing to sneeze at.

Talbert walked behind the curtain on the near side of the stage and emerged, struggling with a large round table. He carried it to center stage and set it down there. He then motioned toward the darkness for Will to come up, though he still couldn't see even a shadowy image of the man. He returned again from behind the curtain a second time with two chairs that he placed on opposite sides of the table and then stood, waiting.

He remembered Will as a sad but handsome young man. He remembered him as a failing doctor who was deeply depressed over an abrupt turn of events that made him question his personal philosophy about life.

The very first time Talbert had met him, he had offered to introduce Will to a spirit guide. Will had laughed it off, turning down his offer and saying he must have been crazy for coming in the first place, and abruptly left. But the spirits had a way of getting what they wanted.

Thanks to Talbert's new assistant, Felicia, the following week the man had come back to see him after the apparent death and revival of a patient. He requested a spirit guide's help in understanding such things. In addition, he requested help in dealing with the impending death of a close friend. The confused and searching doctor had been a man looking for answers to nagging questions that stabbed constantly now at his heart and mind.

Will had confided in Felicia, whom he'd known for quite some time, that for the first time in his life he'd had an unexpected and insistent desire to go to church somewhere because of all these events. But Felicia had given him Talbert's card and raved about his psychic abilities, urging him to come in and see the man once more, telling him that he could always go to church some other time. So he had come in to see the psychic, a lost soul in need of a map of life and a spiritual guide to help him read it.

Will Jefferies dropped the large sack he was carrying, and it fell to the floor with a deep thump and a soft moan. He approached the stage, gradually emerging from the dark like a dreadful apparition from a Shakespearean play.

Marcus Talbert felt something leap within him when he saw the man—a joy, excitement, a craving that he couldn't explain. It was a craving to hear news, but news of what? That he didn't know.

Dr. William Jefferies approached the steps at the far end of the stage at a deliberately slow pace. He wore a dark green London Fog coat. He moved tediously and purposely, like a man in a trance. The coat was buttonless and inexplicably flapped slowly around the young doctor as if caressed and tossed by invisible winds, though the air conditioner was not on and not a single window existed in the auditorium. Under the coat, the doctor wore green scrubs and white floor-gripping hospital shoes that squeaked eerily on the freshly waxed hardwood floor of the stage.

There was a deep silence that seemed to seep into the auditorium, filling every seat, covering every wall, hanging like the black drapes themselves, thick and smothering from the ceiling.

Talbert noted with a tinge of uneasiness that Will seemed to float to him from across the stage as he slowly approached, though he could plainly see the man was walking. Try as he might, however, he could not shake the illusion or the shroud of fear that appeared to issue forth with it.

As Will Jefferies finally emerged into the bright circle of light on center stage, he could see month-old bloodstains on the man's filthy scrubs and a beard that teemed with things never meant to be near human flesh.

Shocked, he noted that the man's unkempt hair moved and seethed with lice and tiny broods of maggots and other parasitic life. Patches of hair were gone in several places, and in its place were ticks, fat and egg-shaped, gorging on blood, their pincers gluttonously buried deep beneath the sore-filled scalp. The doctor's right hand was pus covered and swollen beyond belief; a tattered brown rag that had once been a clean bandage covered it.

Will Jefferies stood on the opposite side of the table from the psychic and leaned forward, the fingertips of his left hand resting lightly on the dark wood.

Talbert gripped the table suddenly to keep himself from fleeing as he fought down the heaving of his stomach.

How could someone change so drastically in only a month and a half? The young man he met weeks ago was gone, and in his place stood a revolting figure that was so disgusting it entranced him with the staggering implausibility of it all.

Will grinned evilly. "I lied," he said.

Talbert's face fell. "Lied?" he squeaked.

"Yes," Jefferies replied, fixing him with his gray, murky eyes. "I didn't come here to speak with my spirit guide."

"You didn't?"

"No. I came here to speak with yours . . . ."

"What?" Now Talbert was terrified—this was getting out of hand. What would he do? The man was crazy; he had to get away! But where would he run to?

"Did you hear me?"

"Yes, I heard you," Talbert mumbled fearfully, jarred from his thoughts. He couldn't get away. The man was only three feet from him and would catch him in no time. Then, sudden inspiration struck him. His spirit guide! His spirit guide would help him!

"Yes, of course I'll bring up my spirit guide for you," he said as he sat down, then added in his mind, *And he will drive you and your filthy person from my auditorium!*

Jefferies licked his dry and cracked lips every few minutes like a dog in heat. The tongue, thick with a coat of white mucus, sent shivers up Michael Talbert's spine. It was obvious that the man was controlled and manipulated by negative spirits, but why hadn't the man's spirit guide protected him from them?

Talbert began the summoning of his own spirit guide, and he inwardly felt relief at the protection it would afford him. He felt confident his spirit guide was at least equal to any evil spirit that was manipulating this poor man. He quietly prepared himself for what could turn out to be a royal battle.

Jefferies sat down across from him and stared. "Don't you want to hold my hand?" a deep and evil voice belched out at Talbert and then laughed a strange and unsettling laugh. It was the oddest thing that Talbert had ever heard. It was a deep, round belly laugh, with a high-pitched, almost girlish titter at the end.

He wasn't about to hold the man's hand; he was no fool. He ignored the remark and began his personal summoning of his faithful guide.

"Sebassssstiannnnn . . ." Jefferies suddenly began to mock, his chin resting on the table. A trail of saliva dribbled from his mouth and crawled across the table toward the psychic.

"Don't call me that," ordered Talbert. He hated his middle name.

"Thank you for my new home, Sebastian. I can't thank you enough," said the crazed man in a voice that didn't sound quite human. He laid his head down on the cool tabletop, sideways like a child, and began to lick up his own saliva.

Talbert had had enough of this. He hurried through his summoning, praying silently that his spirit guide would hurry and come.

Suddenly, to his relief, he felt his presence. Without a word from Talbert, Jefferies jerked upright, ramrod straight, his head snapping left and right as if he sensed an unseen presence.

"Yes, now we will see who is frightened!" mocked Talbert, pointing an accusing finger across the table. "Now you will have to deal with my spirit guide, and you and your negative energy will have to leave! We are for the light, and we reject you!"

Jefferies suddenly jumped up from the table so quickly that the chair flew backwards and flipped off the stage. His head continued to snatch this way and that. He could feel it, feel the presence! Where was it coming from? Which direction?

Now it was Talbert's turn to laugh, and he did.

Finally in the midst of the dark auditorium, a dim form like a gray mist could be seen, forming in midair over the empty auditorium chairs. The form slowly swirled and took shape.

A figure in a Revolutionary War uniform with a gold sword

at his side could be seen walking toward the stage with long, slow, purposeful strides. The translucent figure walked up to the stage, stood stock-still at the very edge, and stared malevolently at Will Jefferies.

Marcus Sebastian Talbert opened his mouth to address his beloved guide and mentor when the madman Will Jefferies rushed at the ghostly apparition—and fell at its feet!

Michael watched in surprise as Jefferies greeted it with salutations and apologies and bowed deeply.

"General Washington, this—" began Talbert.

"Silence!" roared the general at Talbert so loudly that the curtains shook with the refrain.

Jefferies continued to grovel as the general looked at him and said, "What can you possibly offer by way of excuse for your dismal failure?"

"My lord Thullus, I-I have no excuse. But I will find the girl. Slean and the others are already using the human host Pitt to track her. I will join them immediately and put an end to this."

"See that you do. For the sake of your own hide! You know the master is intolerant of failure—and so am I," Thullus said with particular venom.

"Yes, lord Thullus, I was regrettably delayed by an unforeseen circumstance—a meddlesome pest of a policeman, a photographer who fancies himself a detective. He tracked me, and I had to . . . deal with him."

"Is he dead?"

"No, my lord Thullus. I had no time to deal with him properly, so I had to bring him here. He is unconscious and bound."

"Is he a believer?"

"No, sire."

"Then he is no threat. Leave him where he lies, and waste no more time."

"Yes, sire," said Jefferies.

Talbert was aghast. What was going on? They–they knew each other! *Knew!* They acted as if they were in cahoots with each other, and Jefferies responded to the general as if he had been a subordinate in the man's army! And who was in that sack that they spoke of?

Suddenly, he noticed that the conversation had turned to him.

"And, my lord Thullus, what about him?" Bellinus said through Jefferies' lips with a jerk of the head in Talbert's direction.

The general's eyes turned red and luminescent, like blood on fire. He locked his eyes on Talbert, and they narrowed to satanic slits as the uniform he wore dissolved slowly away to reveal powerful but warped and deformed demonic muscle encased in sleek, black leather, V-shaped vest, and black breeks.

A slow grin, like snake oil, spread across his face, and short piranha-like teeth quickly bared themselves. "Don't worry about him. I have his replacement already. His usefulness to me has finally come to an end. Go, do your bidding and leave him to me."

"Yes, my lord Thullus," answered his demented servant. The vocal cords were those of Will Jefferies, but the deep and grating voice was that of Bellinus, ruler and prince of legions. He turned and flashed a knowing smile to Talbert and said with a frightening diabolical grin,

"Nice knowing you, Sebastian," and left.

The auditorium was deathly quiet, and Marcus Talbert backed away as the general, turned demonic leader, approached him, walking on thin air.

"Who are you? And what have you done with my spirit guide? The forces of light are stronger than the forces of darkness and will overcome them!" he shouted as he stumbled backwards toward the stage door exit.

"That may be," said the apparition, relentlessly moving closer, "but you'll never see it. Do you know why? Because gray only looks like light to those who live in darkness."

"Oh, help me! George! George Washington, help me! Help me!"

"There is no help for you . . . not in the names *you* call on," and he chuckled as Talbert's back thumped up against the wall next to the stage exit. Thullus stopped, alighted on the stage, and closed on the man until he was only a frightening six feet away. He cut his eye at the exit, then back at the psychic.

The doorknob—and freedom—was only three feet from the man's left hand.

Talbert stood flattened against the wall in sheer panic, whimpering and trying to remember every enchantment, summons, and incantation that he could against evil spirits. Nothing worked. He glanced at the doorknob, his key to freedom.

"Go ahead; try for it. I'll give you a sporting chance," Thullus lied.

The psychic weighed the offer.

"Ohhh, I see," mocked the satanic prince. "You can't make up your mind. Let me help you. Let's see who we can find to help you decide. Maybe your dead father, perhaps?"

The evil entity suddenly transformed itself into a stern man in his fifties, holding a pipe and wearing a gray smoking jacket—the spitting image of Marcus's father.

"Sebastian! Try for the door, son," he coaxed, gesturing with his smoking pipe. "You'll never know till you try." He grinned, then morphed back into his own form. "Oh, still not convinced? Perhaps a visit from your dear departed mother will convince you."

Thullus then morphed into the matronly and statuesque form of a woman in her forties, impeccably dressed. She spoke in perfect English with just a hint of a Canadian accent.

"Now, Marcus, don't let this nasty old demon scare you, dear. You just listen to Mother, and you just run along now and get away, all right?"

"Why are you doing this to me? All I ever wanted to do was help people, and yet you mock me and terrorize me. Why me?" He was hurt, angered, shocked, and confused. The demon's mimicry of his parents had been exacting! Perfect! Had the sessions he'd held with his parents over the past many years actually been with them or . . . or this thing?

Thullus laughed a deep, guttural laugh, an obscene noise that sounded for a moment like he was retching. "I know what you're thinking," he said in mock pity. "'Was I really talking to Mommy and Daddy on the other side all those times, or was it this ugly and repugnant thing before me?'" He howled suddenly with laughter and, without warning, leaped at Talbert.

The terrified psychic screamed and leaped for the doorknob with a superhuman effort fueled by complete panic. Suddenly he had the knob in his hand when he felt fearsome claws, like harpoons, striking deep into his back, down to the spine. The pain was excruciating!

Thullus wrenched him backwards to the floor with such sudden force that Talbert found the nails of his left hand torn and bleeding and the doorknob itself still clutched in his fingers.

Thullus flipped him into the air and slammed him face-first to the floor with a demonic strength that shattered both cheekbones and the man's left shoulder. The entity lay on top of the bleeding man, then leaned down toward his left ear and snaked a hot, wet, sticky tongue deep inside to lick out blood and wax that oozed grotesquely from the impact and said, "They're all me, you ignorant fool—from your dead mother to General Washington to Mabel Rogers this morning to the six-year-old child yesterday—everyone you have ever summoned. They are all me. We have been around for thousands upon thousands of years," he said, smiling, "and have learned to mimic humans perfectly. Every speech pattern you have, every mannerism, every tone, every idiosyncrasy, every experience—we watch, we study, we duplicate—perfectly. You have yet to speak to a single dead relative, you idiot," he mocked and laughed again with a horrendous retching sound.

"I–I don't *believe* you . . ."

"Ha ha ha ha ha! Do you think I care what you believe? What you believe doesn't matter to us, Sebastian—as long as it is not the truth."

"You–you lied to me," the psychic said through bleeding lips, then choked on the blood in his mouth.

"Does that surprise you?" Thullus retched several times, then feasted again on Marcus Talbert's blood. He then smiled and said, "I'm going to do you a favor, Sebastian, before I kill you. I am going to tell you a secret, a secret you will remember for all eternity."

"But I worked for you. I helped you! Doesn't that count for anything?" he bargained.

"We find it amusing that you, who were made in the image of the Creator—a spirit—are so willfully ignorant of the true nature of spiritual things. Your assistance has been greatly appreciated, but you are like cattle—predictable, breedable, and abundant. You are willing to sell your souls for a little power, a little fame, a little pleasure, a little sex . . ."

Talbert tried to buy time. "I never agreed to sell my soul. If I had known—"

"A mere triviality. You are done here. I have already raised up Felicia to replace you. She is doing nicely and, like you, should be useful for many years."

Talbert was desperate. His eyes searched for another way out while his mind searched for anything, any excuse, to keep him talking. For, in spite of the pain, every second of conversation, at least, was another second of life.

"But I thought—I thought your aim was to help people!"

"No, Sebastian. That was your life's aim and mission. You were a bleeding heart, like your mother, only when it came to spiritual things, she chose wisely. You picked the wrong side. Your absolute destruction is our life's mission," he said, and the single light that was high in the ceiling exploded the auditorium into pure darkness.

8 THE BLUE DOOR . . .

MAHATIEL SWUNG the blue door open slowly, his jaw set and mind fixed, and though exhausted, he stood equally prepared to deal with friend or foe.

The room exploded into a brilliant display of blue-white light. Before him stood a tall figure who turned suddenly and faced him. The figure had shoulder-length hair, and light radiated from what appeared to be holes in his hands and feet.

Mahatiel's eyes narrowed under the startling burst of radiant energy. His arm went up reflexively to shield his eyes from the blinding glare.

In the middle of the raw yet exquisite light, a voice that moved the whole room drove him to his knees by its very power and thunderous force.

"Take off your shoes, for the very ground you stand upon is holy ground."

The voice rolled around the room several times and echoed as if they were in a room ten times the size of the Grand Canyon.

Mahatiel immediately removed his shoes and fell prostrate to the floor.

"Stand upright on thy feet!"

Mahatiel stood to his feet and wavered unsteadily, inundated by the power emanating through him from the Figure backlit by tremendous glory and omnipotence.

As he rose, he noted that he was no longer in the twelve-by-twelve back bedroom of Big Mamma Melbourne of Harewood and Taylor Road, but he stood in the throne room of the almighty God of heaven and earth . . .

Around him, billions and billions of angels rose to their feet, rising in circular waves from their seats, their hands raised in worship. Their wings snapped open and clapped in appreciation and praise of the great God. The praise was thunderous, continuous, spontaneous, and magnificent.

The Lord Jesus Christ turned and walked toward a huge elevated dais that rose two hundred or more feet in the air.

They were in a huge natural amphitheater. Rows and rows of angels—seraphim, cherubim, archangels, war angels, angels of judgment, ministering angels, messenger angels, guardian angels, angels of every kind—stood and worshiped as the Lord Jesus Christ ascended the snow-white marble steps overlaid with a startling bloodred carpet to sit upon the solid gold and white marble throne that sat atop the dais.

He saw now that the Lord was clothed in a lightning-like garment that flashed brilliance even with the slightest movement.

The very air above the dais was filled with powerful cherubim and guardian angels who cried: "Worthy! Worthy! Worthy is the Lamb, who is, who was, and who is to come! As it is written: Blessed be You, O Lord our God, for Your mercy endureth for ever!"

The surrounding atmosphere itself was alive with praise

and worship and the very power of God! Mahatiel noticed that at the right hand of the Lord Jesus, with his writing instrument in hand, stood Ximen—the recording angel!

What was this? What was about to happen?

Slowly the Lord Jesus' eyes panned all that was about Him and then locked on Mahatiel so strongly that he felt as if he had surely been gripped physically by the hands of God Himself. Then, held by that power and the intensity and the solemnity of that gaze, the Lord slowly spoke to him.

"I have heard your prayers. I have seen your tears. I have watched you learn the bitter lessons of life in such a short time, and I am pleased and moved by your repentance.

"Let all of heaven know that as of this day, your disgrace is removed and your position restored. So says the Father, and so saith the Son. So let it be recorded. For it is now fulfilled.

"From this point on, you will no longer engage the forces of darkness as a guardian angel, but once again as one anointed to mete out justice and judgment.

"You are once again received as an Ariye—a Lion of God. Bear your honor well, Mahatiel Ben El. My Father and I bid you well."

Mahatiel lifted his hands and wept in appreciation. He fell to his knees in humility and gratitude and bowed his head to the floor. When he raised his tear-filled eyes, he was back in the cramped but clean blue bedroom at the foot of a modest twin bed.

Upon the bed sat a stranger he knew—a black man, dressed in a brown shirt and matching slacks and shoes. Even though he had a different form, he knew who it was—his dearest friend and supporter, Uriel, his eyes ablaze with delight and joy for his friend.

"What are you doing here—and in the form of a black man—like me?" shouted Mahatiel in surprise.

"I requested it, that I might be allowed to assist you," said his friend. "Welcome back to the ranks of leadership." His comrade grinned and rose from the bed to embrace him. "I told you I was just keeping this position warm for you. I always enjoyed serving under you, and I admired your leadership."

Mahatiel embraced his friend tightly and wouldn't let him go. Uriel had been the only one to believe in him through all the millennia of years. He was the only one to believe that he could come back, the only one to rally Michael to his side and, finally, to appeal to the Lord Himself on his behalf.

Mahatiel owed Uriel everything. But he suddenly stood back from his friend as he heard him say, "I have the Lord's permission, so I am resigning my position immediately so that you can assume comm—"

"No, Uriel, you must not do that!" Then, after a pregnant pause, he added, "At least, my old friend, not yet."

"But why?" Uriel said, puzzled.

"I have something that I yet must do," he said, looking off into the distance.

"Alone?" Uriel's voice quizzed him disapprovingly.

"Yes, but only for a short while." He then took his friend by the shoulders, looked deeply into his eyes, and said, "I promise you."

Uriel's eyes searched Mahatiel's and radiated their concern.

"I give my word as an Ariye that I will call for help."

Uriel finally nodded his agreement. "Okay, and what do you want me to do?"

"Stay here with Mama Melbourne and guard Virginia."

"And what are you going to do?" Uriel's face became a picture of bafflement.

"I'm going after Pitt."

"You mean Slean and his cohorts? I was told to inform you that the detective Marcellus is dead. Pitt killed him. He did it sacrificially. Slean's dark master was so pleased that more dark things were dispatched and placed under Slean's command. The original fifteen have now swelled to over two hundred. They inhabit Pitt and are headed here, seeking the girl."

"And Bellinus?"

"He awaits word from Slean as to the whereabouts of the woman, and then he too will come. I am informed that their plan is to attack en masse, in great numbers. He possesses the body of the young doctor—completely. The man gave him entrance, and now he cannot get rid of him. Slean and his two hundred cohorts are acting as scouts. He has been ordered to locate us. Bellinus wishes to make sure that the woman does not survive—neither the woman nor her child. He will arrive with—"

"They know about the child?" Mahatiel gasped.

"Yes."

"But how?"

Uriel's jaw tightened. Then he spoke. "Slean had the man Pitt torture the detective before he killed him. He managed to gather as much information as possible in an effort to figure out why we were so interested in the girl, and why we were sent to protect her. Marcellus apparently had stolen a file that contained the results of a pregnancy test that the woman had been given."

"By the stars of God . . ." Mahatiel exclaimed, and his face turned grim.

"They still do not know why we wish to save Virginia, but they believe that it must have something to do with the child. So the orders they have received from Thullus are to kill them both—as horribly as possible—to send a message."

"We will not let that happen."

"Not for one moment," agreed Uriel. "So, my old friend, knowing that—now, how do you wish to proceed?"

"Still alone," said Mahatiel.

Uriel looked at him incredulously.

"But only for the moment. When I need help, I'll call for reinforcements," Mahatiel assured his friend.

"Mahatiel," Uriel said and put his hand upon the angel's shoulder, "do you really think that once they engage you in combat they are so foolish as to let you call for reinforcements?"

"But I can—" Mahatiel began in protest, and then caught himself. Had he forgotten all the hard-fought lessons of the day already? Such pride had been the cause of Lucifer's downfall.

"You're right, my friend," he corrected himself. "All right, Uriel, what do you suggest?"

Uriel leaned in close and said to his friend and mentor, "I have a plan . . ."

9

LIGHT SHINES BRIGHTEST IN THE DARKEST HOUR . . .

"BUT YOU WERE THE ONE that called us and said they were here! Does the phrase 'obstruction of justice' mean anything to you, Father?"

The MPD captain of detectives was furious. The priest sat before him in the massive sanctuary of the Shrine and said nothing. All the wasted manpower, all the wasted time. They had to be here somewhere! Maybe the guy had threatened the priest, and that's why he wasn't talking. But that was still no excuse for—

"Captain Hanley!" an officer called, poking his head in the door of the giant cathedral.

"What?" said Hanley, still fuming.

"Call came in from dispatch—all units, officer down. A riot's erupted in Southeast!"

"What?" He checked his watch. "It's two o'clock in the doggone morning! Everybody should be asleep," Hanley complained, walking toward the officer.

"And Captain, they uh . . . they found Marcellus."

"What do you mean, 'they found Marcellus'?"

"Just that. They found him at the reservoir up the street a few minutes ago, and it's not a pretty sight."

"*My God* . . . what is going on in this city tonight? Is everybody gone crazy?" He stopped at the door, visibly shaken, and then added, "Get me Trumball."

"And, uh, what about the press, sir? They're waiting for a statement."

"Tell 'em I said there'll be no statement tonight. We're continuing the investigation. Do they know about Marcellus?"

"Not yet, sir, but you know the press. It won't be long till they find out. The call went out over Tac 2 when the body was found, so none of the press with scanners would find out what was going on and beat us there."

"Good. We're done here for now. You guys go ahead to the riot. Trumball and I will handle . . . the . . . Grimes crime scene," he said sadly. "The man was a pain sometimes, but nobody could deny that he was a darn good cop."

"Yes, sir."

Hanley turned and shouted to the priest, "I'll be in touch, Father, so don't go anywhere, and don't go gettin' yourself reassigned to any new parish or anything in the meantime," he cautioned. "Come on, Phillip, let's get outta here."

They closed the big oak doors and left. Father Barnaby walked to the ornate altar and knelt quietly and prayed.

Arthur Pitt plodded along Harewood Road like a Louisiana bloodhound on the trail of an elusive deer.

He got down on all fours and loped along. He had stripped down to his filthy sweat-stained tank top and an equally filthy pair of blood-splattered gray pants. For the first time in years he had left behind the huge winter overcoat that had been his constant companion on the sweltering days of summer and the most frigid days of winter. He had used it to cover the mutilated body of Detective Marcellus Grimes. His voices had wanted him to travel light for the hunt.

His callused, bare feet thumped dully on the pavement with each galloping step. The run-over leather shoes had been jettisoned too.

He jerked upright briefly, sniffed the air delicately, and then crouched low and held to the shadows, stopping every few feet to sniff and lick the air.

His voices urged him on and heightened his senses to such a degree that he fancied he could actually taste the scent of the girl ever so faintly in the crisp night air. He drooled at the thought of being able to finish what he had begun with the girl.

He carefully avoided the gaggle of police cars and the Channel 7 news crew as they were rushing off to leave the Shrine. They were rushing off to a sudden riot in Southeast like a small cloud of bees off to protect a hive under attack.

He clung to the long shadows the length of Harewood Road like a spider clings to his web, leaping quickly from one strand of shadow to the next in anxious pursuit of his furtive prey.

Then, he lost the scent. "Don't panic," his voices told him. "Be patient. Search. We shall find it. We must."

He seemed a deviant and strange creature, even more so than before. His face was splattered with the war paint of Marcellus' blood. He breathed heavily and grunted with each footfall. His grunts kept cadence as he ran. He seemed half animal, half aborigine, eyes blaring, mouth agape and slack. Small silver strands of spittle hung from his half-open mouth and chin. They glittered weblike and eerily in the stark moonlight.

His nostrils suddenly flared like the hood of a cobra as

he caught the strong scent of the woman again. "Pregnant . . ." he said slowly as he trotted along, turning the lustful thought over in his mind like roast pig on a spit.

"That's right," his voices answered. "The detective said she carries a baby. It must be . . . our baby."

"Our baby . . ." Pitt said and stopped on the deserted street. He gazed upward at the full moon, a bright and solemn witness to the ominous events that were about to take place.

He suddenly looked past the moon into the dark sky and straight into the heavens and laughed. "You think You have won? You thought You could outsmart us?" Slean said through the lips of the deranged derelict. "You thought we did not know about the woman and the child! We know," he said with a deeply evil grin. "We know . . .

"You think You are wise because You are Creator? We are wise too!" he said proudly, thumping his chest, apelike. "That's why the master trusts us. We may not know what You want with the woman and the child, but . . ." Pitt pulled the huge nine-inch hunting knife from its bloody place in his waistband. "But that does not matter. Because it is our baby, and we will have it back," he whispered fiercely and spat.

He licked the blade clean of every ounce of Marcellus' blood. He smiled and looked upward. The moonlight struck the blade, and the reflection flashed like lightning for miles.

He slipped the knife fondly back in its place and loped off slowly toward the distant intersection and the apartment building at the corner of Taylor Road and Harewood . . .

Mama Melbourne got on the phone and called Sister Wiley in her church, the president of their prayer circle.

"Mary? Dis is Lulla. I'm sorry; I know it's late, but we need to pray, baby. Yeah. We got to go into warfare. I ain't got time to explain, but call everybody and tell 'em I said to start prayin' in da Spirit. . . . Yeah, dat's right. Da Holy Ghost will lead 'em in how to pray, 'cuz dat's what da Word says. 'When we know not what we should pray for as we ought.' Tell 'em I said to pray for Matt and Virginia, and, oh yeah, da baby. Yeah, da Devil is after all three of 'em, but especially da baby . . . Okay, yeah, dat's good; git 'em involved in it too, and tell da pastor . . . Okay. Bye."

Mahatiel and Uriel emerged from the blue bedroom refreshed and smiling. They closed the door and walked to the center of the living room.

"Lawwwwd," said Mama Melbourne, "if you two don't look radiant! Faces juss shinin'! Ya look like angels!"

The two looked at each other and smiled.

Just then, there was a soft knock at the door.

Mahatiel's expression changed in a heartbeat. "Is there another way out of here?" he said quickly.

"No, other dan out da winduhs. Da kitchen one is da closest to da ground. But we still three stories up," said Mama Melbourne.

"Were you expecting anyone?" asked Uriel.

"No . . ."

Again the soft knock at the door. Softly, gently, childlike.

"Where is Billy?" snapped Mahatiel.

"In da kitchen," whispered Mama Melbourne.

Uriel suddenly went back into the blue bedroom.

"Take him and go into the bedroom with Virginia, lock the door, and pray," snapped Mahatiel.

"Okay," she said and raced off to the kitchen. She returned seconds later with her grandson and a huge black cast-iron skillet.

"Are there any windows in that bedroom?"

"No," said Lulla Melbourne.

"Good." Mahatiel felt a little better about that.

A long pink and slimy tongue snaked its way up under the front door and slid slowly back and forth, from one side to the other. Then it rose and reared itself, hissing like a cobra, licking the air and collecting splinters as it slid along. It seemed impervious to the pain of the tiny shards.

Uriel returned with a long tan shroud wrapped around something hidden.

Lulla and the boy watched the tongue slowly lengthen and lick the air, tasting it.

"Lord Jesus!" she gasped, grabbed her wide-eyed grandson, and snatched her Bible off the coffee table. She then raced into the rustic bedroom where Virginia lay sleeping quietly, slammed the door shut, and locked it.

The two angels then heard the woman admonishing the young twelve-year-old to have courage. Soon they heard their voices rising in strong prayer to the God of heaven.

The tongue suddenly snapped from under the door and disappeared, as if it had been singed with fire.

Uriel quickly unwrapped the tan cloth, revealing two gleaming golden swords. One of them was Mahatiel's own.

"How did you—?"

Uriel smiled. "Special permission. I thought we could use these." He winked.

They tossed the cloth to the side and freed the glittering weapons from their scabbards. The swords glittered and flashed like lightning. The handles were of pure gold studded with precious stones, which doubled as grips for the weapons. The blades themselves were of pure lightning in the shape of three-foot-long blades, which could be lengthened at will.

Mahatiel took the wrist thong attached to the hilt of his sword and wrapped it around his wrist.

"I know the woman is in there with you. Give her to me, and we will spare you . . ."

The voice came from the other side of the door.

"If you have a death wish and a desire to meet your master with the smell of crushing defeat on your foul breath—come take her!" growled Mahatiel.

"Screeeeeeeeeeeeeeeeeeee." Daggerlike nails suddenly scratched their way up the length of the door, from bottom to top and back down, over and over and over again. It was nerve-racking.

Mahatiel suddenly stepped forward and drove the point of his sword through the door up to the hilt at the exact spot he estimated their antagonist's head would be.

"Ayyeeeeeee!" There was a tremendous pounding on the door, then the floor, and then down the stairs as their unseen visitor thrashed in howling pain and horrific agony.

Mahatiel snatched back the sword. It was covered with blood and gore. He used the tanned cloth to clean the dazzling weapon.

"Well, that took care of him," sighed a relieved Uriel, and he started to the door to peek through the new peephole the sword had made.

"Don't," said Mahatiel, restraining him.

"You don't think he's gone?"

"I know he's not," cautioned Mahatiel. "It's not that easy."

Moments later they heard thunderous and enraged feet pounding their way up the stairs, down the hallway, and toward the apartment and the door like a stampeding elephant.

"Arrrggg! I am going to kill you and ravage your flesh, you—" A huge string of obscenities followed as the pounding noise grew in intensity until the floor, the walls, and the furniture shook with a sound like that of charging rhinos.

They heard a neighbor open his door and step out into the hallway, cursing loudly about the volume of noise. Then they heard his strangled scream cut short by the grisly sound of him being crushed by the mad charge of their enraged visitor. Hearing the bloodcurdling scream, no one else dared venture from his apartment for the rest of the night.

Uriel placed a hand on the couch to steady himself and watched his friend.

Mahatiel stood like a rock, unmoved, and rode the trembling floor with a steadiness that was impressive even to Uriel. But he knew that this was Mahatiel's element. This was what he was bred for.

The sound drew nearer and nearer to the door. Uriel watched unsteadily as Mahatiel walked to the locked door and listened to Mama Melbourne and her grandson screaming to make themselves heard over the rising crescendo.

He suddenly heard Virginia's voice crying out weakly, "Matt? Matt! Where are you? I need you!"

Mahatiel reached the bedroom door, but instead of entering, he turned and placed his back up against it and faced the front door, which shook with each thunderous footfall.

Just at the moment when the intruder must have been only feet away from crashing through the front door, Mahatiel's whole face seemed to harden into pure indignation. He exploded from in front of the bedroom door, leaped across the living room, and crashed through the front door and into their unseen antagonist!

The movement was so sudden and explosive that Mahatiel was through the door before Uriel could stop him from this unexpected and high-risk maneuver.

The door shattered into a thousand splintered pieces. Mahatiel hit the man on the other side of it with all the impact of an Abrams tank. He took the demon-possessed man completely by surprise.

The man had been going full bore toward the door when

the angel blasted through right into his chest. It was the age-old problem of an irresistible force meeting an immovable object, because Mahatiel was bound and determined he would not be moved.

The two antagonists thundered down the steps head over heels and landing after landing until they crashed at the bottom of the stairwell and then exploded out into the street—a street that was now filled and teeming with millions of demon spirits. Even the sky was thick with clouds of them circling above—leathery wings blocking out the moon.

Mahatiel quickly leaped to his feet, snatched his sword up by its wrist thong, gripped it, and sliced his assailant across the chest. The demon-filled man leaped backward at the last second, but the blade slashed through his open coat and green scrubs into his chest.

Blood now ran from two wounds on the body of Will Jefferies. The wound in the man's throat showed the accuracy of Mahatiel's earlier guess. But the angel had no time to gloat.

Mahatiel caught his breath as he realized that he was completely surrounded.

He had never before seen so many demons in one place at one time. How had so many managed to gather so quickly and undetected?

He stood, sword at the ready, as the demonic hordes, both in the air and on the ground, circled him. They were in constant movement. The effect was dizzying.

He stood facing down Harewood Road, the way Virginia and he had come earlier. Suddenly, the huge demonic horde on the ground opened up and formed two long rows that stretched the length of both sides of the street. They formed a gauntlet down Harewood Road stretching off into the distance, as far as the eye could see, even extending past the distant Shrine of the Immaculate Conception.

Then, he heard them—running and chanting in the distance, coming closer. Then he saw them, heavily armed, running in formation, chanting a cadence with every step. He recognized them—they were known as the Fornicators—hell's finest.

"Huh! Uh! Huh! Uh! Huh! Uh! Huh! Uh! Huh!

"Unto-unto the battle! Unto-unto the battle! Unto-unto the battle!"

They ran in twelve groups, phalanxes of four hundred bodies deep and one hundred bodies across. Their armor clanked and jostled menacingly as they beat their breastplates rhythmically with their curved battle swords.

Not a single demonic soldier was out of step. They ran as one man. Fierce, loyal, and merciless, they were doomed to hell and knew it. Their aim was to kill and drag as many others down with them as they could.

Flying just above them with military escort—two heavily armed fallen angels keeping pace—was Thullus.

So that was why these others had not attacked yet. They were waiting for their commander.

Bellinus watched Mahatiel take in the awesome scene. "That's right, Mahatiel! Fear! See!" Bellinus said gleefully like a kid at Christmas. "The Leader comes! He who is on the great council of Satan himself! He comes to deal with you! Tell me, slave of heaven, tell me! How will you stop us now? One way or the other, we will have the girl and take her unborn child."

"Mahatiellllll!" It was Uriel.

He was in trouble.

Mahatiel dashed back into the building and raced up the stairs three at a time.

The first blow caught him on the head as he neared the second floor landing, stunning him briefly, but he recovered, and his sword penetrated the dark body and dispatched it with personal vengeance to the pit.

Vengeance belonged to the Lord, and since he was now reinstated to his original position, he was now the arm of that vengeance. He fought and hacked his way through dozens of dark things, which had found their way secretly down from the roof.

He heard a scream and knew it was Virginia. He forged his way through, his sword carving a path through bodies and demon swords like a crazed lumberjack through a forest of dark trees. Just then, the power went out, and the stairwell plunged into total darkness.

Mahatiel snapped out two words in an angelic tongue, and his sword glowed a deep golden flame that lit his way as he fought fiercely past the second-floor landing up to the third.

Dark things dressed in light armor, scouts, fought to block his way and hold the line while their compatriots stormed the apartment in huge numbers.

Ting! Ting! Ting! Clang! Ting!

Mahatiel's sword cleaved through iron and bone and demon flesh. Dark weapons like serpents bit at him and nicked and cut at his own flesh and tore his coat to shreds. He spun, kicked, chopped, slashed, hacked, charged, ducked, lunged, and stormed forward like the judgment of God.

He had to make it through before the phalanxes arrived.

A dark thing climbed atop the back and shoulders of another and leaped at the angel, weapon first.

Ting! He blocked the blade aside with a vengeance, but the weight of the thing carried them both to the floor and back down the stairs like tumbleweeds to the second-floor landing with the hairy and putrid-smelling thing roaring and baring its fangs, snapping and snarling for Mahatiel's exposed throat all the while.

Mahatiel spun as the two were falling to the second-floor landing so that the demon thing landed under him and felt the full impact of the angel's three hundred chiseled and well-muscled pounds. They landed with a powerful thud, and the demon lay momentarily stunned.

Mahatiel heard a murderous war cry behind him and deformed feet pounding toward his rear. A disease-ridden crooked sword sliced past his ear just as his reflexes jerked him out of the way and against the wall. The weapon missed him by inches and plunged deeply into the chest of the thing that had lain beneath him. He hacked clean through his cowardly attacker, and the thing crumpled, mortally wounded, on top of its compatriot in an awkward mutual embrace of agony. Their bodies too mortally wounded and destroyed to continue, soon they too were translated to the pit.

The bodies of fifty or more dark things lay in Mahatiel's thunderous wake. The way was now clear to the third-floor landing. Bleeding and exhausted, he forced himself to bound up the stairs two at a time, over twisted bodies and past severed limbs. He could hear the sounds of Uriel's glowing sword steadily ringing in battle like a steel bell.

"Matt!! Help me!"

It was Virginia!

"In the name of Jesus I rebuke you!" *Bong!* It was the voice of Mama Melbourne and her frying pan.

Mahatiel hit the third-floor landing running. The scene before him brought him to a screeching halt and made him catch his breath.

The splintered doorway he had crashed through was now packed with demon spirits who trod each other down trying to get at Uriel. The living room was a pile of bodies and broken swords and writhing limbs crawling and scratching their way across the floor, looking for the torsos that belonged to them.

Uriel stood atop the couch, a battle gleam in his eye, fighting like the expert swordsman he was—and Mahatiel should know, for he had taught him. His glowing sword cast surreal shadows on the writhing scenes of carnage.

Just past him was Mama Melbourne, frying pan in hand, sweat pouring, swinging left and right. He could hear her voice above the din, still praying in the Spirit. Just past her through the shattered bedroom door, he saw Billy on the bed with a baseball bat at the ready, and behind him Virginia, looking terrified.

"In the Name of Jesus—" *Crack!* A demon spirit fell-and his sword went flying as the bat connected.

Suddenly rising from downstairs came the dreaded sound that Mahatiel knew would come.

"Huh! Uh! Huh! Uh! Huh! Uh! Huh! Uh!

"Unto-unto the battle! Unto-unto the battle! Unto-unto the battle!"

The Fornicators had entered the parking lot of the apartment complex. In ten seconds or less they would be in the building and up the stairs to the third floor.

The dark things that crushed their way through the narrow front door of the apartment had no idea Mahatiel was behind them, assuming that their murderous companions had taken care of him.

It was time for Uriel's plan. Mahatiel waved his glowing golden sword—the signal. Uriel caught sight of the sword of his friend waving and weaving an intricate battle pattern in the darkness of the hallway outside.

It was about time.

His friend liked to live a little bit too close to the edge sometimes for his taste.

Uriel then got Mama Melbourne's attention, in between his slashes and her swings.

"Thank You, Jesus!" she said under her breath. *Bong!*

It's about time!

She had been purposely holding back in her use of the Name as part of their strategy. Mahatiel and Uriel had pointed out to her and showed her in the Bible that every time the disciples used the Name, it was immediately followed by a specific order or command. "Rebuking is good, Mama Melbourne, but that's only half of it—that's not enough."

"Well, if it wuz good enuff for Jesus, baby, den it's good enuff fo' me."

Uriel had dropped his head in slight exasperation.

"Mama Melbourne, do you know what the word *rebuke* means?" asked Mahatiel, taking over. He had explained to her that it was vital for her to understand in this battle how to effectively use the Name.

"I think it means, uh, well, it means . . . it—" It dawned on her that she had never really thought about what it meant before. She just grew up hearing her mother do it, and other saints in church do it, but had never really thought about what it meant herself. "Uh . . . I think it means shut up, doesn't it?"

"Correct. It means to reprimand or criticize sharply. Notice, Mama Melbourne, that every time the disciples used the Name, or even when the Master Himself dealt with an evil spirit, they did so by following up immediately by issuing a specific command that ordered the evil spirit to do something—come out, go, or enter no more into him, or bind the spirit."

"I don't understand . . ."

"Most believers that Uriel and I have seen over the centuries have used the matchless name of the King of kings like a lucky charm or talisman, something like what you would call a rabbit's foot, hoping that something will happen when they use the Name, or they simply rebuke in the Name and that's all. Notice, whenever the Lord of Lords, your Savior and our Master, rebuked an evil spirit, He did so by immediately commanding the spirit. That's how you rebuke. An example of this is in the Book of Truth, in the opening chapter of the book of His servant Mark: 'And Jesus rebuked him saying, Hold thy peace and come out of him!'"

"Ohhhh! I see, baby! So I need to command somethin' when I rebuke! Woo Lawwd! Between dat and da blood, dem demons don't stand a chance! I got it now!"

It was with that understanding that Mama Melbourne now implemented the critical first part of their plan. She took two steps back and dropped her frying pan, where it fell to the floor with a metallic clang. She drew herself up to her full height, and with a gleam of anger in her eye, she opened her mouth and bellowed at the top of her lungs with a voice that sounded like thunder: *"In da name of da Lord Jesus Christ, I bind every demon spirit under the sound of my voice, by the blood of Jesus, da LAMB of GOD!"*

"Screeeeeeeee! Screeeeeeeeeee!" The reaction was immediate.

The hordes in the apartment and those jammed in the doorway panicked in sudden confusion and oppressive pain at the powerful and emphatic use of the Name and the dreaded blood of Jesus Christ.

The blood was to them what sunlight was to a vampire; it would literally dissolve their repugnant flesh and immediately dispatch them to the pit, the dreaded Abyss, till Judgment Day. So just the mere mention of it was enough to sear them with fear. And the Name used like that was smothering! Oppressive! They couldn't breathe. It was like being in a room where all of the oxygen had abruptly been sucked dry. They turned and jostled each other in confusion and anguish.

Then, out in the hallway, Mahatiel quickly covered his eyes.

Mama Melbourne suddenly turned her back quickly and closed her eyes.

In the ransacked bedroom, Billy, on cue, threw a heavy blanket over his head and Virginia's and told her to get down and close her eyes tightly shut.

Uriel rose to his full height and quickly brought his sword upright before his face and in the full volume of his voice shouted, "**It is written! And in the name of the God of heaven, I say again, 'Let there be LIGHT'!**"

The angel's sword exploded in a blast of radiant energy that blinded the eyes of the snarling and confused demons in the apartment and those packed about the door. The concussion from the discharge rocked the apartment and floored every demon spirit in it. The explosion of pure energy was so sudden that there was no time for even an outcry of pain or surprise.

The blast pierced the ceiling of the little apartment and continued through the roof into the heavens and sliced through hordes of evil spirits circling above the building. They were sliced clean through and shrieked in pain as they fell to the earth like stones, crashing into their compatriots on the ground far below . . .

"Hey, thanks for going with me, man. After we run by here, I'll drop you off back at your place," the driver said, heading up Pennsylvania Avenue from Silver Hill Road.

"No problem, man. You know me—I'm a night owl anyway," said the younger man, putting on his seat belt. "So what's going on? Where are we going?"

"Over to Mama Melbourne's house."

"Oh, good! It's been a while. I had a dream about her. How's she doing?"

Terrence's face clouded over as he turned onto the on-ramp of the Beltway, 95 North, and headed for her place. He was in a hurry, so he took it up to sixty-five miles per hour on the lightly traveled expressway. "Well, that's what that meeting was about at church. We were just leaving when you arrived. Something's going on. Mama Melbourne called Sister Wiley and asked the prayer group to pray for her, her grandson, and two other people that were staying with her."

"I didn't know Mama M took in boarders."

Terrence glanced at his twenty-two-year-old brother meaningfully. "She doesn't."

"Oh . . ."

"It was a man and a woman and—"

"And was the woman pregnant?" interrupted Mark.

Terrence looked surprised. "Well, yeah," he said slowly. "How did you know?"

Mark turned pensive and reflective before he answered. "Hmph. It's funny. Had this dream for the past two weeks I couldn't shake. At first, I thought it was, you know, one of those pizza dreams. But I keep having it. Same dream every time."

"Well? Don't just sit there and make me guess. Tell me what it is!"

"Okay, okay." Mark chuckled. "It's probably nothing, but . . . I dreamed there's this pregnant woman drowning in this really turbulent sea, in this Cimmerian water. And—"

"In *what* kinda water?"

"Cimmerian—it means really dark."

Terrence continued, "You can sure tell a reporter. Gotta use them big words, huh? Just gotta throw one in there *somewhere* every now and then, just for the fun of it, huh?" he chided with a smile.

"Okay, okay. Anyway, even though she's near the shoreline, since she's pregnant, she can't get all the way up out of the water, 'cause the baby is really, really heavy. There's this guy on the shoreline, or actually on this dock, holding on to it with one hand and reaching out to her with the other. Mama Melbourne is there, but she's standing on the dock, praying. The guy tries to pull the woman out, but she's so heavy he can't do it by himself, so he looks at me, real desperate. He stretches his other hand out to me and says, 'Help me . . .' Then all of a sudden, I fall in too!"

They drove on in silence. After a while, Terrence said, "And?"

"And what?"

"Did you save her? Did you help the guy? Did *you* get out?"

"Oh, sorry. I dunno . . ."

"What you mean, you don't know?"

"I dunno," Mark said, shrugging his shoulders. "I keep waking up before the dream is over."

"Did you pray about it and ask the Lord to tell you what the meaning of it was?"

"Naww, it probably don't mean nuthin'."

"Mannnn, you should always pray after a persistent dream and ask the Lord for the meaning. It could be a warning or something. And you'll never know if you—"

"Look out!" yelled Mark, pointing out a black Corvette that shot out of nowhere and cut across four lanes and directly in front of them, causing them to swerve out of control toward a steel guardrail . . .

"What was that light?" said Thullus in great surprise.

"I—I don't know, sire," said Gaderian, a member of his military escort.

"Well, go find out!" said Thullus, kicking him forward.

"Yes, sir," said the evil spirit. He then flew ahead to find out what had transpired.

"Sire," said Slec the Hammer, his other military adjutant.

"Yes, what is it?" Thullus ejected irritably.

"We have a report from one of our Watchers that a prayer group has dispatched two believers to the scene to attend and assist those inside," he said, nodding toward the besieged apartment building.

"Well, stop them! Do not bother me with such trivial details. See to it!"

"Yes, sire. I already have. There has been a terrible . . . accident. And in addition, I took the liberty to dispatch Rinc to create a small riot in Southeast. This should keep the police occupied till we have finished our little business here," he said meaningfully.

"Good! Good! That's what I like—efficiency! Well done."

"Thank you, sire," said Slec, as he bowed away gracefully.

Thullus turned his attention again to the apartment building in the distance and watched with pleasure as his first phalanx of shock troops entered the building and stormed their way up the stairs, headed for the third floor. "Slec!"

The fallen angel was instantly at his side again. "Yes, sire."

"Report! Any sign of reinforcements?"

"No, sire, not a single angel has been spotted headed this way. We have a string of Watchers from here to the stars. If so much as a feather leaves from the gates of heaven, we will see it from afar."

"Good, goood, Slec! You may yet have your brother's place."

"Thank you, sire. That is the general idea," he confided with unbridled pride.

Thullus smiled and clapped him on the back and then laughed heartily. "I like your ambition, Slec!" He then abruptly grabbed him by the throat and jerked him so close that their noses touched. "But if you try to feed your hellish ambitions at my expense, and think to replace me, I will kill you dead before you even have a chance to bleed. Do I make myself clear?"

Slec swallowed his pride as his true ambitions lay totally exposed. He answered softly, "As they say, sire—crystal."

Thullus kicked him away and turned his attention once again to the battle . . .

Mahatiel uncovered his eyes in time enough to see dark things screeching, moaning, cowering, and rubbing blinded eyes. One creature—who had been looking directly at Uriel's sword—screamed in pain as gray ribbons of smoke ascended like incense to the heavens from black and empty eye sockets.

Mahatiel watched as Uriel leaped from the couch over writhing bodies and ran toward the blue bedroom door for the final part of their plan. Up the stairs behind Mahatiel, coming up from the second-floor landing, he heard hell's storm troopers. Better armored than their forerunners, they came like a flood tide up the narrow stairs seeking vengeance.

Phalanx number one was led by a tall bull-like creature with huge twisted horns whose looks were as revolting as his name—Vomit. He led the charge that rose and pounded their way up the stairs—a flood tide of evil beasts running to a slaughter of lambs.

Mahatiel realized that he had to hold them until Uriel reached the bedroom door. He placed the tip of his sword downward just inches from the floor, the hilt up. He called this posture the Earth Style. It was an invention of his own. He called the technique behind it the Ascension, in honor of the Lord. Some of his order had considered it childish to name his sword techniques, but he had had the Lord's permission, and he enjoyed having techniques that were uniquely his own.

They came stampeding up the stairs to the third floor full of bloodlust, and once they reached the third-floor landing and saw him, poised, they charged down the tight hallway in desperate fury, like a herd of hungry tigers in the Roman Colosseum.

The narrow hallway forced the huge and hulking creatures to fall in behind one another single file as they rushed to get at him. Behind him he heard some of the other dark things beginning to regain their sight and clarity.

"Hurry, Uriel," Mahatiel whispered under his breath as he edged his way slowly backwards, sword at the ready.

Uriel was nearly at the bedroom door, just a step away from it, when a dark thing that lay on the floor grabbed his leg as he felt him rushing by and held on for dear death. Locking his arms around the angel's leg, he then sank tigerlike teeth into his flesh. Uriel screamed and raised his sword to cut the thing from his leg. Just then, as if the attack were coordinated, another demon, who had been smart enough to look away before the intense explosion, dove across a chair and caught the angel's upraised sword arm and held it in an iron grip as Uriel screamed in pain from the ferocious bite.

Mahatiel heard his friend scream but dared not turn as Vomit himself charged him. Their swords clanged, and sparks flew from the strength of their blows.

Vomit charged with a series of successive overhead blows that he called the Wheel of Death. The demon's strength was considerable, and Mahatiel knew why. They drew their strength from humans foolish enough to worship them, and he knew that by this time witches and satanic worshipers up and down the Eastern seaboard would be called upon to offer prayers and incense for the success of their mission, not knowing that their only reward would be the privilege of suffering the same eternal punishment as their masters.

He ducked under the last blow, and the maneuver brought the two antagonists together chest to chest, face-to-face, muscles bulging, swords locked.

Vomit bared his tiger fangs and opened wide his mouth. He smiled. Mahatiel was inches from his face and found the creature's rancid breath was suffocating in its revolting stench.

"I see why they call you Vomit," said the angel.

Vomit took offense and tried to lean closer—fangs pointed at Mahatiel's face. The evil spirit suddenly squirted venom from his needlepoint fangs, intending it for the angel's eyes. Mahatiel jerked aside, and the acidic liquid seared his shoulder. He shifted his weight suddenly to the left, and the demonic leader fell for the trick. Immediately Mahatiel shifted his weight back to the right, spun suddenly, and flipped his sword hilt up, blade down, and swiftly up again in a lightning-quick move—the Ascension Maneuver. The upward stroke of the razorlike blade was so powerful that it instantly made the satanic leader now capable of being in two places at one time.

Uriel strained with his left hand to reach the knob of the blue door. Veins protruded from his neck like steel cables as more and more spirits clung to him like evil lint, all striving to pull him down to the floor and overwhelm him.

But he had to reached the door! It was the next critical part of their plan!

Finally, he summoned all his strength and half surged, half leaped the last two feet to the door, turned the knob, and collapsed to the floor. The door exploded open, and through the open door poured—

"Ariye! Ariye! The Lions of God! The judgment angels of Jehovah! Of the Lord and of His Christ! We are doomed!"

cried dark things as they fled in stark terror for their lives.

Their reputation was known throughout all of hell. The high council of hell itself feared the Ariye—the Lions of God. They were the ones who had fought the Egyptians in the Red Sea. Just one of their number had slain 180,000 Assyrians in one night! They were the angels that were sent when the great mercy of God had come to an end! They were the bowl angels of the book of Revelation, who will one day pour out the wrath of God and judgment on the earth when time itself has come to an end. And they were here!

Their creed was that those who showed no mercy received none.

Mahatiel heard what sounded like a frightened herd of buffalo behind him, thundering up the stairs to the roof.

Ting! Ting! Ting! Slash! His sword found demon flesh and bone, and another huge demon fell to the floor on the two pieces of the first. The rest of the horde below pushed and shoved forward, forcing those in front of them to charge into him, blades flashing.

Suddenly behind him he heard a most welcome sound!

"By My God Have I Run Through a Troop! By My God Have I Leaped Over a Wall! My God, Who Teaches My Hands To War! My God, Who Teaches My Fingers To Fight!" The *Battle Song of the Ariye!* His companions had at last arrived! Uriel had made it to the door!

The colossal war angels wore specialized armor—winged lions with crowns—on their breastplates. They were heavily armed and wore visored helmets, gold leatherlike breeks, and boots with shin guards made of gold. They carried gold swords, the Word of God, and gold shields of faith that were light as a snowflake, but harder than diamonds. Across their backs they carried glistening golden spears, the aggressive prayers of the saints!

They poured into the apartment like water from a broken levy. The lesser demons fled up the stairs for the roof where, in stark terror of facing the Ariye, they leaped! Others were trapped inside and were given the same treatment and dispatch they were prepared to dispense. They fled or were dispatched to the pit in droves.

The Ariye—or Golden Lions as they were also known—charged out into the hallway to assist Mahatiel. When the first few Fornicators saw the Golden Lions, they choked in fear. One dared to charge them and was instantly cut down for his efforts. The host of gold-clad warriors turned back the sea of shock troops and slaughtered those who tried to stand and fight. The time of God's judgment against hell's intrusion had begun.

The phalanxes coming up the stairs were unaware of what transpired on the floors above and continued to push forward, unwittingly driving their compatriots before them into the whirling blades of the attacking angels.

It was a classic battle—the Lions of God versus the tigers of hell . . .

Finally the flood tide of golden warriors broke the back of the demonic rush. Alarm filled their ranks when word spread like hellfire that the Golden Lions awaited them upon the stairs. A total panic seized them, and they tried to turn, but being so tightly packed, it was practically impossible, and the beginnings of a chaotic rout began to fill the air.

All twelve phalanxes had been ordered forward and were stacked and packed in a long line from midway down Harewood Road all the way into the building and up the stairs. As the Fornicators were attacked, panicked, and driven back, they fell backward down the stairs and over the railing. The effect was as devastating as it was dramatic, for they fell like dominos backwards, row by row, one upon the other like a tidal wave. They fell down the stairs, landing to landing, landing to ground floor, ground floor to parking lot, and parking lot to the street and beyond.

"Hothiel!" Mahatiel yelled excitedly as he saw his old comrade leading the golden tide.

"Ho! My friend!" Hothiel responded in greeting.

"Drive them back while I see to the girl!"

"With pleasure, old friend! Yahhh!" he yelled and charged past Mahatiel into the lead contingent of Fornicators, followed by a flood of his warriors.

A high-pitched scream pierced the air, and Mahatiel's head snapped in the direction of the apartment. Over the heads and helmets of the Ariye he saw a flailing hand in the bedroom where Billy was guarding—Virginia!

Mahatiel shoved and pushed his way against the swarming flood tide of his comrades and more reinforcements that poured forth from the bedroom like the waters of the Red Sea. Finally he made it into the apartment where another angel was attending to Uriel's wounds.

"Go after her, Mahatiel. I tried to stop him, but he caught me by surprise, and I was too weak—"

Mahatiel shoved his way into the rustic bedroom, and Mama Melbourne was on her knees tending to her grandson, who was out cold.

Virginia was nowhere to be found.

In front of him, directly beside the bed, was a huge hole in the wall, large enough for a man to fit through.

Mama Melbourne was crying and praying.

"What happened?" Mahatiel demanded.

"Lawwd, dis man punched a hole in da wall from da bedroom of de apartment next door. Billy and I tried to stop him, but he was through 'fore we knew it. He was like a crazy man, had dis big ol' knife, just punched and kicked his way through da wall and took dat po' girl, and—"

Mahatiel was already gone.

He was through the hole and into the bedroom of the next apartment before the woman realized he was gone. All the time he was muttering to himself, "No! Not another one. No! Not another! I swore it!"

Thullus surveyed his massive army as it was crunching its way up Harewood Road with all the precision of a colossal drill team—focused, synchronized, and single-minded.

There were twelve divisions of shock troops, 480,000 strong, not counting the powers of the air—fallen angels placed under his command for this operation by Satan—Lucifer himself.

It had been over ten thousand centuries, but he still had to keep reminding himself not to refer to the master by his fallen name. The master hated the name Satan. He preferred to be addressed by the name he had held in grander times, before the fall.

Thullus would never admit this to anyone, and especially not to the master himself, but Satan was looking older now than he ever had before.

There was something going on all around the world, and it was worrying him. It was something slow, something subtle, something so imperceptible that for the longest time it had gone unnoticed and under the radar screens of the legions of the damned. There were little things, so minute that alone they seemed totally random and insignificant. But when added up, they portended ominous events.

A night clerk, a nobody, in a small motel out in the middle of Nowhere USA gets saved—becomes a Christian. Who cares? No big deal. We never needed him anyway.

Three thousand miles away, a bellboy—with a little encouragement from one of their own number assigned to promote alcoholism—drinks himself into a stupor. Fine, no problem.

The nobody night clerk, it turns out, has a cousin out in California, and of course they don't find this out until later. The cousin invites the nobody night clerk out to LA for a visit. He disappears off their radar screen in Nowhere USA, but he's a nobody, so again—who cares?

Then Joe Nobody shows up in California and just happens to get an inkling to go job hunting while in LA. On the last day of his stay in LA, he coincidentally turns up in the four-star hotel just after the drunk bellboy gets fired. The rest was bad news and ancient history, as the next week a famous producer, who was on the verge of bankruptcy and suicidal, booked himself into that very hotel while in town to try and pitch a movie project to some investors. This producer was so down on his luck that he was desperate enough to try anything.

Anything.

Even let a nineteen-year-old nobody bellboy pray for him and his picture deal, and then eventually lead him to the Lord.

The rest was box office history. And now, curse it, to top it all off, the producer had started a weekly Bible study.

There had been too many such incidents over the past several years, and they had multiplied in number like rabbits—all over the world.

In response to this, all incidents that bore even the minutest chance of having the slightest potential of long-term impact were now met with massive firepower. The strategy was still relatively new, so the jury was still out on the results, but the massive destruction they caused made it all worth it, if for nothing else.

The master had an aeons-old death sentence hanging over his head from the Creator of the universe, and he was paranoid that the noose was closing in. From now on, his orders were: massive response and overkill at every opportunity.

Sure, it made their resources thin sometimes, but with millions of evil spirits at his beck and call, he wasn't worried.

But perhaps he should have been . . .

Things were going so well that Thullus decided to move a little way from the battle scene. He found himself over the reservoir floating above the crime scene and watching with smug satisfaction as officers went about the sad duty of recovering one of their own. He inhaled and savored their grief like a drug. He felt invigorated and high with the deep agony that poured like oil from the open wounds of their hearts.

He smiled. With the way things were going, he'd have much more to savor tonight.

"Master! Lord Thullus! Come quick!"

"What is it?" he demanded irritably, resenting the interruption.

"You must come and see this for yourself! Hurry! Slec sent me to get you!"

"What is this?" roared Thullus, as he arrived and watched his sardine-packed troops tumble like dominos, while others leaped from the roof to their immediate dispatch to the Abyss or severe injury.

"My Lord Thullus, I don't know!" said Slec.

"Well, find out, you worthless idiot!" He kicked the fallen angel with a steel-toed boot that sent him sprawling to the earth. He watched as his prize troops scrambled like frightened children before the bogeyman and burst screaming in terror from the bowels of the Taylor Road apartment building. Some dropped their weapons, and others trod over their own compatriots to flee from whatever terror was within. He watched in alarm as the effects of the melee spread like one of their most virulent cancers.

The troops in the street and parking lot still strove to enter the building, but those that fled the interior blocked their way. They were in such desperation that they fought and cut down their own to escape to safety. Thullus watched amazed, angered, and appalled as phalanxes one and two fought with phalanxes three and four to force them out of the way!

Preposterous! "Turn and fight, you cowards! Stand and hold your ground! Turn and fight the enemy, you fools! Not each other!!" What in the name of hell's flames could make the most feared contingent in hell act in such—

"By my God have I run through a troop! By my God have I leaped over a wall!"

Now he knew!

"Flee!" his troops shouted. "It is the Lions of God and His judgment!!"

The Golden Lions burst from the entrance of the apartment building in a storm of swords and fury.

Gaderian returned nicked and blood-covered, his shield gone and a deep gash in his right arm. "My lord Thullus! They are Ariye! And they are everywhere!" he said, pointing to the growing swarm of golden warriors who flowed from the building like a tidal wave.

"I know. I can see," snapped Thullus. Quickly his mind sought a solution to turn the tide of battle in their favor again.

Just then above them the wind began to blow. Thullus looked up concerned as the dark sky grew darker still with strange, red-tinged clouds. He looked around him, then said to Gaderian, "Quickly, bring me Scur."

Gaderian pointed his cracked sword at the melee and growing rout ahead and beneath them and said, "But sir, the battl—"

"Now, you insolent piece of hell scum!"

Gaderian was gone like a shot, and moments later he returned with a spent and harried-looking evil spirit clothed in battle-scarred, chipped, and dented armor.

"Scur! Is this your doing?" demanded Thullus, pointing at the sky.

The fallen angel in charge of hurricanes, floods, earthquakes, and destructive storms looked skyward, his face betraying his surprise. "No sire," he said quickly, "This is not *my* doing. I called forth no such storm for today."

"I don't like this," Thullus said, scanning the skies with his eyes. "The clouds are low and reddish colored. I've never seen clouds like this before."

"My Lord, the battle," interrupted Gaderian desperately, arresting his attention back to the situation at hand. "What should we do? Where did the Ariye come from?"

"Through a portal in the building, no doubt. That's why we didn't see them. He opened a portal inside one of the rooms in the building, and they've come pouring through, directly from heaven, like fire ants from a ruptured nest."

"My Lord, in all the years of the Great Rebellion I've never seen Him do that before!"

"It is foretold in the Book that in the last days, He would do a new thing, and I fear He has more such surprises in store. Humph. After all, in spite of all our posturing," Thullus said, glancing upward again and continuing with a certain bitter resignation in his voice, "He is God. He can do whatever He likes."

Everyone looked up as a rumble of thunder like a cannon's roar startled them.

"I don't like this," Thullus repeated cautiously.

"Tell the troops to—arrrrgg!" The leader screamed in horrific pain as the first drops fell.

"Psssssssssss . . ."

"What is *this?*" screamed Gaderian and Scur in pain as drops fell on them, eating like acid through their armor, uniforms, and skin.

Thullus rubbed the caustic substance between his fingers, watching it eat clean through the fingertips of his gloves.

"**Blood,**" he said with disgust.

"Those cursed Christians have prayed through! This battle is lost," he said with even more disgust and finality. "Sound the retreat. Let us save ourselves and as many of our troops as we can. Well, hurry! Don't just stand there writhing in pain like fools! Go! Sound the retreat and be away from here while we still can! The sun will be up in an hour!"

With that, he flew off, saving himself from the drenching, warm, bloodred rain . . .

David King, pastor of the young but growing one hundred-member Spirit of Grace Tabernacle, prayed with deep earnestness of spirit along with thirty other members of the prayer circle. They had all roused themselves unselfishly from the comforting arms of warm sheets and husbands and wives to gather at the church and pray, as each of them had received an urgent call from Sister Mary Wiley.

Pastor King had even called his good friend Pastor Paul Robertson of the Kingdom Warriors Outreach Center, a church ten thousand members strong. The two were like brothers. They loved to kid each other about what it had been like being in seminary together. They had both originally gone to the distinguished Lambano School of Theology in Baltimore, but that had not turned out to their liking. What's the use of going to a school of theology, they had reasoned, where the students had more faith in the Bible than the professors did?

David was new at pastoring at the time. Paul had been a pastor for ten years but felt pressed to return to seminary for additional courses in New Testament Greek. There he had met David, and the two had become fast friends.

They had both decided to return to D.C. and there enrolled in a smaller but equally prestigious seminary. Six years later, they both graduated with honors.

"Hello, who is this . . . ?" Paul's voice had been as hoarse as a bullfrog's when he took David's call.

"Hi, Paul. I'm sorry to call you so late, but I was really impressed of the Spirit of God to call you."

"David? David, is that you? What in the world could be so urgent that you'd be calling me at . . . Hey, man! It's three o'clock in the morning!" he had said, looking at his clock.

David had gone on to give him a brief explanation of what they knew and of what had occurred so far, and then what he had been impressed with in his spirit. "I really sense danger with this, Paul. You know Mama Melbourne—she's no alarmist. And if she asked for prayer, she really needs it. Check this out—her phone, and all those in her area, have been out for two hours. The two men we sent over to check on her were killed in a car accident on the way. There's a riot going on over in Southeast D.C., and there was a special news bulletin that there's been a power outage over a twelve-block area in Northeast D.C. near the Shrine of the Immaculate Conception—"

"Over there where Mama Melbourne lives," Paul said with dawning realization.

"Exactly," snapped David.

"I'm on my way. I'll call my prayer leader and have her rouse our prayer group. I'll also call some other pastors I know. I'm sensing that this is no minor battle, David. We need to get the body involved in this. We need to cross denominational lines. It's time the body of Christ started taking these battles out of our own little sandboxes and get the entire body of Christ involved in praying and confronting this enemy. Call every pastor you know who loves God and knows how to pray—Baptist, Methodist, Pentecostal, Lutheran, C.O.G.I.C, Church of God, Assemblies of God, etc. You know what I mean?"

"Gotcha."

"We've gotta hurry, David, because we're behind the curve on this one."

"What do you mean, Paul?"

"Based on what you've told me," he said, throwing back the covers and swinging his feet out of bed, "the battle has already been engaged, and we're lagging behind. We need to get to praying, and praying now."

"Man, Paul, the Lord was pressing me for over an hour to call you, but I hesitated because it was so late. Man, I could kick myself! I feel so bad for those two young men. If I had just been obedient and called you earlier, we could've done this sooner, and those young men very well could have still been alive!" He felt as if a massive stone, heavy and weighty, was placed on his chest.

"Don't blame yourself, David. They're with the Lord now. Satan and his minions have been at this for centuries, and we are still learning. But it emphasizes the fact that this is a deadly serious game, and that when the Lord tells us to do something, we have to be obedient. Right then. Lives can depend on what God tells us to do."

"Okay. Thanks, Paul. I'll start calling folks right away."

"Now listen. This is warfare, so we need to present a united front. The Lord said, 'If two of you shall agree on earth as touching any thing they that shall ask, it shall be done for them of my Father.' Remember that the word for 'agree' in the Greek means *symphonize,* like when various instruments in an orchestra come together in harmony and bring forth melodious music."

"Gotcha, Paul, so what's your point?"

"Ask everyone you call to pray *aggressively* and in their prayers to *apply* **the Blood of Jesus** to this situation."

"Okay, okay, I see! I get it! We're all in one accord!" shouted David.

"That's right, and you know what happened in the book of Acts when that happened."

"The room was shaken where they were!"

"Exactly. So we present a united front, apply the **power of the blood of the Lord Jesus Christ.** And this time, we don't just rock the room. We rock Satan's **world.**"

"Good deal, Paul. I'll get right on it."

"And David?"

"Yeah?"

"Give my condolences to the families of those young men."

"I will," David King said sadly. "They were brothers, you know."

The heart and spirit of Paul Robertson suddenly filled with indignation, much like the heart of the Lord Jesus when He found the money changers defiling His Father's temple.

"David, Satan's minions drew first blood, and they're going to have to pay. God's Word says, 'Touch not my anointed, and do my prophet no harm.' If it's a fight the minions of hell want, then it's a fight they're gonna get."

Pastor King had hung up the phone rejuvenated and called all the pastors he knew. A concerted wave of power and prayers rose to the heavens and touched the very throne of God. The Holy One of heaven was moved and pleased to see such unity. The awesome power of unity among His people touched the very heart of God and then began to move His hand . . .

"We apply the power of the blood of Your Son upon our capital city of Washington, D.C. Dear heavenly Father, may Washington, D.C., be washed by Yyour Son's holy blood and let it cleanse our mired streets like a warm and threshing rain! We beseech you, O God, in the mighty name of Your Son, the Lord Jesus Christ!"

Prayer rose like incense to the throne of God from all over the Washington metropolitan area—from churches, from kitchen tables and bedrooms and basements, from workrooms and prayer rooms.

Messenger angels carried the petitions from all the churches and homes directly to the great God Himself. Beside Him, in phenomenal splendor, and also well pleased, sat the Son.

"At last, My people begin to understand the power in unity."

Ami-el, the mighty war angel of God, came and knelt before the throne of God and the Lord and reported, "Now that members of the body of Christ in the city and surrounding area have begun to pray thus, the battle is fully engaged on all fronts. The enemy is surrounded . . ."

10 DON'T . . .

MAHATIEL WAS FURIOUS with himself for not anticipating such a maneuver. What he hadn't realized was that Mama Melbourne's building buttressed up against the back of another building, its cxact twin in every detail, including the bedroom layouts. Pitt had simply entered the other building, which couldn't be seen from the street, disposed of the occupants in the two adjacent apartments, punched and clawed his way through their thin walls, and finally broke through Mama Melbourne's bedroom wall. He then had taken Virginia.

Mahatiel found himself first in one apartment and then another, following the large holes in the walls and Virginia's cries.

Finally he emerged into a hallway and caught a brief glimpse of a struggling Virginia disappearing around a corner ahead of him. "Virginia!"

"Matt! Help me! He's crazy! Pleeeease, help me!"

Mahatiel bolted down the hallway after them. He turned the corner and caught sight of Pitt dragging Virginia up a flight of stairs, headed to the roof. "Harm her, Slean, and you will answer to me!"

"Threats! You threaten us! We are not scared! We have the woman! And soon we will have our baby too! Eeee hee hee heee," he laughed sadistically.

Mahatiel's legs couldn't carry him fast enough as he bounded up the stairs after the two of them. He reached the last landing before the roof, when around the corner he heard a great wrenching noise and crash. He made it to the landing and looked up.

Pitt was on the roof. The padlocked and chained door to the roof lay twisted and discarded to the side like a bent aluminum can.

Mahatiel took the last seven steps to the open doorway in two great bounds. He emerged onto the dark roof, sword drawn, eyes scanning, prepared for anything. Shadows on the roof danced deceptively in the golden glow of his sword. He held it high like a lantern. There was no way down but through the door or over the edge.

"So, you haven't told her yet, have you?"

He spun around, and slightly behind him and to his left stood Pitt, his knife at Virginia's throat, tottering on the very edge of the roof itself. He was threatening, with a single step, to ruin the angel's life all over again.

"Wait! No! Don't do it! Don't! Please!"

Pitt glanced down at the street, four stories below. In the distance, he saw his compatriots toppling like bowling pins and Ariye swarming over them like killer bees. All was lost, and he knew it . . . But then again, maybe not . . .

"You surprise me, Mahatiel. You sound like you actually care for these things now."

"I do. I realize the true value of them as honored creations of God." He edged closer.

"Stop right there! No heroics! Drop the sword, or I will drop her!"

"Matt!"

"Awww, it even has a pet name for you too . . . Silence, woman! He may care for you now, but all you are to me is a piece of flesh."

"Shhhhh . . . It's okay, Virginia; stay calm. It's okay," Mahatiel said slowly, laying down his sword.

"Well, it seems I won't be going anywhere for a while—unless I decide to jump and take her with me," Slean said, smiling evilly. "So I may as well enjoy this."

"What are you planning to do, Slean?" Mahatiel said in concern, his hands held out away from his sides.

"Whatever I like," he said, and Pitt licked the face of Virginia. "Maybe I'll rape her again, right here, now, and make you watch."

Mahatiel made a sudden move toward him.

"Uh, uh, uhhh!" Slean warned. "Jump like that again and I'll slit her pretty little throat!"

Mahatiel was enraged, but he controlled himself and held his position.

Slean placed the cold blade on Virginia's cheek as she whimpered in terror.

"You really do care for this thing, don't you?" he said mockingly. He nuzzled his mouth against Virginia's ear and said, "Let me tell you about your friend Matt. Did you know that he was an Ariye before, a Golden Lion, like those down in the street, slaughtering my friends? He was sooo good at it that every demon in hell knew him, by name. He destroyed some of our best work. Did you know, Virginia, that it was he who was sent against Joseph Stalin? Yes, your little angelic friend.

Ohh, the grand plans we had for Stalin. Most of your historians don't know that, being a good communist, Stalin was planning a brutal purge of all Christians from the Soviet Union. It was our most ambitious plan to date against the church in Russia. Then, the night before Stalin was supposed to sign the order, Christians started praying."

Here he spat on the ground and then pointed the knife at Mahatiel.

"And your little friend over there was sent to deal with him. God had had enough of our most prized possession . . ."

Mahatiel was fuming.

"But you know what? Your little friend over there started to like his job just a little too much—"

"Shut up, Slean!"

". . . and the Lord took note of that—"

"Shut up, Slean, and give me the girl, and I will let you go."

"Sure you will. The Lord noticed that Matt had grown so used to being a judgment angel that he began to lose his sense of the value of human life. I mean, even though you're a judgment angel and it's your job, you're not supposed to like it. Are you, Matt?"

"Shut up, Slean!"

"Ohh, but he liked it all right. Too much. And the Lord removed him. We thought he was going to be kicked out and come to our side, but no." Slean spat again. "But God, in His despicable infinite mercy, decided to give him another chance, and you know what He did? He made him a guardian angel so that he could learn the value of human life, by having to protect it."

"Slean, I'm warning you!"

"And you know what? He hated it! Hated it! Then you know what happened? On the second assignment he had, he was so unhappy—obedient, but unhappy—that we were able to steal his charge right out from up under his nose. Kathleen was her name, wasn't it, Matt?"

Mahatiel was so furious that he couldn't speak. His fists were so tightly clenched he thought the nails might puncture the skin of his palms.

"Yes, we were able to get her to commit suicide, right under his very nose. He was disgraced. Did you know that? Did you know that you were his last chance to get back into the redeeming graces? Word has it that if he failed at this one too, he would have been through. Hmmph. We still may get you yet, Matt, after I tell her this next thing."

"I despise you, Slean, and there will be no place on earth or hell for you to hide," Mahatiel said with pure vengeance.

"So you see, Virginia, his first protectee committed suicide, and you very well may too after I tell you what I have to tell you." He smiled, then put his cracked lips to her ear and locked his eyes on Mahatiel to watch his reaction as he said, "Virginia . . . you're *pregnant.*"

"With **my** baby."

The thunderbolt took her completely by surprise. And Slean began to laugh.

A tornado of emotions rose and fell within her soul. She felt physically sick.

Pregnant! Pregnant by a *rapist! A monster! Pregnant!* Then she saw her career going down the drain, the look on her mother's face, her father, friends and neighbors, the whispers, the shame of something that had not even been her fault.

Her eyes locked onto Mahatiel.

"You *knew!* And you didn't tell me! I thought you were my *friend!*"

Mahatiel was mute with conflicting emotions. "I—I couldn't . . ."

"You couldn't!" she screamed in anger.

"Jump with me . . ." cooed Slean. "That can be your greatest revenge. Ruin him, and spite the awful God that let such a terrible thing happen to you."

Mahatiel saw her whole expression change and fill with hate. He remembered then their first encounter and her emotional defense system, that whenever she became terribly frightened or dismayed, she became dreadfully angry.

"I'll scratch your eyes out!" she screamed and leaped at the angel.

Slean grabbed her and tottered perilously on the lip of the roof. "Easy, easy, girl. You'll kill us both!" he said, restraining her. She fought to get at Mahatiel, much like the first time they had met when she remembered she had been raped.

Raped! Wait a minute.

Booommmm!

Sudden thunder rolled in the heavens above them, and everyone jumped and looked skyward at the strange and gathering clouds.

Everyone but Virginia. She had indeed felt betrayed by Mahatiel, but—

Pssss! Pssss! Psssss!

"Arrggghh! What is this?!" screamed Slean in pain. He released Virginia as the first drops began to fall. He looked at it and caught two sizzling drops in his palm that promptly burned through the skin.

"Blood!" Slean knew instinctively that somewhere Christians were praying and applying the blood of Jesus against them. He looked up just in time to see Virginia slowly turning to face him with a gleam of pure hate in her eyes.

Crack!

With all the fury of a hurricane, she punched him flush in the face so hard she instantly broke his nose and burst his chapped and cracked lips.

Slean tottered on the roof edge, swinging his arms to regain his slipping balance. His bleeding face was full of fear that melted into fury as he fell, grabbing a handful of her hair to take her with him.

Mahatiel leaped across the roof with the speed of a cheetah and grabbed her legs and held on for dear life. Virginia screamed, and just then a torrential downpour fell, searing demonic flesh far and wide. Pitt screamed in agony as her wet hair slid through his fingers and he fell to the wet red pavement four stories below.

Virginia sat up and embraced Mahatiel, weeping. The rain soaked them through to the skin, but neither one minded. He laughed and cried with joy and thanked the Lord that she was safe.

She pulled away from him briefly, and when he looked at her, she slapped him hard across the face and left a blushing red handprint there.

He fell back on his haunches, surprised, his hand going to his stinging face. "What was *that* for?"

"For not telling me I was pregnant!" she said angrily.

"Okay . . . I guess maybe I had that coming. I thought for a while with the look you gave me that you were really going to scratch my eyes out."

"I was," she said matter-of-factly.

"What happened?"

"It dawned on me . . ."

"What did?"

"Well, that little small voice—and thanks to you I know who it is now, the Holy Spirit—said to me, 'You may feel angry at Mahatiel, and maybe you have a right to. But remember, it was Pitt who raped you.' And this time, unlike six weeks ago, I listened. I'm not saying I like what you did. I'm not saying I like being pregnant either. Nobody asked my opinion or my permission—least of all Pitt. But at this point in my life, I really don't have a choice. I mean, I do have a choice, but I don't. You know what I mean?"

"Yes, I understand."

"I don't like it, but I'm in it for the long haul. It's something I definitely have to get used to, but . . . I listened to all the things you were telling me, Matt, and I don't understand it all, and I don't agree with it all, but with everything I've seen, I know there's a God, and I'm going to give the Lord control of my life and learn more about this whole spiritual thing. Will you help me?"

"Of course I will. Just don't hit me anymore, okay? That *hurt!*"

She laughed. "Okay. Matt, tell me something."

"Sure, come on. Let's get you out of the rain."

"What was Pitt, uh, Slean, or whatever the heck his name was, screaming about—*blood?*" She stuck her hand out, and water filled it and overflowed her palm.

"Virginia, right this moment Christians throughout the whole Washington area and all across the country are praying for you and your baby."

"Really?"

"Yes. They are praying for your protection through the blood of the Lord Jesus Christ. Right now, as we speak, to you and me, this falls as harmless rain, but upon the minions of evil, it falls as the awesome, all-powerful blood of the Lamb of God."

"Wow . . ."

"Now, let me tell you who your son is going to grow up to be . . ."

Moments later, they heard feet pounding up the stairs toward them, and limping out onto the roof came Uriel.

Virginia sat collapsed and in a daze at the news Mahatiel

had shared with her. "Me, the mother of the first black president! Oh my G—"

"Virginia . . ."

"Gosh," she corrected herself.

Uriel limped over to Mahatiel. "The enemy has been routed, the streets are clear again, and Billy is conscious and going to be all right. Mama Melbourne and he are going to spend the next several nights at the home of some friends. Hothiel sends his greetings and says, 'See you at the next good fight.' We can leave now, and Paltiel is well again and ready to be reassigned as her guardian angel."

Mahatiel looked at Virginia and felt a twinge of sadness.

"The Lord Himself commends you for a job well done. Your old job awaits, and it is time for us to leave. Paltiel is on his way."

"Uriel . . . I . . ."

His friend searched his eyes. "You don't want to leave, do you?"

"No, my friend. Not like this. I want to see this through. What about Jefferies?"

"He's dead, and Bellinus is banished. Thullus had to take his wrath out on someone. Word is he will report to Satan that the entire defeat is Bellinus' fault. You know the story—no honor among thieves. And Pitt and Slean?"

"Over here," said Mahatiel. "You should have seen it."

"How did you do it?"

"I didn't—Virginia did it. She caught him completely by surprise—and me too—when she punched him so hard he went off the roof. He's right—"

"Right where?" said Uriel, scanning the empty ground below.

Virginia jumped up and came to the edge with them and scanned the wet pavement below. There was no sign of Pitt anywhere.

"Uriel, petition the Lord for me. I'm going to stay."

"I understand," the angel said quietly.

Seven-and-a-half months later, in a renovated St. Michael's Hospital, a ten-pound, perfectly healthy baby boy was born. Virginia's mother and father were in attendance, along with Uncle Uriel and Uncle Matt.

Uriel had looked at Mahatiel with a raised eyebrow and mischievous grin for a moment when Virginia announced that she had named her son Matthew Sills, or "Matt" for short.

Grandma Melbourne also was there and rejoiced with Virginia and a crowd of hospital staff that were amazed at how well Virginia's life had turned out.

Mildred Hartley had dropped by to see mother and child. After seeing them both and how well they were doing, she remarked on her way out, "There truly is a God . . ."

The next night Virginia was resting comfortably and the baby was fast asleep, well fed and satisfied, swaying in the arms of a wonderfully attentive nurse as she carried him back to the nursery.

Mahatiel walked in.

It was well after visiting hours, but the staff had standing orders from Virginia herself that no matter what time it may be, he was always to be allowed in.

Virginia was nearly asleep but struggled to sit up when he walked in.

"Hi, Matt. I missed you; where have you been? It's not like you to leave me alone like that all day," she said, rubbing sleep from her eyes.

"You were never alone." He smiled and nodded toward the far corner of the room.

She turned her head and looked in the direction he'd indicated and after a few moments said, "I don't see anyth—"

Out of the corner as if through the very wall stepped a tall and powerful figure, almost as tall as Mahatiel himself. He was dressed in an immaculate blue suit and matching light blue shirt and tie. He smiled at her as he walked by the end of her bed and out the door down the hall toward the nursery. He was handsome and well built and strode with purpose and poise, yet with all the athletic ease of a panther.

"Who is that?"

Mahatiel smiled at her amazement and wonder-filled eyes.

"That . . . is little Matt's guardian angel. And if for some reason I am not around, rest assured, he will be."

"Why would you not be around?" Concern spread a growing shadow over her soft features.

"I may have some unfinished business to attend to."

She searched his eyes, looking for answers.

Not wanting to worry her, he quickly looked away.

"Matt. What is it you're not telling me?"

"Well," he said, changing the subject, "speaking of unfinished business, I have something to show you."

He quickly went to the door and looked up and down the hall to make sure no one was coming, then returned to her bedside and sat on the edge of the bed.

"I don't know what you're being so secretive about. You should just go ahead and tell me whatever it is you're hiding. I mean, with everything I've been through, I can handle anything now."

He ignored her.

"You know, Matt, I like you, and you're a good angel and

all that, but me and the Lord are going to have a talk about your propensity to keep secrets and—"

Mahatiel took his finger and drew a fourteen-by-fourteen inch square in the air in front of her. He then slid his hand across the invisible square as if wiping a screen of some kind, and it instantly became one.

"Matt!" gasped Virginia, "you didn't forget!" she said as scenes unfolded on the crystal screen, picking up where the story had been interrupted in the silo those many months before.

"As you said, so you can get to see Satan get kicked out of heaven and the creation of man and—"

She hugged him suddenly, forgetting all about the other secret he was keeping.

"Thank you, Matt. Thank the Lord for you and how you saved my life, and the life of my baby." She quickly lay back down to watch the ensuing battle unfold, wishing she had some popcorn, while Mahatiel looked for a tissue, claiming he had something in his eye . . .

Fifth District Police Headquarters was pretty quiet at 11:00 p.m. as the late-shift personnel were just starting to come in.

"Hey, Darrell!" said a police sergeant walking by.

"Yeah!"

"So how's married life?"

"I love it!" said Detective Darrell Gibbons.

Trumball rushed up to Darrell's desk and dropped a file on it.

"What's this?"

"Our next case, partner. This is the guy who killed Marcellus and raped Virginia Sills. Seems no one had seen or heard from him in quite a while. Then someone said they saw him snooping around St. Michael's the other night. They're sure it's him. It seems he picked up a severe limp from somewhere and some serious third-degree burns. But there's no mistake; it's our guy. And I want him—*bad.*"

"You and me both," Darrell said, grabbing his coat off the rack. "Marcellus could be a pain in the butt sometimes, but nobody deserved to go out like that.

"Let's go check it out . . ."

Pastor John P. Kee, from the Grammy-nominated CD, "Not Guilty, The Experience," has written the message behind the music. This page-turner will keep you on the edge of your seat from start to finish.

"Pastor Kee has captured the very essence of victory in the face of an adverse life situation in this compelling, true-to-life drama."
—Fred Hudson, legal counsel, New Life Fellowship

Not Guilty
by John P. Kee
ISBN: 0-8024-1517-2
ISBN-13: 978-0-8024-1517-2

The Negro National Anthem

Lift every voice and sing
Till earth and heaven ring,
Ring with the harmonies of Liberty;
Let our rejoicing rise
High as the listening skies,
Let it resound loud as the rolling sea.
Sing a song full of the faith that the dark past has taught us,
Sing a song full of the hope that the present has brought us,
Facing the rising sun of our new day begun
Let us march on till victory is won.

LIFT EVERY VOICE

So begins the Black National Anthem, written by James Weldon Johnson in 1900. Lift Every Voice is the name of the joint imprint of The Institute for Black Family Development and Moody Publishers.

Our vision is to advance the cause of Christ through publishing African-American Christians who educate, edify, and disciple Christians in the church community through quality books written for African Americans.

Since 1988, the Institute for Black Family Development, a 501(c)(3) nonprofit Christian organization, has been providing training and technical assistance for churches and Christian organizations. The Institute for Black Family Development's goal is to become a premier trainer in leadership development, management, and strategic planning for pastors, ministers, volunteers, executives, and key staff members of churches and Christian organizations. To learn more about The Institute for Black Family Development, write us at:

15151 Faust
Detroit, Michigan 48223

Since 1894, *Moody Publishers* has been dedicated to equip and motivate people to advance the cause of Christ by publishing evangelical Christian literature and other media for all ages, around the world. Because we are a ministry of the Moody Bible Institute of Chicago, a portion of the proceeds from the sale of this book go to train the next generation of Christian leaders. If we may serve you in any way in your spiritual journey toward understanding Christ and the Christian life, please contact us at:

820 N. LaSalle Blvd.
Chicago, Illinois 60610
www.moodypublishers.com

DARK THINGS TEAM

ACQUIRING EDITOR
Cynthia Ballenger

COPY EDITOR
Tanya Harper

BACK COVER COPY
Elizabeth Cody Newenhuyse

COVER DESIGN
Lydell Jackson, JaXon Communications

INTERIOR DESIGN
BlueFrog Design

PRINTING AND BINDING
Bethany Press International

The typeface for the text of this book is
Weiss